Face of a Bigamist

Yve Gibney

Published by Mind and Body World Publishing: www.mindandbodyworld.com

Cover by Peej Bruce: www.peejbruce.com

ISBN 9798729160365

www.yvegibney.com

This book is dedicated to the memory of my friend Sam Nolan, whose generosity of heart and spirit was as large and unforgettable as the sound of his laughter.

Acknowledgements

To enable me to thank those who accompanied me on this journey; that took just a few steps by my side along the way or held me up to reach the finishing line, I would need to add another chapter to this book. There are too many names to mention but they could all be found in the dictionary as examples of the meaning of friendship. Most importantly, you know who you are and I hope you also know how appreciative I am of all you did for me and how much I thank you from the bottom of my heart.

Contents

Preface

I have been an avid reader for as long as I can remember, but I have to admit as a first-time author, I had to go online and research what is suitable content for the preface of a non-fiction book.

So, I learnt that this is where I should explain to you when and why I decided to write this book, but first, I am going to give you a glimpse of the content of Face of a Bigamist to enable my reasons to be put into context. I met my husband in 1995 and after a whirlwind romance we married and almost lived happily ever after, except that in 2013 he chose to marry another woman, while he was still married to me.

I initially embarked on an investigative course of action to discover the truth behind his duplicitous lifestyle, but the biggest discovery and most shocking of all, for me, was the realisation of how I had been manipulated and controlled by him for so many years without realising it. Admittedly he proved to be a master of his craft, but it is still difficult to accept that as a strong and independent woman I had not recognised my husband's coercive behaviour.

I have written honestly and openly on this issue, although that was not easy to do; and while this is my individual story it has to be shared, as it does not just belong to me, it belongs to all women who have experienced coercion and control in any form. I hope this account of my experiences will go towards challenging the stereotypes and perceptions we have about the hidden abuse in domestic situations. Your love for someone can be used as a weapon against you, no matter who you are.

During the divorce proceedings and the bigamy trial I had to navigate the flawed systems of family law and criminal justice, I was miserably failed by both. My story exposed the biases and injustices against those that cannot afford to pay for the loudest voice.

I have changed the names and locations of those individuals who appear in the book and with whom I have no contact. The real names are used of those who have given me permission to use them. As Maurice Gibney and Suzanne Prudhoe's names and details are widely available online, they are named in the book.

Once I discovered that my whole marriage had actually been a lie, I stopped saying Maurice's name because I no longer knew who that person was, so he is referred to only as M, in the chapters that follow our marriage.

From the very beginning of my emotional and legal journeys I kept copious notes and it is these notes, along with my legal paperwork, text and emails that inform the content of this book. All correspondence sent by me is reproduced in its original format; but for legal reasons this is not possible for all other texts, emails and letters, these have been recreated in as close to the original format as possible. Any exceptions to this are marked accordingly.

I hope that by sharing my story it inspires others to peel off the victim label and live their lives as the person they truly are and not who others expect or want them to be.

Part 1

Chapter 1

Their wedding at Gretna Green, Scotland on 6 November 2014, was the third time they had married each other in 19 months and gave a whole new meaning to the phrase 'third time lucky.' When he first married her on 20 March 2013, he and I had been married for more than 18 years. When he married her for the third time, we had been divorced for just seven months.

I had met him in Lagos, Nigeria in 1995 just after we had both arrived in the country. He was working as a quantity surveyor for an Italian construction company, I was with the Foreign and Commonwealth Office (FCO) on a three-year posting as a nursing officer based in the British High Commission (BHC) health unit. I had travelled out as a single parent with my 4-year-old son Josh. We had been given diplomatic passports but were far from the traditional diplomatic family. I had never married Josh's dad, Joe, an African American from a middle class, professional family in Chicago, and cousin by marriage to the tennis player Arthur Ashe. I was four years his senior, a second generation British white, working class cockney from East London.

Joe and I met in Swaziland. I had backpacked around Sub Saharan Africa with my friend Jo and having studied tropical medicine decided to stay there for a short while and find work, I eventually left four years later. I had worked at a refugee camp, in a mission hospital, and spent a year at the first private multiracial clinic in South Africa, on a 10 night on/10 night off rotation; after my last night shift, I would take the local bus back across the border to Swaziland. Working and living under a system of apartheid has, rightly so, had a lasting impact on me. I will never allow myself to forget what I witnessed during that time. I came back to Swaziland to work full time with the American Embassy, Joe was a Peace Corps volunteer, but we also knew each other socially. Our relationship developed and I followed him back to America at the end of his tour. But that's another long story; in short we separated while I was pregnant, and I returned to London.

I was determined that I was not going to let being a single mother stand in my way of going overseas again to work. The opportunity with the FCO was a godsend: recruitment was for nursing officers for four specific locations, Shanghai, New Delhi, Karachi and Lagos. The choice for me was obvious: it had to be Lagos. I wanted to return to Africa, but no more backpacking or travelling on the cheap and taking risks, which were the modes of travel I had been used to. If we were to go overseas it had to be an organised venture with a secure job and a guaranteed lifestyle. At that time, Lagos was far from the safest place to be, Nursing Officers were only posted to the most difficult locations in the world. I knew we would be well looked after by the FCO, otherwise I would never have considered going. My initial priorities were to settle Josh into this new environment, throw myself one hundred percent into my well-paid job, and enjoy our new lifestyle. No way was romance part of the plan.

There were very few singletons at the BHC, and I soon realised that if I had had dreams of romance they were not going to be found in the workplace. Everyone seemed so odd, yet their eccentric behaviour was very much accepted as the norm. We had a weekly postal allowance that came by 'Diplomatic Bag.' Daily essentials were scarce in the shops and there was nowhere to buy clothes. Most of the women ordered outfits via catalogues, and the outrage on 'Bag' delivery day when two of the same dresses were unwrapped was extraordinary. In the end it was agreed that all potential planned orders would be shared to ensure no-one duplicated your choice. I used to think that, surely, there were far more important issues to be discussed.

Cathy, a recently arrived Visa Officer sported a number 1 blonde crop and wore a fantastic wardrobe of loud and sexy clothing. She was older than me, and was the other misfit. I was not alone; we became instant friends. An outgoing Scouser, Cathy was frequently chatted up and in my second week she secured an invitation to the Canadian Club, from a particularly dull Danish diplomat whom I was convinced was married, although he vehemently denied it. But his wedding band was the clue.

The Canadian Club was part of the Canadian Embassy and had an 'open night' on Fridays. Once there we soon ditched the Dane. Cathy had her eye on, one of the few black guys there who was playing pool with a short, tubby white guy with thick lensed glasses. They were Dick and Bert; I told Cathy this was not going to be a case of 'I don't think much of mine.' We thrashed the pair of them at pool and as the losers they had to buy us a drink at the bar. Perched on the bar stool trying very hard not to engage with Bert, I spotted him: alone, leaning against the wall drinking a beer and staring directly at me. I could have sworn I knew him from somewhere, but where? Tall, good looking, slim with dark hair, Dick introduced him as the 'third flatmate,' Maurice. Maurice? I remember thinking what is it with these old-fashioned names? Why wouldn't he have attempted to disguise it by calling himself Mo or by acquiring a nickname?

He asked if we had met before, as we both had an undeniably strong sense of familiarity. Cathy, who like me, was into spiritualism, was convinced we had known each other in a previous life. While I wasn't that convinced, I felt myself being strongly drawn to him. There was no chance we had met before: he was from Liverpool and in those days coming from London I would never have dreamt of going 'up North.' For what purpose? Later, whenever we recalled that night, he reassured me that it had not been a chat up line, he genuinely thought he knew me, as I had him.

Maurice had arrived in Lagos the week before me, and on completing an orientation programme, was scheduled to join the Abuja office 450 miles away. Good, I thought, no chance of romance here then, although I still gave him my newly acquired phone number after an evening of non-stop talking where the conversation had flowed effortlessly. We had adopted the stance of two people who were obviously attracted to each other, the shuffling around on the same spot, conscious not to touch, feeling that shock of pleasure when you accidentally did. He told me he had a daughter, Jessica, whose photo he showed me within the first 30 minutes of meeting. She was three weeks older than Josh and his pride in her was apparent. He asked me a couple of times if I was married, seeming to find it difficult to accept that I had come to Lagos as a single parent to do what was an incredibly demanding, and at times, dangerous job.

The guys dropped us home and in spite of myself I hoped Maurice would call, but he didn't. I checked daily with our receptionist at work, but he hadn't called there either. The communication network in Nigeria was dire and we were often without phone lines; maybe he had already moved on to Abuja. A few weeks later Cathy and I attended a charity event at the BHC club. I was ordering drinks at the bar when a familiar voice asked how I was doing. I was surprised but pleased to see him and I couldn't help myself from blurting out:

"I thought you were going to call?"

He explained he had called the number I'd given him, but it was the wrong number. I had only just got the phone and must have jumbled the number. He had thought it was intentional so hadn't called the BHC to track me down. Though the three of them had agreed to come that evening for the fun aspect and cheap drinks, he admitted he'd hoped I would be there.

I agreed to a 'date,' a word not usually in my vocabulary. I used to go out for drinks or to see a film, a play even, but a date? I was not meant to be getting involved. However, we met at Frenchie's, a popular expat bakery which had a very limited menu in the eating area upstairs. We chose pizza. I wanted a drink to calm my nerves, but it was not licensed. It transpired he had walked there and, on the way, fallen down a storm drain, leaving the hem of his left leg trousers stained and damp. I drove him home in my CD (diplomatic corps) number plated official BHC car. A far cry from my battered Ford Sierra the last time I'd seen back in Hackney it had lost its side door, ripped off by a passing refuse collection truck driven by an L plate driver.

We parked outside his apartment and talked for hours, neither of us wanting the evening to end. We kissed. I don't remember that first kiss now, I guess I must have done once, and had probably thought it wonderfully romantic but time and events have obliterated such things from my memory. When I look back at how I fell in love with him there is no joy or happiness in those memories. They now have no worth at all.

Our romance moved very quickly, especially for me who had no intention of getting involved, and it seemed like destiny as his role had changed, and he was to stay full-time in Lagos. On my first visit to Maurice's flat, I noticed on his bedside cabinet two photographs. One was of his best friend Tracey and the other of his daughter's mother Jane. Even then, on reflection, I had thought that a bit odd. As much as I love taking pictures, I have never been one to frame people's faces, let alone to have them stare at me while I slept or made love.

So, what was the story of those two women according to Maurice?

Firstly, let me introduce Jane. The story I was told at the time and that he never deviated from, was that they had been together for a couple of years before his infidelity, mostly with one-night stands, had led to their splitting up. The final straw was that while they were living together, Jane had found Maurice with another woman in their bed in the house he owned in Liverpool. He and Jane had at some point got back together, and Jane had fallen pregnant, which according to him had been a deliberate act to 'trap him.' Years later, his mother, Isabel, told me the story of how none of their family knew Jane was pregnant until her own mother, trying to locate Maurice to tell him that Jane was in labour, had called his father to get the message passed on. Neither I nor Isabel ever found out the reason why the pregnancy had been concealed from Maurice's family.

They had tried to stay together but he had not been willing to change his promiscuous behaviour, so they had finally split up shortly after Jessica was born. The day after her birth he had gone on a stag do in Manchester and ended up sleeping with a girl he had just met that night and Jane had somehow found out about it. He explained he couldn't commit to full-time parenting or to a monogamous relationship. He had arrived home from work one day to find an empty house, Jane and Jessica having gone, to live with Jane's mother in Cheshire. Eventually mother and daughter moved into a housing association property, and Maurice had care of his daughter every weekend.

The second photograph was of Tracey. Who knew then that she would always be the shadow lurking in the background of our relationship? Maurice and Tracey had met at college in Liverpool, became engaged and stayed together for three years until Tracey broke it off and moved to London. Maurice had told me she had started using drugs, became a sex worker to support her habit and was in such a 'bad way' that he had gone to London to be her knight in shining armour and rescue her from her troubled and dangerous life. After she had settled back in the North West with her small daughter, he would take Jessica to visit them at weekends, secretly as Jane despised Tracey. Apparently Jane was jealous of Maurice and Tracey's friendship and also of their previous relationship. Yet here they both were, their images side by side, witnesses to his bedroom activities over 5000 km away.

The following weekend was the Caledonian Ball, a highlight of the Lagos expat social season. At great expense a large Scottish ceilidh band was flown in, men donned kilts and women tartan sashes, and they danced many Scottish dances including the ubiquitous Gay Gordons. The BHC had several tables and we single people were seated together. For most of us this was our first Caledonian ball, and also our last. Maurice's company had a table, and he was there accompanying a contractor from England, a pleasant young woman in a very revealing dress. Cathy and I unkindly referred to her as the 'undressed woman.' He told me she had got very drunk and came on to him, but he had politely declined her offer. At the time I believed him, just as I believed everything he told me, why would I doubt him? We had a few drinks together, I wanted him to myself, and was unhappy he was escorting someone else to the ball.

Despite everything, my determination not to get involved, the inherent differences in our backgrounds and the fact he was a 'Northerner' while I was a 'Southerner' we fell in love with ease. The weather was glorious, and there were parties or events to attend virtually every night either officially in my diplomatic capacity or as part of the expat scene. Lekki Beach, a 45-minute drive away, was our Sunday destination provided I wasn't on call, and it all made for a great social life. The beach was wild, and we eventually built a beach hut there in partnership with Cathy. The only downside was that some of the huts were company owned and were filled with European men working on single status (married or partnered men whose families remained in thier home country), who brought sex workers to the beach. I never failed to be sickened at the sight of those older, married, white men lusting after the young, beautiful girls, some of whom they would have paid to be topless and to serve their food and drink, and no doubt provide additional services as the day progressed.

Our favourite nightclub, which was owned by the then President of Nigeria's son, Ibrahim Abacha, was on the busy Awolowo Road in Ikoyi. We loved to dance and The Real Thing's 'You to Me Are Everything' became 'our song.' In what we believed to be a coincidence, as you so often do when you are in love, they were Liverpudlians and, oddly, Eddie and Chris Amoo were the nephews of my 'aunty' Audrey, not a blood relative but one of my parents' oldest friends.

Within a few weeks, after seeing how comfortable he and Josh were in each other's company, I agreed to his suggestion that he move into my home which was in a six-house compound in Ikoyi, one of the more affluent areas of Lagos, and managed by the BHC. We had, like most residences, the necessary 24-hour security; we were very well protected on every level – others were not so fortunate as us. Lagos was a violent place, with poor law enforcement; it was an unfamiliar experience for many expatriates to be in a white minority in a black environment and some people felt intimidated by that. But I also knew a lot of people outside of the diplomatic community who had been attacked, carjacked or held captive at gunpoint while their houses were robbed. It was not unusual to hear gunfire at night.

A couple of weeks after Maurice moved in we went out for drinks with a colleague from the BHC, Lesley, and her Geordie husband, Stuart, whom she had met in Germany shortly after she was divorced from her previous husband. I told Maurice how they had married within months of meeting each other; having both been through failed relationships they knew that what they were experiencing was very real and that they would always be together, and they still are. Neither of us had married our child's parent, but this relationship felt so right, he said maybe that's what we should do.

"Do what" I asked.

"Do what Lesley and Stuart did. Get married" he said.

It seemed the most natural thing in the world, of course we should. I never took this to be a marriage proposal as such; it was more a statement of fact and that's not being unromantic, it just seemed the path to follow, the way to go. At this point we had been together TWO months.

As Josh was going to spend time with his father in the States in August, we decided that would be the perfect time to get married. Josh had quickly settled with Maurice; I think at the age of four he had concluded that Maurice must have come with the house as all these new things were introduced to him all at once. I believed Maurice would be a good stepfather to Josh, otherwise I would never have considered marrying him; and

I believed Josh would benefit from having a more constant male presence in his life. I knew how much Maurice loved Jessica and had no reason to doubt that he would grow to love Josh a§lmost as much. I now sadly know I had probably never been so wrong about anything in all of my life.

So, Maurice never actually proposed to me, although he did tell me that on the flight back to England, he had planned to ask the captain if he would announce the proposal from the cockpit that passenger Maurice Gibney had something very important to ask a fellow passenger. The captain was then to say Maurice has asked 'will you marry him'? But it never happened. He had had such bad diarrhoea on that flight, and had worried that the captain would make the announcement, there would be a reaction and he would be locked in the toilet throughout the whole thing. While it would have been a really romantic gesture it could also have been hideously embarrassing, the captain proposing on his behalf I mean, not him being locked in the toilet for most of the journey. Although in those days British Airways crew were generous, and I am sure we would have got a free bottle of champagne out of it, as I often did when I escorted medically evacuated patients back to the UK.

We both booked time off but due to the limited amount of leave we could only marry in Scotland where just 15 days' notice was required. We were unsure of our options; I thought Gretna Green might be a possibility, but when I shared my dream of marrying in a romantic setting over the phone to the registrar there she strongly advised against Gretna, explaining how touristy and unpleasant it was. She recommended Comlongon Castle 17 miles away. And so, it began...

The castle was booked, one of my closest friends, Chris, home on leave from his job in Kazakhstan, would be my matron of honour. My Scottish friend Caitlin, who helped with the organising and with whom we were going to stay en route, was also invited. Maurice asked Tracey as his best friend to be his best man; her partner Jason would accompany her. We told very few people in Lagos or at home because it was to be personal and very much about us, without the worry of looking after other people on a day that was to be so special.

After arriving in London, we had met my parents, who were overjoyed, if surprised by our news. Their delight was also rooted in their desire to see me settled with someone to look after me, as well as Josh, and of course for us to be happy, which is exactly what we all thought married life would be like. The ceremony took place in the afternoon of 15 August 1995, conducted by a non-denominational minister in the tower of Comlongon castle, lit only by wooden torches, with music from M People and Delibes's opera Lakme.

The reading was from The Prophet Kahlil Gibran on Marriage:

You were born together, and together you should be forevermore,
You shall be together when the white wings of death scatter your days.
Yes, you shall be together even in the silent memory of God.
But let there be spaces in your togetherness.
And let the winds of heaven dance between you.
Love one another but make not a bond of love.
Let it rather be a moving sea between the shores of your souls.
Fill each other's cup but drink not from one cup.
Give one another of your bread but eat not from the same loaf.
Sing and dance together and be joyous, but let each one of you be alone.
Even as the strings of a lute are alone though they quiver with the same music.
Give your hearts, but not in each other's keeping.
For only the hand of Life can contain your hearts.
And stand together yet not too near together:
For the pillars of the temple stand apart,
And the oak tree and the Cyprus grow not in each other's shadows.

These thoughts perfectly summed up the type of marriage we wanted, to be together but to maintain our independence, to love each other but to have space in that love to have our own opinions, be ourselves and retain our identities as individuals as well as a couple.

Before the ceremony we had drunk Lanson's champagne with our guests, and we were then joined by the minister. That morning we had realised we didn't have a wedding cake, so a quick trip was made to Marks and Spencer in Dumfries. As I'm not a lover of fruit cake we looked for an alternative to the typical wedding cake. We chose a Lion King sponge cake which, as we had met in Africa, seemed the obvious choice. The cake was put on display in the lounge area of the hotel ready for our post-wedding celebrations, alongside the triple-tiered, ornately decorated cake that belonged to the other, much larger party who were also being married in the castle that day.

Chris was approached by the mother of the groom of the other wedding to ask if we would like to have our photograph taken with their much more splendid, and conventional, wedding cake. She must have felt our cake was inadequate and would not have realised the significance of the lion nor the fact that we were totally happy with it, after all it was a serendipitous find in Marks & Spencer's and it reflected the unconventional nature of our own wedding. In response, Chris asked if her son and his bride would like to have their photograph taken with our Lion King cake. Needless to say, no photographs were taken.

After the ceremony we drank more champagne and then went for the wedding breakfast in the castle dining room where we occupied a single table. The other wedding party sat at the remaining tables where a number of men dressed in kilts drank a lot and got louder and louder as the evening progressed. At one point, Tracey followed one of the men into the gents' toilet. Curious, Chris followed Tracey. He heard some unexpected noises from one of the cubicles and rapidly retreated.

M spent a large part of the evening talking to Tracey, and only Tracey, which upset me. I told him how I felt which resulted in an argument, I threw my wedding ring back at him, and he spent the first part of our wedding night sleeping on the floor before I let him back into our marital bed. The following day after breakfast as we were saying goodbye to our guests, Tracey took me aside and asked me why I had married M when Chris and I were so obviously in love with each other. She claimed she had seen all the signs: the way we looked at each other, spoke and laughed together. She was so wrong. I explained to her we had a close and strong friendship, and unlike her and M we did not have a romantic history that had culminated in an engagement; Chris and I had a solid and caring friendship, one that I still cherish today. On that day, in less than 24 hours of marriage Tracey had cast her net and it had landed a place in our married life where it stayed until the very end.

From Comlongon we headed north to the coast to visit M's father Ronnie who had a hotel on the edge of a loch, catering primarily for fishermen. It was a beautiful location and we stayed for two nights. We found his father, who was not expecting us, in the kitchen. The first thing he said after briefly hugging his son was that M's brother John was now divorced from his wife: it seemed that while he was working in the Middle East, she had cleared the whole house, leaving behind a solitary plate, mug, knife and fork. (I actually thought I like your style girl, but of course didn't say that). He went on to say that he would disown any child of his that came to him to tell him they were marrying. Behind his back I saw M take off his wedding ring and slip it into the pocket of his jeans.

He went on to introduce me as a friend from Nigeria, not as his wife. He had an odd relationship with his father whom he had hero worshipped from childhood, although from what I learnt about him over the years he was not somebody to admire and certainly had a warped sense of morality. I only ever met him once more, in the December of that year, by which time he was aware of our marriage. He completely ignored me, barely spoke to M, did not acknowledge Josh, whom he had never met before and also ignored his granddaughter Jessica, whom he obviously knew well. M remained estranged from his father for 12 years until he became terminally ill; on his diagnosis M and his brother John returned from Nigeria and Germany respectively where they were both working to visit him in hospital. On their arrival at his bedside his father mistook M for a friend of John's; so much time had passed since they had last seen each other he did not recognise his own son. I saw his father only one more time, after his death, when he lay in an open casket; my lasting memory of him was that he looked small with enormous hands. He had died without ever meeting his grandson Sebastian. I never understood then the reason behind his anti-social behaviour, but now I am better placed to take a guess at the reasons why.

From Scotland we drove south to Liverpool and M's terraced house close to the Liverpool Football ground. At the time his mother Isabel was staying there. She was between houses, having sold up in Liverpool to move closer to his sister Stella, and before meeting her I was again told not to say anything about the wedding. M said he needed to explain everything to her and his family; he speculated that she would be upset that he had married without her knowledge and that she had not been present at the ceremony. He would tell Jane when he saw her the following day, which sounded reasonable. I went back to London to see my friends and family and to help organise a post-wedding party my parents were hosting for us at my older brother Larry's house.

In the first year after our marriage, there were problems between Tracey and M. I understood, because Joe too had married when Josh was three and I was aware that the transition could be difficult. However, a couple of years later Jessica came to live with us in Lagos, and she and Josh grew very close. Life was good and got even better when in 1998 Sebastian was born and I felt our family was complete.

Most of the time during those years M worked in other parts of Nigeria, coming home at weekends; we rarely travelled to visit him due to security issues. When Sebastian was born in London, M was working on a short-term contract in Norway. I returned to Lagos alone to a very demanding job which sometimes necessitated my being on call 24/7 for weeks on end with a new-born, Josh and Essi. Essi became our nickname for Jessie, because Essi was one of the first words Seb ever said, and the name stuck. My newly retired mother-in-law came out to live with us, to train the nanny and also to support me. As an additional incentive we paid her £400 a month which we knew would help supplement her state pension when she returned home. She had no expenditure in Lagos as we covered the cost of everything. She quickly settled in and also got a job filing as a locally engaged member of staff for the BHC, which gave her an additional independent income and a great social life. This meant that in reality she had little time to support me, although it did give her a chance to bond with the children, especially with Sebastian, this was a bond she chose, 14 years later, to sever and never to return to.

Those early years of our marriage set the pattern as we often found ourselves working in different locations. Eventually Seb and I came back to England when both Josh and

Essi, who were at school in the UK, were 16. M continued to work in Nigeria for another two years, then did a short stint in Japan before moving to France where he spent two years working and lived in a rented apartment on the Cote d' Azur. It was a great location to visit and he flew into Liverpool airport most weekends. No matter where we were located, we spoke every day, and emailed and texted constantly. Our way of life suited us, I trusted him as he did me. We looked forward to and enjoyed the time we spent together, but we also retained a sense of independence, which was important to both of us. His being in France made communication much easier and I enjoyed frequent visits to Nice.

During Christmas in 2010, he told me that he was being transferred from France to Abu Dhabi. He was disappointed, the last place he wanted to work was the Middle East. I never understood why he had been uncomfortable working in an Arab culture, but that, coupled with an 8/2 rotation, coming home for two weeks every two months, prompted him to resign. I understood but I wasn't happy that he had made a unilateral decision. In early January 2011 we hired a van and drove back to the South of France and cleared out the apartment. It was there that I discovered, by overhearing a conversation between M and a work colleague, that management had not renewed his contract and that he had never had the choice to continue. Yet why could he not have told me? In hindsight I think that would have been to admit defeat or failure, something that, it transpired, is anathema to him. That trait fuelled his behaviour in the latter years of our marriage and the court cases that followed. When most people, given the circumstances in which he had found himself, would have accepted defeat, but not him. He would do things his way, regardless of the consequences.

Chapter 2

After finishing in France, M at stayed home for the first couple of months of 2011 and did much needed work on the house. We had not spent so much time together since the four years we spent on Bonny Island, when we returned to Nigeria in 2003. That time he was working on an oil and gas project and given that accompanying spouses were not allowed to work, I was fortunate to obtain a job at the Shell plant's hospital. Having him home was great and we easily slipped into a new routine; most importantly he and Seb finally had the opportunity to do things together without the time constraint of his leave or our holidays. It became apparent to both of us that this was where we wanted our life to be but work locally was limited, and he was not prepared to take such a big salary cut compared to his ex-pat salary. So, we agreed perhaps just one more stint overseas.

In March he landed a short-term contract in Oslo and began a weekly commute, regularly changing hotels to the cheapest options. I would send him back with a goody bag of food each week and the occasional jigsaw puzzle. He found the Norwegian work culture stress free and very much to his liking, but the weekly commute very quickly became exhausting, as he would regularly have to transit through Edinburgh on his way to and from Liverpool. A job opportunity arose in Oman, and although he was not keen on being in the Middle East, he accepted it reluctantly . It was a well-paid senior position and we agreed on a six-month tour and then a rethink.

He travelled out in early July, and I followed the next month for our 16th wedding anniversary. From the first moment I arrived I loved Oman. It was a wonderful blend of Islamic and European culture with traditional architecture: white buildings against a bright blue sky. There was a feeling of mutual respect among the Omanis and with everyone you met and of course, there was the stunning coastline. There was a feel to it that instantly ticked all the boxes for me. M had just moved into the apartment; it was well placed above a small shopping mall and just a block from the beach. As he had to work, I spent my time wandering the streets; it was very, very hot but that didn't deter me from exploring. At other times I lay on the beach and caught up on my reading. For our anniversary he bought me the most beautiful emerald green and black hijab trimmed in diamante. We ate our celebration dinner at a local Italian restaurant, and back at the flat we drank a bottle of Lanson's, our wedding champagne, that I had brought out with me.

Our wedding bands had hurriedly been bought from a stall in London's Covent Garden market before we left to marry in Scotland in 1995. Having found his suit almost immediately in Liberty, we had walked our feet off looking for a wedding dress. Just as time was running out, I had found a plain beige A line dress that skimmed my ankles in Wallis for £40, and a pair of slingback Mary Janes in dusty pink suede in Next. His suit had cost three times more than my complete outfit, but cost was immaterial to me, it was about finding the perfect dress and I was happy with what I had. I knew a designer jewelry store, Electrum, in London's exclusive South Molton Street; and when we peeked in the window our real wedding rings called our names, they were an unusual design in white and yellow gold, his much chunkier than mine. We were fitted for them but had to be patient while they were made in Germany and couriered out to us the following month.

Sixteen years on he had reverted to wearing the original ring, having lost the real Electrum one while working on a building project at his mother's house before the Norway stint. He had removed it as he always did when laboring, and could only conclude that it had somehow ended up in debris that had been transported to the dump. He had been so upset. So, secretly, I set about ordering a replacement. Fortunately the designer was able to recreate the original ring design and I gave it to him for our anniversary. He was delighted with it. We were a pair again!

I saw him next seven weeks later when he was home on leave. We grabbed a few days away together on a romantic break in Northumberland and stayed in an old castle and overindulged in every possible way, except for the planned hiking. While home he had heard from his ex-colleague and friend Steve, about a possible job with him in Rotterdam. Steve, who lived close by, was bringing his American boss home that weekend, so they scheduled an interview which would roll over, it seemed, into a pub crawl. It all went well, except for maybe M's hangover the next day, but he was offered the job and we were so happy. He would finish in Oman in January 2012 and would resume the weekly commute again, easier this time as the flight was short and direct to Liverpool. I looked forward to frequent trips to the Netherlands; having lived there many years before, I was ready to start practicing my Dutch and looking forward to eating chips with mayonnaise again!.

However, a few weeks later, just before he was due to fly back for Essi's graduation in Leeds, the job offer was withdrawn, the department had been restructured and the role no longer existed. He was bitterly disappointed, as reluctantly he would now have to stay on in Oman until he could find a better alternative. I was doubly disappointed over the job and that I was not able to attend Essi's forthcoming graduation; there were only three tickets available and they had been allocated to her mum, her nan and her dad. Even though I understood that they were the priority it didn't stop me from wanting to celebrate her achievement. I suggested that I collect him at the airport with the boys and then we could all join together for the celebratory meal after the ceremony. But no, it had been arranged and Jane was picking him up. OK I thought, this is about them as a family on that day and I had to accept that.

He had sent me a text on departure from Muscat to tell me that there was something important he wanted to discuss, and that we should set aside some time. He had an irritating habit of doing this and never giving a clue as to the topic, and annoyingly he would not be drawn on it. I guessed it was about the job. He texted again on arrival, he had his usual 'travelling upset tummy' and was not feeling well. Essi's nan was unable to go as she too was unwell, but as he didn't suggest I took her place I wasn't going to. He sent pictures from the graduation and Essi looked lovely. The plan was for Jane to bring him home after an early meal; he hadn't been planning to drink as he still felt rough. But he didn't arrive home that night nor did he reply to my texts; his phone went straight to voicemail, and there was no reply from Essi either. I started to become worried, the weather was awful, there was torrential rain and fog, so I barely slept, because he would always text, I had an uncomfortable feeling, I was sure something was wrong. I tried again early morning, no luck, until Essi texted around 9.00am to say he had fallen asleep on the sofa drunk and his battery was dead, so she was messaging to let me know that he and Jane would be leaving soon, and that was that.

I pottered about and went for a shower, but on coming downstairs I saw him standing in the kitchen. He was surprised to see me, as he had forgotten I had taken the day off work, but I was equally surprised by his appearance, he looked awful: ashen and drawn, and he had visibly lost a lot of weight in the short space of time since I had last seen him. He looked really ill; instantly I thought that this was what he wanted to discuss, he was going to tell me he was very unwell, possibly seriously going by his appearance.

He stepped forward and took my hands in his and placed them on his chest,

"I have to tell you something that is going to be really upsetting."

What was he going to tell me?

He continued, "Once I say it, I'm going to leave, I won't be able to stay."

"What is it? Just tell me."

"I want a divorce!"

"What?"

Where has this come from? I don't recall if I said that out loud or just thought it, I was in a state of shock.

"What are you talking about?"

He led me by the hand to the kitchen table and sat me down. He made coffee, although his remained untouched. What followed was a long one-sided conversation, which I wouldn't let myself interrupt. He spoke with an honesty of emotion I had never heard before: he felt useless as a father and husband, he was never home and never with us when we needed him the most. He described stacks of boxes in his head where he stored all the things he had done over the years to hurt me, in particular, but also our relationship. They had, he said, been locked away for years but the lids wouldn't stay closed anymore the contents were spilling out, and he couldn't cope. He felt sick all the time, he wasn't sleeping, he loathed himself for who he was and what he had done. He didn't elaborate on what that was, but I could guess; it must be in part about his friendship with Tracey, whom I knew he sometimes met in secret.

In 2001, we returned from Nigeria and he started a job in London and would come home on weekends. Without fail the then single Tracey, and her children, came to our house every Saturday which gave us little family time together. I had asked him to tell her that while she was always welcome, she couldn't visit every week, but she never actually visited again. Well, not when I was around anyway. He would not always tell me that he was meeting her, that suited him. There was something about his personality that made him do things without my knowledge, I had learnt that early on, and I was initially perturbed by it, but my thought process was: if it is so important to him, and as long he never puts anyone before his own family, then do it. I knew his friendship with Tracey was important to him, I trusted him and I would not let it become an issue.

He tried his best that morning to assure and reassure me that when he had met female friends without my knowledge it had only ever been platonic and he had never been unfaithful to me. He told me how that was his benchmark, because if he ever went beyond it there would be no coming back to me. As he knew, I would never forgive the betrayal of our love and respect in that way, and our marriage would end.

He asked if there was a way forward; given what he had shared, did I still want him? He knew I did. We had so much invested in our marriage and we were such a part of each other. I felt overwhelmed by the sense of relief that he had finally come clean and was purging himself of the deceitfulness which he had kept concealed for so many years. If only that was it, his telling me what I actually already knew, then I could manage that and help him to understand how proud he should be for having taken the first step, and that we would work through it to a happier ending together. We ended up in bed, as always, our way of proving our love for each other. Lying close he had told me he had felt there was no other option but to leave the marriage and the family, as he felt so unworthy of us. That was not going to happen; as long as we loved each other and recognised we had a rocky road ahead for a while to come, he wasn't going anywhere. Or so I thought.

I dropped him at the airport the next morning. He would arrive back in Oman on a weekend, but he couldn't stay longer as he wanted to work it to make up for the time away. We would be together again in less than a month when Seb and I would fly out for Christmas and New Year. In the interim he promised he was going to try to write down his thoughts and share them with me so we could make a plan on how to help him, to regain his sense of self-worth and belonging in our family and begin to talk about how he had to be more open and honest, but as I later discovered he had no concept of either.

Years before, in 1997/98, with the exception of holidays, we only saw each other alternative weekends, as he was working on the early construction of the Bonny Island camp that we later lived in when we returned to Nigeria, while I worked in Lagos. Without fail, by 9.00am, on every workday Mr Musa, the fax room operator at the BHC would deliver a fax to me. Every missive would contain a message of love and every day he told me how much he missed me. Mr Musa could never contain his smile as he regularly handed over a fax covered in hearts; it was adorable. So, from past history I knew he was capable of writing openly and honestly about his emotions, and I hoped he had not lost that ability or the inclination to do so.

Around a week later he told me his letter was ready, should he send it?

"Yes, send it," I told him and braced myself.

He didn't want me to be upset, he asked me to read it and reflect on my feelings, and we would continue to talk and talk some more at Christmas. Hesitantly, I opened the attachment. I knew the three-page A4 document would be difficult to read, but it had to be done. Inevitably, I cried my way through it, we had indeed reached a turning point in our relationship.

He began by thanking me for my patience and the time I had given him to enable him to process whatever was going on in his head, he appreciated it. He wrote that he had struggled in trying to analyse his role within our relationship from when we had first met to the present day. That while we had grown together in so many positive ways, he perceived me to be the stronger character and had learnt a lot from me through the years.

He explained how he had tried to live up to my expectations of him but had to admit he had failed when it came to being honest and open or in achieving a sense of integrity. He apologised for his failures. M referred to the *'negative times'* in our relationship and accepted sole responsibility for the disharmony at those times, he described a deep rooted need in him to rebel against the marriage, he had no control over when that need would surface.

He recounted his feelings from around the time we had first left Nigeria in 2001, and that he believed was when our relationship had changed and started to go awry, it had deteriorated. He felt ashamed because he had chosen to *'disrespect'* me at that time. The reasons for doing so escaped him, and his shame was compounded, he explained by my being the mother of our children or simply for me being the person that I am. He went on to explore the differences in our upbringing as a possible explanation for his destructive behaviour and compared my having been brought up in a close and affectionate family while his? He told me I knew what his family life had been, but did I really?

I had always felt his family was deeply fractured. When I first met him, he had little contact with his siblings or his parents, and I would have to suggest he called his mother. It seemed like the siblings were on a constant rotation of bickering and falling out with each other only to re-unite to divide different pair of siblings. His parents followed the same pattern. They reunited after divorcing, only to separate again. His mother had to take his father to court to retrieve her divorce settlement which she had invested in his business, as he had denied all knowledge that she had done any such thing.

M had told me early on in our relationship how as a child every Sunday afternoon he would accompany his father to the boat he was repairing. While he was considered by his siblings to be the 'favoured one' he was far from it. Sat on the deck with a bag of sweets he was the cover for his father who would be below entertaining whatever woman he was currently having an extramarital relationship with. Ronnie had, according to M, even had a longstanding affair with one of Isabel's friends while she worked alongside Isabel in the office of the family business. There were, according to M, many affairs and episodes of unpleasant behaviour that all occurred simultaneously with his father's regular attendances and donations to the local church.

However, the most disturbing thing he ever revealed to me was that he had no childhood memories prior to the age of nine years old. He said it just once, he had never questioned why, and he had no desire to do so. As if his dysfunctional family life was not enough to deal with there was also an unspoken trauma in his past that would remain just that. I could not begin to contemplate what he had suffered. It was no wonder that his behaviour in the context of our relationship was sometimes difficult to understand.

He wrote of the highs and lows in our relationship and how he had been drawn to others, (who I could only presume were women), in a way that he knew was wholly unacceptable even though he implied it was only for friendship and guidance which he referred to as a form of escapism. Only recently, he wrote, had he allowed himself for the first time to acknowledge this behaviour for what it was and he now deeply regretted it all. He stressed that while his intentions were never to hurt me or to cause me pain, he had still been willing to take that risk. As a form of self protection, all of these thoughts and actions had been packed away in boxes in what he described as the dark place in his mind. But, now there was no space left, both boxes and space were at full capacity, so he now had no option but to open the boxes and try to deal with all he had concealed from me during the past 16 years.

He reflected on how he should have been stronger and dealt with issues as they arose, and shared more instead of attempting to manage issues in secret and away from me.

> *I am so very sad as I do not believe we will be able to be as happy again as we once were. And even sadder when I think about how that is predominantly all down to me. We have an amazing family and share a deep love for our children and we have had many, many wonderful times together. But, Yve, if you put all of that aside, I ask myself if you are truly content with me? Your answer has to be straight from your heart, and not for what is best for others or the easier way for the future.*

> *I no longer recognise the person I have become. In part, this is due to my work related lifestyle; it is also about our relationship. I don't understand how I could have done the things I have done, how I could have betrayed you, the person I love so much. I haven't shown you the respect or the honesty you so deserve. I have deliberately hidden even the most inconsequential things from you, because it was easy to do rather than deal with it together.*

He was right, about the secrecy which over the years was the main issue that had triggered arguments. For example, giving money to his family who used him as a bank for non-repayable loans. I would never have begrudged them financial help if they truly needed it, but he would give them large amounts of money regardless of our financial situation; on one occasion he gave one of his brothers an £8000 loan, when at the time it was the total amount of our savings. That debt was repaid but not until five years later. Even if we had discussed these loans at the time, and I had said no with what I considered to be a reasonable rationale, he would have opposed me and accused me of not caring about his family, this was wrong. I just wanted to protect my own family first. I had always thought he needed to impress them and that he needed them to need him, and I stand by that still.

He also favoured Essi financially and would buy her things without my knowing until I spotted an email detailing delivery instructions or Essi let slip that dad had bought her this or that, forgetting that she had been briefed not to tell me about her latest acquisition. But I tolerated it, I excused him and put his behaviour down to guilt, to compensate for treating her and her mother so very badly in her early years, when he had abandoned them in favour of Tracey. But what I could not forgive was that he was teaching Essi to be dishonest, to lie, to me in particular and the inexorable outcome that would have for her relationship with me. Latterly, I felt strongly it was as though he had groomed her in the art of deceit and trickery from an early age enabling her to perform her final act, to be his special pawn to validate his ultimate deception, albeit unknowingly.

He couldn't say how or why or what had caused him to change. Inherently he was, he claimed, someone who had always wanted to love and to be loved and to be there to help others. Yet he felt he had done the opposite of that, he had failed us, let us down and had not been there for his family at times when he had needed him the most and he carried a heavy weight of guilt as a result.

He then referred to an incident that had happened in 2008, which involved a mutual female friend. Scrolling through his phone for the delivery notification for parts for the bathroom he was remodelling, I couldn't help but notice a text conversation between him and Myra, fairly innocuous at first sight: It had been on a Sunday evening after he had returned to the French apartment, she was enquiring if he had had a good weekend at home. There was nothing unusual in that, but she went on to tell him she was in the bath, and that her '*tits looked really big even though they're not.*'

I could not believe what I was seeing. Only the week before, after helping Myra choose a dress for a work event, I had told M how 'prudish' she was, as rather than try dresses on in front of me in her bedroom, she had got changed in the bathroom. The next text described her bath ritual, his response was to tell her he was having a beer and watching a DVD. Innocent so far on his part . However, when she described washing between her legs, he replied he would clean her with his tongue. I was so shocked; in that flash of a second, I concluded that they were having an affair.

I had charged upstairs and while he lay on the floor fixing the sink, I had confronted him. He tried to lie his way out of it with a series of outlandish excuses, so in front of him, on his phone, I called Myra and asked her why she had been sexting him. She sounded very nervous, she was in the car with her family, she told me she couldn't talk, so I told her I would screenshot her husband the texts. She stayed on the line and tried to laugh it off as a joke before terminating the call. An hour or so later she had texted that she had shown her better half the message chain; allegedly he had found it hilarious and accused me of being the prudish one for not seeing the funny side of it. M apologised profusely and acknowledged how unacceptable and wrong it had been. He did his best to reassure me it was the two of them simply messing around, and nothing more. I let it go, as my gut feeling told me he was now telling the truth. I was so disappointed in both of them, he as my husband and her as a friend, especially as I had been her main support for several months prior to that incident when she was convinced her husband was having an affair with his P.A. Our friendship with that couple ended that day.

The following week I flew out to join M in Abu Dhabi where he was temporarily on assignment. His hotel suite was fantastic. Waiting for me was a vase full of red roses, a day booked at the luxurious hotel spa and a pair of slippers encrusted with Swarovski crystals, (to this day still in their box as they are too good to use). He would do anything to ensure I knew how sorry he was. The gifts were all very nice and I knew he regretted his actions; but while some would have considered his actions as micro cheating, an impulsive flirtation, it meant more to me. Was I right to have the level of trust in him that I did? I still struggled to understand why it had happened in the first place and why he had not considered the consequences if he had got caught. I then found myself reading that sexting incident in 2008 had been the turning point for him:

> *This part is very difficult for me to write and I am sorry that it will be hurtful for you to read, it is about the incident with Myra. What happened that day was a turning point for me, it left me with no hiding place. It forced me to take hold when I saw how much I had hurt you and made me realise how easily I did what I did without a thought for the possible consequences. I am ashamed to say that was the first time I had experienced guilt even after all the things I have done to you in the past. The guilt I carry from that incident is all consuming, it has impacted on my physical and mental health. I have to stress, and please believe me, that I never had any physical contact with Myra, what I did was inappropriate but it was 'just' a flirtation, and believe me when I tell you I know how very wrong it was. I have to say though it only happened with Myra because she was available, it could have been anyone. Because, at that time, I was compelled to press the button marked 'self destruct', to push our relationship to the limits, I needed to know what would happen if I did. Don't ask me why as I do not have the answer.*

The part of this I struggle with the most and you won't know this, is what I would have done if the opportunity had occurred to have a sexual fling with her, I would have taken it. Not out of attraction or desire or lust but purely to commit the absolute betrayal of our marriage vows and above all to defy you. Who am I Yve if I could consider that, let alone do it, to someone I love? I knew how devastated you would be if I would have allowed that to happen, yet, I'm sorry , it would not have stopped me.

He continued to explain how he had tried to tell himself 'that it meant nothing, that he should move on, put it behind him' but that he hadn't been able to.

What followed was written with an unfamiliar sincerity as he described how he had no self-respect or sense of self-worth for the person he had become, and how that particular act of disrespect dismayed him the most. He had never thought that he could become this person and yet he had to accept that this deceitful person was who he had sadly become.

The next paragraphs referred to the ups and downs in our relationship and how we had got through them but how he felt each episode had eroded our relationship that little bit more; which was exactly the expression I would always say to him. He went on to write:

Our relationship only needed one last nudge for it to fail and I ask myself is that why I would have let it or made it happen?

M continued; the last thing he wanted to do was to continue to hurt me but given his past behaviour he could not reassure me or guarantee that he would not be able to stop himself from doing just that, no matter how hard he tried not to. What he had considered to be bouts of depression he now knew to be 'highs and lows' instead and he felt most vulnerable when at a low and that was when he would lash out and hurt. M was sure he had been in a 'low' for several years and asked if I had felt that? How physically and emotionally he was not the man I had loved for all of these years. It was painful to read that he could no longer look at me without feeling overwhelming guilt, and that while there was the occasional respite and he felt happy in being with me, he felt overall we could not recover the happiness we had once had. His all encompassing feelings of guilt would not allow him to.do that. He had resigned himself to accept that the only role he was capable of was as a provider, and as such, would always be here for me and the children, but he could do no more than that for fear of continuing to hurt the ones he loved.

M struggled to understand how I could look at him as my partner and he felt that if I searched deep inside of myself I would no longer be able to. He closed by telling me the time had come for me to consider my emotions and how I felt now I knew the truth and to contemplate the options so we could talk them through. He made it clear he did not want to lose me, but he feared if we carried on with our relationship, if not now then later he would lose me completely.

This was distressing to read, but I was also confused by its content. He portrayed our relationship differently to how I perceived it or felt that we had lived it. If he had truly felt it had deteriorated, his word not mine, to such a degree so early on circa 2001, why ten years later were we still together? Why did we text each other constantly, speak daily, enjoy each other's company so much? Why was he so keen to work closer to home, to spend more time together, if he no longer believed we belonged together? I knew I had to stop and re-assess, that was true. He had caused me heartbreak over the years, but again, these incidents were always centred around his secrets. I don't believe he knew I actually knew so much about them. But it was apparent his guilt and loss of sense of self-worth was all consuming, I was staggered by just how much he had opened up and his newfound sense of clarity. But this was certainly his epiphany and not mine.

His self-realisation had hit him hard; I hated the thought that he had been in a low for so long, how had I not seen it? Was it because it had become the norm? I struggled to grasp the idea that our relationship was doomed, unless he had not been as honest with me as he said he had. Unless there was somewhere else, he wanted to be, somewhere that didn't include us? After ten days of talking, mailing, sleepless nights and too many glasses of wine we decided to draw a line under the topic which had rapidly become all consuming.

Now that he had acknowledged and owned his harmful actions that had been the cause of so many problems between us, I felt the road ahead was clearer, but his behaviour would have to change as we could not end up back where we had started. I told him I felt we could make that happen; he was hugely relieved that I hadn't abandoned him when he needed me the most. We could talk more at Christmas. The immediate future looked challenging, but as we both wanted the same outcome, I knew we would get there. But it transpired there was a disparity between our outcomes that I could never have anticipated.

Chapter 3

S eb and I were excited to be spending Christmas 2011 in Muscat with M. Josh and Essi had their own plans, which worked well logistically as the apartment only had two bedrooms. I looked forward to a quieter, more relaxed Christmas in the sunshine and the opportunity to catch up with M face-to-face. He had known for a while it would be a busy time at work and while he would be unable to take extended leave, he would be off work on the 24th/25th which made for a four-day weekend.

In the lead up to our arrival he was, with little notice, dispatched to a project still in development in the desert, as the contracts manager there had been promptly dismissed for drinking on the job. I mailed him the day he travelled and my actual mails are reproduced below:

From YG To: MG Wed Dec 14, 2011

So, have you survived and arrived safely? Or have you woken up at an oasis in a Bedouin tent being fed figs and sheep's sweetbreads? Must be hot there and I suppose cold at night? I don't actually know anything about the desert weather, only what I've seen in films! Guessing a problem with email or getting a desk as take it would've heard from you by now?

In Liverpool tonight for Seb's last drama club session, I'll go in and wander, will go to M n S as still to get a few bits for your mum's Xmas hamper as well as cake and Xmas pud to bring out and a few more pressies. xx

From: MG To: YG 14 Dec 2011

Uneventful journey for once! Really hot now but it was cold last night, they reckon it can be freezing some nights. Am sat at my desk, which is the one that belonged to the contracts guy that just left, but lacking on the comms side: no phone but I have a computer and the usual problems with internet connections.

This morning was spent on a boring induction which is why I haven't been able to mail yet. Lunchtime here, so I am off to explore the canteen and see what delights await.. I had breakfast in my room, ate leftover fruit, couldn't let it go to waste, I am turning into you ! …

So, you are in town tonight, I suppose there is late night shopping so you will be able to keep warm as no doubt you will be in all of the shops..

Meeting with the head of site later on so I will have more info as to my schedule between being here and in Muscat and also get definite dates for Christmas time. Fingers crossed it works out ok.

Ok, can't stop off to look for the loos! xx

From: YG To MG Wed 14 Dec 2011

Don't you mean hole in the ground and the spade with your name on it? Sounds like a totally new experience, hopefully a short one! Good luck with the grub – hopefully, something suitable, also guess you'll meet some other expats there? Take it no bar or social club? But maybe a social area? Good luck with meeting later, fingers crossed the dates work out. xx

From MG To: YG Wed 14 Dec 2011

No, there are real western loo's. Lunch is over, same menu as Muscat: pasta, salad, rice, chicken, beef, bread.

Remember, cheap pressies only this year. Happy I'm in the desert, no shops here, although I might barter on a camel XX

From MG To: YG Wed 14 Dec 2011

I'll send a pic of the accommodation centre area, serif you can find the social club and bar! It's not only the desert that is dry !

Enjoy shopping, one way of keeping you out of mischief! Xx

From: YG To MG: Wed 14 Dec 2011

Just thinking how you're going to shop for Xmas pressies in the depths of the desert and no I don't want a tube of coloured sand or a sand sculpture thank you!

From MG To YG Wed 14 Dec 2011

All sorted. Buy pressies for yourself tonight, so I only have to wrap them! X

To: MG From: YG Wed 14 Dec 2011

No not good enough, accost a passing Bedouin or Tuareg for silver or a cloth made of desert jewels. X

M was finding it expensive to live in Muscat as he received a salary without perks which meant he was responsible for the £1,000 per month rent, cost of utilities and his car lease. This expenditure was eating into his salary, which at first glance had seemed impressive but now he was not so sure. We had agreed to try to economise until he could find a job with a similar salary but with a remuneration package that covered these expenses and making family separation worth the sacrifice. So, we agreed we would not be as extravagant as we usually were at Christmas, he always bought me the best presents and seemed to have a knack of always 'getting it right'. The previous year he had bought me a Prada handbag, if I had stood in a shop of one hundred bags, that bag would have been my first choice.

The next day our emails were not as light-hearted. He had managed to get a call out to me which was not welcome news: he was expected to go back into the desert for four days from December 24, Christmas Eve. It looked like he might be in the desert for the foreseeable future and more there than in Muscat, or at least until they could recruit a new contracts manager for that post.

From YG To MG Thu 15 December 2011

Morning, I tried to call you back, when it cut off but no luck! So, I know now you are not a happy bunny but if that is the best you can get off, which is bloody rubbish, we still just have to manage it best we can. I was thinking maybe I might hire a car while you are away for the 4 days or so or can I get put on yours? Probably not, just so Seb and I can do a bit more than just the beach and flat. xx

From MG To YG Thu 15 Dec 2011

Hello

Bit of a late mail sorry, the net has been down yet again, seems it's a bit of a regular occurrence. Seems problems with phones when out of the office area too so it's like being back to the good old Bonny days, depending on radios. You can call me via the Muscat office reception though, once I know my extension number I'll give it to you, hopefully later today. .

The Christmas break situation is crap. To be honest, I'm unsure how we will sort this out. I can't see you being able to hire a car in Muscat, I would prefer you not to as the roads are so dangerous here, I don't think it's safe. I should be back in Muscat in the evening of the 21st so don't worry I will be waiting at the airport for you. Do you think it's worth looking at postponing by a few days and coming on the 27th? Just so you are not here alone, I don't think you would enjoy it. I know that means less time together but given the lack of transport, the poor internet and phone connection in the flat, and the possible transports problems I think it won't make for the best time. Anyway, lets try and catch up later today, hopefully the bloody phone will be sorted by then,

Back soon going to get lunch. There won't be any surprises there . xx

From YG To MG 15 Dec 2011

I think it will cost a fortune to change the tickets and then it will give us just 4 days together as we leave on the 1st. I've already told Seb and he is ok with it, obviously disappointed, but we'll have to make the best of it. If we can't hire a car, we'll just have to manage. I've told him he and I will go out for dinner on xmas day he can open his pressies and then we'll have Xmas dinner on the 27th when you come back. If we can't

I wasn't in a position to consider postponing the trip: it would have been impossible to reschedule our flights which were non-refundable, over the busy holiday period and it would have been unfair on work colleagues to ask to change my leave at short notice. I felt I was familiar enough with Muscat from my trip in August to be able to go to the beach and the shops, and we could occupy ourselves for the time he was away. After all it was only really two whole days.

We arrived on the evening of 21 December at a hectic airport as the schools had broken up that day and expats and their families were travelling home for Christmas. We were surprised not to find him in the arrivals hall to meet us; but then he texted that he was struggling to find a parking space. So, we met him in the warm night air of the car park, where he had parked a few hundred meters away in spite of there being many closer, empty spaces. I was puzzled and even more so when, as I moved forward to hug him, he backed away. He reminded me it was illegal to demonstrate affection publicly, but I had witnessed people embracing in the airport, physical contact being acceptable in public between married couples. He walked on ahead of both Seb and me and left me pushing the luggage trolley; I remember thinking 'what's up with him? He was behaving as if he didn't know us.'

However, once we were settled in the car, he seemed chilled and pointed out illuminated landmarks to Seb including the beautiful Grand Mosque as we drove to the apartment. We arrived to find a mezze supper waiting for us and, in spite of being tired after the long journey and the three-hour time difference, we ended up having a lovely evening. That night in bed he showed me just how pleased he was to see me, it felt so good to be back in his arms. Unbeknown to me, my space there, in his arms, on his chest, had in my absence not been empty for long, Someone else had been held there, laid there, filled that void. I never suspected for a moment that his arms would be wrapped around her again, so soon after our night of passion and lovemaking.

The following day we all went to the Mall, ate our favourite Cinnabon's, went bowling and enjoyed a Chinese takeaway for dinner. There had been an unfortunate last-minute change of plan and he now had to go to the office the following morning, in spite of it being the weekend, and was to fly to the desert that afternoon, a day early. I wasn't happy but what could I do? Maybe he would get back a day earlier in return?

He left super early the following morning. Around mid-morning Seb and I set off to spend the day at the beach; on our return he had mailed:

From: MG To: YG Friday 23rd December 2011

Hi

No mobile phone signal so have popped by the office to mail you, all ok here, hope all ok there? Will mail you in the morning . Enjoy your night.

Take Care and sorry I had to leave today xx

From YG To MG on work email 24 December 2011

Oh well, we're off to the Intercon for the day will see how long Seb lasts! We will be back around 4 – 4.30 I suppose. Have a good day, Missing you.

xx

From: MG To YG 24 December 2011

Hi

Well, I hope your day's been good. The net has only just been restored so back up and running again, so sorry for the late reply. I have been out to the rig and the contractor's offices so no chance to call yet, and now you are out. I will plan to stay late in the office and keep trying to see if I can get through.

Ok I have got work mails to catch up on, so will check back with you in a bit. I hope the intercon worked out and Seb lasted long enough for you to enjoy it.

Back in a bit. xx

Seb and I sat around the pool at the Intercontinental Hotel opposite the apartment, it was too hot to do much else. Seb had chatted about England for ages to a lovely elderly, Omani gentleman while in the pool and enjoyed his company. We ate an overpriced lunch there: chicken burger and chips for Seb and the inevitable salad for me. We bought ice cream from the diary parlour below the apartment block on the way home, which we ate while we watched TV. Such was our Christmas Eve. There was no further contact from M.

On Christmas day we took a taxi back to the shopping mall and I bought Seb an X box game. I felt so bad for him not having a proper Christmas, but M would be back soon, and we were only postponing for a few days. We mooched around the shops and in fact it felt like any other day, and why wouldn't it? We were in a Muslim country after all. We ate our Christmas dinner at the nearby Italian restaurant where M and I had celebrated our 16th wedding anniversary five months earlier. They served wine, which was a treat, and I thoroughly enjoyed several glasses. M didn't have a liquor licence and so the flat was dry. I thought Seb and I might appear an odd couple, but no one really noticed us. We ate three courses each and were back at the apartment by 9pm.

I managed to get online and so, my Christmas entertainment while Seb played his new game, was to go on Facebook and wish friends happy holidays. From Eammon, an old friend from Bonny Island, I learnt that our old friends, also from Bonny, Vicki and Sam and their daughter Anna, were heading to Muscat from Qatar the following day. I messaged Vicki, who said they were staying with friends who lived close by M's flat which was perfect, and we arranged to meet on the 27th. M was due to return that day, but not till late afternoon. I was excited to see them again, Seb would see Anna, and we would have some company at last. It felt lonely just the two of us over Christmas. The idea of meeting up lightened our mood; as much as I tried, I had no Christmas spirit, M's phone had gone straight to voicemail, there had been no Christmas text, mail or missed calls, this was not exactly how I had thought the holiday in Muscat would pan out.

I woke to an email:

From: MG To YG 26 December 2011

Subject: Ho ho ho Merry Xmas

Hi

Hope you are ok, and that things aren't too difficult without a car. I tried calling a few times yesterday but the lines are just not connecting to local Oman numbers for some reason, seems it is easier to get international so I will try your UK mobile a bit later. Am sorry, as I know this is not what we had planned for and is far from ideal, I hope it hasn't ruined yours or Seb's Christmas.

I had a Christmas dinner, well of sorts. I went to one of the American company' canteens and got turkey with some decent vegetables, and don't get jealous but I had American apple pie and ice cream afterwards. How was your dinner?

I know you are out now so will mail later and try calling again. Xx

My reply was to the point:

From YG To MG 26 December 2011

I just turned on the laptop and hey presto an email from you. All very frustrating and disappointing especially as we never got to talk to you on Christmas day. Seb never opened one present yesterday which I think is very special. It's really disappointing and I'm getting a bit peed off to be honest… not one working phone in the whole camp? I know the house phone works as Josh called yesterday and so did Jeff, so I got to speak to dad.

Plan today is to take a taxi to the old town and wander around, market, giant incense burner, etc follow the guide I downloaded to my phone. Ok let's see how today pans out, I'll mail again later.

Let me know what time to expect you tomorrow. x

There was nothing from him that night, but first thing the next morning, he had mailed to tell me he had been bumped off the flight, his seat taken by a senior manager, at the last minute. We should now expect him the following day. Needless to say, I was upset, my disappointment compounded by the poor communication. Had he even tried to call? Or had he avoided it to prevent any potential confrontation over his delayed return? I had received a call from my friend Astrid back in the UK the previous evening, so I knew my UK mobile was working OK.

I mailed him back and asked him to confirm:

Do you know for definite you are on the plane in the morning? If that falls through can you come by car?

Inevitably, I did not receive an answer.

We met our friends at the Souk and it was so lovely to see them again and to meet Julie and her family, their friends who had travelled with them from Qatar. At one of the souks many jewelry stores I fell in love with a chunky silver bracelet, with large citrine and amethyst stones. but at £150 it was out of my price range, but it was so 'my style'. I teetered but thought it best to leave it behind. We had a very long lunch in a café at the entrance to the souk that served the best warm hummus with pomegranate and hot almonds I have even to this day ever tasted.

Sam was hoping to get transferred to Muscat from Qatar in the new year and their positive first impressions meant they were keen for the move to happen. That would be fantastic, I thought, I would get to see them whenever I visited, and I was sure Sam and M would resume their golfing partnership at the earliest opportunity. It would be good for M, who seemed lonely, as he never once mentioned any friends or even a work colleague who he saw socially. While the wall fans whirled loudly and circulated the warm air around us, we talked and laughed and shared our news. I probably spoke the most as I had only had Seb to talk to in the last few days. This was the highlight of the trip so far, and we agreed to meet once M was back on the 28th at the house of their friends Sarah and Ali.

I was determined to cook the Christmas dinner as planned, more for Seb now than M, who I was annoyed with, as rightly or wrongly I felt he could have made more of an effort to get in touch with us. My annoyance was partly fuelled by having spent time with two such lovely and close families the previous day. I was envious as it was what I had wanted for us, being together as a family on this trip. It just seemed wrong that we had travelled all this way only to be further separated. We decided to walk what we thought was the short distance to the supermarket except it was a lot further and in 30 degrees heat, not a pleasant task. Somehow, we found the only frozen turkey breast in the welcome coolness of the freezers. There were no taxis on the road, so we had no option but to walk back in the searing heat, this time laden down with shopping. We could certainly justify our detour to the ice cream parlour again.

An email the following day said he was definitely coming back but would have to go straight to the office – he would be home around 6.00pm. I was not impressed, why did he have to go to the office? Surely, he should have been coming straight back to us. I rescheduled our meeting with Vicky and Sam until the following day as we were going to sit down as a family and eat that bloody Christmas dinner.

We cut short our time at the beach so I could start the cooking, not an easy task as I then found out the oven didn't work. The turkey breast obtained under such duress had to be chopped up and fried, along with the potatoes that were meant for roasting. By the time the meal was ready I began to wonder why I had bothered, it bore no resemblance to what I had intended, but we still had the Christmas pudding and custard to save the day. M returned without ceremony and was in a foul mood which he blamed on being away from us at Christmas and not being able to talk to us. He felt he had badly let us down, yet again. I couldn't disagree because he had, but I realised I felt more frustrated about the situation as opposed to feeling angry towards him. After all, I had no reason to doubt him, aware the internet and phone access were poor having just experienced it in the apartment.

However, had I stopped to question the communication problem at that time I might have been suspicious that it didn't add up. Given that he had replaced someone removed only days before his arrival and he had taken over his workspace, why wouldn't he have had a phone or known his extension number? The office was well-established, as was the project, run by the country's own oil company so there had to have been a competent communication system to enable the project to function as effectively as it did.

After dinner, we opened our presents. Seb was happy with more games and some new T shirts, and he still had a few small gifts waiting at home. I had given M new running gear, a Thomas Pink shirt and a few little bits and pieces. I opened my Pedro Almodóvar DVD from Seb and waited for my gifts from M. He handed me what was obviously a CD and four separate packages, the three bottle-shaped gifts were Clinique skin products, the fourth was the gift bag they had obviously been purchased in. I was disappointed, he knew I hadn't used Clinique products for years, and was that it? Nothing else? He became agitated and reminded me we had agreed not to spend much on presents, yes, well all the more reason to ensure they were thoughtful gifts I told him. He lost his temper, raised his voice and asked where I thought he would be able to buy gifts in the desert. I didn't, I told him, but the main shopping mall was easily comparable to any European mall, he could have made more of an effort, especially as this was the first Christmas in 16 years that we had not spent together. This behaviour was so unlike him. This is what we had waited for him to come back from the desert for? This trip was going from bad to worse.

The following day was the weekend, fortunately, or I am sure he would have gone into the office. We went for a drive into the desert and had a race up the sand dunes. It was impossible for me to beat him, even if I had been capable of doing so. He was so competitive that I wouldn't have been surprised if he had been practising. We set out our picnic and camels came close; this was what the holiday should have been like from day one, I mused. We met up with Vicki and Sam that evening and had a good time. M planned to meet up with Vicki and Sam again once when they had relocated to Muscat, but that meeting actually took place a long time after it should have done and in the most precarious of circumstances.

We went bowling again, although now Seb complained of M's competitiveness, which spoilt his fun. We went to the cinema, to the beach and ate out, and the remaining three days passed too quickly. On my last day he suggested I return to the souk to buy the bracelet I had wanted as my Christmas present. He gave me his card to withdraw money from the cashpoint, but it didn't work. I had written the wrong PIN, so I paid for it myself, in fact, I am still waiting for him to give me back the money.

We had planned to talk, but the mood wasn't right. M declined on the basis that he wanted to enjoy the limited remaining time we had together and did not want anything else to mar it. I was relieved, as neither did I, lacking the energy to deal with anything more. When we left after New Year, we had expected to see him at home on leave in February, and then Seb and I were scheduled to go to Muscat for the Easter holidays. More regular contact was exactly what we all needed, but it was the opposite of what actually happened.

The day after we had returned home Seb told me that Essi had posted on Facebook that she was travelling to Oman the following week. This was news to me; M hadn't mentioned it. When I asked him, he told me they had only just discussed it that day. She needed time out as she was in a quandary, unsure if she should stay in Leeds at her bar job as this helped her save money toward her Australia trip planned for later that year, or accept an offer of a marketing job in London on a salary that would not enable her to save, but would look good on her CV. He thought a break would do her good and, after all, he did not see her at Christmas.

I was confused as I was under the impression he would be heading back into the desert and was therefore concerned for Essi, left alone in Muscat, with a poor internet and phone service. What if something happened? But it transpired he would now only be away for a few days in the three weeks she was to spend there. I emailed her the guidebook and she used it to go to the souk and other sites; she too had bought some Omani silver jewellery. I was surprised when she told me she had signed up for a three-day diving course; from experience I knew that most of her water-based activity was sunbathing and drinking poolside cocktails. I did ask how handsome the instructors were though, and she had replied that "they would do."

We spoke several times as the house phone was now working, and Essi told me she was enjoying herself. M had taken her to Dubai for a weekend where they had gone shopping and she had bought some swimwear and make up. I did wonder what else?

Essi told me she would take the job in London having negotiated a rise in salary of several thousand pounds, which I very much doubted given that this was her first proper job and that her role was selling advertising space for a hotel chain. I believed that was their 'own code' for dad having agreed to cover the rent, a decision made without consultation with me, of course, as it was Essi, and this is what he did. It didn't seem as if he had made too much effort to change his behaviour as he had promised to do just two months before. What other promises was he going to break?

Chapter 4

Our planned Easter trip to Muscat was cancelled as M had to travel to Australia for work; his plan to detour home on his return journey did not materialise either. He eventually arrived home mid-May (2012) and while we didn't manage to have our usual romantic get-away we spent a lot of enjoyable time together, but in spite of that I still had a niggling feeling that something was not right, I couldn't put my finger on it, but he didn't seem to be one hundred percent present. I thought it might be the aftermath of the emotional pressure he had been under given the pre-Christmas episode, as we still hadn't had much opportunity to talk about it any further, partly, because he continued to shut down my efforts to do so. I decided not to challenge, I would wait and see what happened.

On the final weekend of his leave, he had planned a walk on the North Wales coast, it was an unusually hot day, and as we sat on a group of rocks to have our picnic lunch, he edged closer. He peeled the shell from his boiled egg and asked if I had any salt; while I looked, he told me, almost matter of factly, that he was not coping well. All of those little boxes in his head were now wide open and despite trying as hard as he could to close the lids, they refused to stay shut. His head was always buzzing, alive with constant noise, he was desperate for quiet. He was caught, he explained, in a whirlwind of guilt and self-loathing, spinning him round and round, he could not break out of it. He felt our marriage was squeezing him further, he felt trapped and spoke again of feelings of inadequacy as a husband and father, it seemed he had made little progress in coping with his demons since he had first shared them seven months ago.

I suggested that he stayed home, delayed going back to work, got some psychological support and again considered starting on antidepressants, but he rejected the idea and insisted he had to go back. He elucidated further that while work was stressful it was what kept him sane. But, he continued, he felt caught in a situation he had no right to be in, because he was so hopeless at it, and once again, he asked for a divorce. He needed, he said, to be free of the marriage. According to him, divorce would give him the freedom to deal with the turmoil in his head compounded by the sleepless nights and the ever-present anxiety without the continuing worry of what he might do wrong, how he might harm and hurt me again.

It seemed he had fully researched the options; we could go for a quickie divorce on the grounds that we had lived apart for two years even though that wasn't true. For us, he explained, as a couple getting divorced would not mean we were splitting up, we wouldn't even separate, we would stay together just as we always had been. He continued, between mouthfuls of food, that he felt getting divorced would probably bring us closer together than we had ever been. I could not comprehend his train of thought, I had to suppress a smile as it all sounded crazy, well to me anyway. He told me we must agree to never, ever tell anyone we were divorced, not family or friends and certainly not the children. He insisted his plan would work, there was no reason for it not to, our family life would continue in exactly the same way as it always had, nothing would change at all: except that we would no longer be married. He seemed to presume that I would be in total agreement with his proposal; at no point did he ask what I thought about it. On reflection, it seemed as if he had read from a script. His speech was without emotion; I felt he didn't need to engage with me on the issue, it was a monologue, and he could tick the box that it had been done.

As he bit into his apple he expounded further on his internal battle, how he had tried so hard to work towards never keeping secrets from me again, how difficult it was for him, but yet he knew it was within his capabilities, it would be possible, the sense of freedom he would have after we divorced would enable it. He would no longer feel the need to lie as an act of defiance or rebellion anymore, the divorce would enable honesty and conviction.

I was baffled. What was wrong with him that he thought this was a reasonable request? That he could ask me to get divorced while he bit into his unsalted boiled egg? That between the crunching of a salt and vinegar crisp I would learn that nothing would change except we would no longer be married. Did he really think this was a scheme I was going to agree to? It made no sense to me; try as I did, I could not rationalise it. Was he that mentally unwell that he thought this would be acceptable to me? I hadn't responded to him and he had not requested that I did. I packed up my uneaten lunch, climbed down from the rocks and walked off alone along the beach. Within minutes there was a crunching of stones behind me, he had caught me up and took my hand. I turned to look at him, he responded by planting a kiss on my cheek, what was he playing at?

Knowing the lengths he would go to to avoid confrontation, I had to consider if he had met someone else, with whom he wanted to be so badly that he was prepared to divorce me for her? However, I dismissed that notion; given the 'low' he was in, I doubted that he would have the emotional capacity to be involved with another woman. But I had to ask as it seemed the only plausible reason for his odd behaviour. I told him that if this was the case, he would only have to say it once and that would be it, he could have his divorce. But yet again, he categorically denied there was anyone else and re-iterated how much he loved me, and that nothing in our lives would change. I had to accept that it was his state of mind, his low self-esteem and despair that was the trigger for this bizarre request. When I thought about it how could he divorce me for someone else and still maintain our normal relationship, our marriage? Unless of course he planned to live a duplicitous life? As he wasn't managing this one so well, I knew that would be beyond him.

He again emphasised that I had to agree never to discuss 'the divorce.' It would be our secret as apparently it would reflect badly on him. He had to remain protected from his family who had always, he now saw fit to tell me after 17 years, believed our marriage would be short-lived, and that he had only married me in the first place to upgrade his living situation in Lagos.

On that beach, still hand-in-hand, I allowed myself in that moment to consider, is this what I really wanted? A husband that I now saw so infrequently, whom I spoke to less on the phone for a variety of reasons, and while we still texted and emailed as much as we always had, there had definitely been a shift in our relationship. I had accepted that he had prioritised work over family, and gone along with it to ease the pressure he was already under and as I now understood, he may well have done that not only due to the demands of the job but because it also 'kept him sane' As he was so unwilling to get the help he so desperately needed, when or how was this ever going to end?

The situation was taking its toll on my mental health too. I worried about him constantly, I worried about Seb, as M had, in reality, been very much the absent father that past year. I made a split-second decision to call his bluff and if that didn't work then maybe I should consider separation if not divorce. It was obvious that something had to change. I had shocked myself that I would even contemplate that, but I had the sudden realisation that he was dragging us all, including Josh and Essi, into a state of emotional turmoil, I couldn't let that happen, I had to stay strong to support them all.

"If you still love me as much as you always have, and you only want out because you don't feel worthy of the marriage then you have to think of the implications. Because if we get divorced then we will be divorced. I am not going to divorce you and then continue to live with you as husband and wife. I would not be willing to keep it a secret, especially from the kids. They would have to know the truth."

No reply.

I tried to stay calm as I asked:

"Are you seriously telling me that you would lie to them to save your reputation with your family? Think about the impact such a lie would have on them if or when they found out, because they would find out. Have you thought about that?"

No reply.

"I will do whatever I can to support you and to make you feel better and recover from this low that you are in, but I am not doing that. It's up to you to decide, if you have any other reasons for asking for divorce now would be the time to tell me."

I don't know if his reply was an attempt at emotional blackmail or a plea for help, but I was deeply troubled by his response.

"But you need to understand this," he said as I recall, so this is not precisely what he said, word for word, but rather as I remember it, "if you don't agree to the divorce it's ok, but one day I will get on a bike and ride off into the desert, and I'll keep going until the fuel and the water runs out, and that will be it. You will never see me again. I mean it, I have thought about it and planned it, I know just what route to take, I've plotted it on a map. I will probably never be found, and you'll always wonder where I am. But you'll never see me again."

Back in the car, I was driving but found it difficult to focus, I was so distracted, neither of us spoke. Although, by the time we had picked up Seb, M's whole mood had changed, and he was chatty and suggested a takeaway for dinner as it would spoil the relaxing day if I had to cook. Relaxing day? I barely slept that night as I replayed the conversation in my head, I was no closer to making sense of it. Two days later he was gone, no further discussion, I was so confused. I had not seen this side of him before and I didn't know how to handle it, especially as he continued to further reject all my efforts to help. I was now trying to deal with my own inner conflict too, reluctant to admit it but I knew my feelings towards him were changing.

He had promised he would try to bring his next leave forward to be home for my birthday in July. I didn't hold out too much hope and true to form it didn't happen. However, he did surprise me with a gift of an iPad, in a hot pink leather cover and the biggest bunch of white lilies he had ever sent me; his thoughtfulness made my day. Foolishly, I allowed this to reassure me everything was OK, and I found myself looking forward to seeing him in the next few weeks.

Two days later, a Monday, he called to ask me if Stella, his sister, could borrow our

Range Rover as her car was off the road and she needed transport for work. I was using it that weekend as I was taking Seb and his friend on their annual activity week holiday. We always took the Range Rover for the space and the built in sat nav, I would manage to get lost if I wasn't using it, so daren't be without it. He assured me that she would return it in time, for the Friday evening, but he knew as well as I did that she could not be trusted. Earlier in the year she had borrowed it ostensibly for a few days, but it was not returned for three weeks, and only then after I had asked him to intervene as she had ignored my texts and calls. And as a result of that I had to let a friend down for whom I had promised to help shift furniture. One day I came home from work to find the car, minus the keys, on the driveway. Once again, she failed to respond to my attempts to contact her, not even when I lied and told her I had misplaced my keys and needed the set in her possession to drive the car. M had told me he would chase her, but he hadn't and somehow the issue got buried under all the other goings on.

So, I told him "No," to the Range Rover which we had bought in his name, but she was welcome to borrow my Chrysler, a much smaller and older car. He tried to persuade me with arguments that were easily counter balanced, for example, she has never driven my car before, but I told him, it's the same as driving a rental car, she wouldn't have driven that before either. He was not happy, but then nor was I. Why did I have to defend my position to drive my own car to get our son and his friend safely and comfortably to their destination against loaning the car to his sister for what I suspected would become an indefinite period?

He snapped back "Well, I will have to hire a car, then won't I? How much is that going to cost?"

"Why do you need to hire a car for Stella? She has the offer of a car, if she doesn't want it then it's up to her to hire a car. I'm not paying for a hire car for her," reminding him that it was our money he was offering to spend.

"Why? Because I told her she could have it, I didn't think you were going to be so selfish."

Oh, so, this was him changing his behaviour was it, not doing or agreeing to do things for his family without discussion?

"Well, you can say what you like." I told him, "the answer will remain no, if she changes her mind tell her to ring me."

I ended the call before I said what I really wanted to say: "Fuck off."

Knowing she still had the car key, I went straight to Halfords and bought a steering lock, it seemed extreme but inherently I knew I was right to distrust her and reluctantly, I had to admit, I did not trust him either. I suspected he would be too spineless to go back on his word and tell her she couldn't take the car, and when she did, he would try to explain it away as a misunderstanding. My mother-in-law had spare house keys and she spent a lot of time with Stella. I was unsure how abstract my thought processes were, but I called a locksmith and had the porch lock changed, my perceived level of suspicion ran high. I did not want them in my house. I would simply tell M when he came back that I had lost the door key.

During the following months he came home several times but for short periods only: trips tagged on to the end of travelling for business or else planned two weeks leave would be cut short as he was recalled to the office earlier for an important work issue. We would fall into the same routine we always had when he was home: I was aware he was still not completely present as I fought my internal conflict. I tried to deny that my feelings were no longer of an all-consuming love as opposed to a love that was borderline and could go either way. I had sought counselling and had finally met a woman who challenged me exactly how I needed to be challenged.

After several sessions she drew on a flip chart a Venn Diagram and suddenly it all became clear: the visual impact of the three separate components of M's life; Essi and Jane in one circle, his mother and siblings in another and me, Josh and Seb in the third circle. It was true, for the first time I understood, this was how he justified doing what he does, how he dealt with us all as if we were isolated entities, the extended family totally disjointed, his whole world (or what I knew of it) was fragmented, and he was the common denominator to us all. How had I never seen this before?

December was approaching, the secret divorce plan had never been mentioned again, however, no matter what happened I had the feeling that this Christmas holiday was make or break time. We had to tackle all of the outstanding issues once and for all, no excuses, no retractions, no whahala, it would be difficult but had to be done. It was fortunate that his mother was going to Germany to spend Christmas with his brother John who lived there and that Essi was in Australia, so it was agreed that this year we would skip his family converging on our house on Boxing Day, as they did every year. What a relief. We would have a quiet family Christmas at home with Josh too. I so hoped that for Seb it would make up for the previous Yuletide disaster in Oman.

M was due back on the Saturday 22nd December, so he would have flown out the exact same date that we had arrived in Oman the year before. Two weeks prior to when he was due home, just when I was patting myself on the back for being so organised, the presents bought and the bulk of the food in the freezer or cupboard, the horrible emails started.

Accusatory in nature: "why hadn't I filed for divorce? Our marriage was over. How many times did he have to tell me! Why was I so thick that I couldn't understand that?"

Here we go again, I thought, what is it about the lead up to Christmas? On the phone he told me he was no longer in a 'low' but rather a full-blown depression, he was so full of anger he felt he would explode. He didn't feel he could come home, he feared a breakdown and wanted to protect Seb.

"Come home" I told him, "You have to come home."

I offered to make him an appointment with the GP for the 24th but he declined. However, he finally agreed to look for a counsellor in Muscat, a huge sigh of relief, as he had finally acknowledged he needed to talk to a professional. Time was running out though, he had to come home; for his sake and Seb's, I would do whatever it took. I contacted a recommended solicitor and made enquiries regarding a divorce application and told him so. At this point I was not seriously planning on pursuing the action but would use it to coerce him into coming home, if I had to, if that was what he really wanted. My own feelings were cast aside as I was now more concerned about him than ever before. After many, many emails and telephone conversations he agreed he would come home after all; I was aware how carefully I would have to tread, but I was prepared to do whatever it took.

The morning of the 22nd, the tree was up, decorations hung, and I was in the car park of Marks & Spencer loading the car with the last few Christmas necessities and then would go on to the airport to collect him. I put his favourite Danish on the passenger seat alongside a bottle of juice and told myself it would be OK; we will get through this. My phone rang, it was his Omani number, was his flight delayed? I was acutely aware that for the first time ever he had not texted on departure, but no it was worse than that, he hadn't taken the flight, he hadn't even gone to the airport. The line was awful, there was a lot of background noise, in desperation he had contacted a relationship counsellor at the Relate organisation and spoken to a counsellor for several hours on the phone the day before, she had advised he should not come home. She agreed his fear that he would have a total meltdown in front of Seb was enough to prevent him from flying as it would only add to his already overloaded stress levels.

"So, you are ringing me now as I'm on my way to the airport to pick you up to tell me? Why didn't you ring me last night, I might have been able to persuade you to come? You need to be at home, not alone in Oman."

"I kept thinking about how badly I let you both down last Christmas, I feel like if I was at home now, at Christmas, I would hate myself even more, and I would lose it and it would all spiral further and further out of control."

"So, come after Christmas then, come on Boxing day or the 27th if you have to, you just need to come home" I pleaded.

I felt relieved as he agreed he would be here on the 27th, he would tell Seb work had once again prevented him from coming as planned. He would only be a few days late, but this year we would not postpone Christmas; Josh, Seb and I would still celebrate on the 25th.

I called Isabel that afternoon. I wasn't sure when she had left for Germany; she didn't seem to answer my calls very often, but I wanted to find out if M had spoken to her, and if so, how he seemed and what was her take on her son's mental state. This time she answered, I noted it hadn't rung with an overseas tone, she was at home she told me. I didn't follow up on the Germany trip, my only concern was M. Had she spoken to him? How did he seem? She sounded unconcerned, he was busy with work, otherwise he seemed fine. I didn't want to alarm her, so I told her he seemed a bit low and that he was now not coming home for Christmas, her reply:

"Well, you will have to get used to that won't you? Being alone at Christmas."

I asked her what she meant by that comment, but she evaded the question and spoke of some mundane issue that I had no interest in. I terminated the call as soon as it was polite to do so. What did she mean, I would have to get used to it? "Being alone?" What did she know that I didn't?

M had done as I had asked and emailed Seb, but not until two days later, it was a long, tedious email which described the responsibilities and demands of his role to justify his failure to be with him at Christmas yet again. He told Seb to pack up his bedroom so as soon as he was back on the 27th he would move him into what had been Josh's much bigger room.

When I told him, Josh had already moved Seb, re-run cables and set up his TV on the wall, he was livid as he said, "that was my job," well, as I told him "not when you are not here it's not."

But 27th December came and went without M, as he remained in Oman. The reason this time round was the pressure of work, and his compulsory attendance at a meeting on 2nd January, so he would postpone until later in January. We slipped back into our regular pattern of texting and mailing, and I tried not to dwell on it, but I was not happy.

In mid-January, we lost a precious, young, family friend, and Josh, Seb and I were all feeling incredibly sad and upset. I also had important exams looming, I felt anxious when he, with only a few days' notice announced his planned arrival. I asked him to postpone, as I could not face dealing with him and whatever psychological baggage he would bring with him; we needed to get through the following few weeks without any additional potential aggravation. But he came home regardless for what transpired to be the last time he ever did.

Chapter 5

This day was one of those which started out with a plan that could not possibly go wrong, or so I thought. We woke early, as we always did, in spite of it being the weekend. While he had the capacity to sleep on, I have always felt compelled to jump up as soon as I open my eyes. I was intent on tackling him about his depression. I knew it would be difficult for him to engage, but enough was enough, the impact his behaviour had had on our relationship the past year had been, I now believed, possibly beyond repair. It had to be tackled now before it was too late, no matter how uncomfortable.

"I'll make coffee" I said, "I'll bring it up because I really think now is the time to talk about your depression, Seb's asleep, we have a few hours before we have to think about the rest of the day."

I thought if we stayed in bed, he would feel more relaxed and amenable, not so threatened in the more intimate environment, that he would open up more easily. But he was having none of it though; he was straight up out of bed, jeans on, top on.

"I told you I don't want to talk about it."

"I know you don't, I know how difficult it is for you, but we have to talk about it or it's not going to change, it's not going to get any better. This has gone on for over a year and you are no further forward, if anything, you are in an even more disturbing place." I could hear myself as if I were on repeat mode.

"I've got things to do."

"At quarter past six in the morning?"

"Yeah, I am going to my mother's and I need to do some work before I go."

"Really? I thought you were spending the day with Seb and then tonight we were going to have a family dinner?" He knew this, why did I have to tell him what we had agreed the day before, it was straightforward after all?

"Yeah, well plans change," he said.

"No, they don't," I challenged. "Not when it means letting Seb down yet again. It's obvious you're just saying that because you don't want to talk. How much longer do you think you can put this off?"

"Why would I want to talk to you? I'm not one of your patients, I've spoken to the counsellor at Relate and I'm doing what she told me I need to do. Not what you want me to do."

I doubted he had spoken to a Relate counsellor when he had first told me and after he failed to appear at Christmas I had called Relate. My suspicions were confirmed as they do not offer telephone consultations to clients whom they have never met and who live 3,000 miles away.

"So, what else did she tell you to do then, other than not come home to your family at Christmas?"

I was wound up, but I didn't care, he was not going to put himself before Seb yet again. I tried hard to keep my cool and explained that the upset at Christmas caused by his failure to come home, coupled with his prolonged absences and short visits, was not good for any of us.

"It's work" he replied, "I have to work to maintain this house, pay the bills, do you think I want this? There are no jobs out there, the oil industry is shot, it's not my fault if I can't take my holidays is it? They say work and I have to jump."

"But it's written into your contract so of course you can take your holidays; I think you chose not to come home at Christmas."

I could sense his irritation: "I couldn't come at Christmas, I had a big contract to finish, you have no idea do you, you forget they're all Ragheads, what do they care about Christmas?"

I hated that expression, 'Ragheads,' which referred to the Keffiyeh, the traditional male headwear.

"I thought you couldn't come at Christmas because you were too depressed, remember the Relate counsellor told you not to? Yet you just said it was due to work, were you lying?"

He walked out of the bedroom and slammed the door behind him.

'Oh no matey, you're not going to walk away from this,' it was obvious he was lying about something as he had changed his story. I followed him downstairs into the kitchen and closed the door behind me. I could guess how this was going to pan out and I didn't want Seb to hear any of it. M was sitting at the kitchen table drinking his coffee. I sat opposite him.

"What did you mean" I asked, "that you had a big contract on at Christmas? Are you lying, and playing the depression card with me, because you knew that would give you the OK to stay back in Muscat?"

He stared at me, with that familiar expression of, "do you think I'm going to bother to answer that? It doesn't suit me too, so I'll just ignore you."

"I'm asking you" I continued, "this is really important. It's not just about Christmas, it's about the whole of this last year, you're not the same, something is going on and you need to tell me about it, because this can't carry on. I'm not having you cancel visits, or let us down, like at Christmas, and I'm not having you hardly see Seb. I don't believe it's all work or depression, I am beginning to think it's your choice. You've had bouts of depression or lows before and you know the way out, you know what you have to do. I'm here, but it seems like you don't want to be helped through it this time. You are being incredibly selfish; you don't give a damn about the impact it has on us. I know it's difficult. I know I'm being confrontational, but you need a boot up the arse to deal with this because you're not going to deal with it yourself, are you? You haven't seen Seb for months on end, yet you are going to spend time with your mother instead of spending time with him like you promised. I know why, because she won't challenge you, she'll make it OK, but it's not OK is it?"

The rhetorical question was answered.

"I've not got time for this" he said, "I'm going to my mother's and she is expecting me." His voice was raised, I could anticipate he would try to shout me down.

"Your mother is expecting you at 6.45 in the morning'? And what about Seb?"

"Well, I'm not spending the day with him, now am I?"

"So, what are you going to tell him then? That you are going to go to your mum's instead of spending time with him?"

"That's what I just said wasn't it?"

"Well, while you are there ask her what she meant when she told me we will have to get used to being alone at Christmas, because that's what she said when I called her to tell her you had cancelled your trip home for the holidays?"

"She never said any such thing, she said it's a shame you are alone this Christmas!"

"And you would know what she said would you? better than me? Even though she was talking to me when you were in Oman or were you in two places at once?"

He was angry now, he would have taken that comment as a criticism against his mother, in spite or that not being my intention.

This conversation was going nowhere, and I had really had enough of him and needed to tell him. So, I did.

"If you choose to walk out of this house and go to your mother's then don't come back, because if you think your mother is more important than your son and you're going to let him down again, then you don't belong here. He is better off without you, like he has been for almost the past year."

I meant it too, I had had enough. He was behaving as if he just didn't care about Seb and that was not good enough. Maybe it was his depression or maybe it was just him, but I couldn't hear the excuses any longer, Seb came first, and if he was really going to see his mother instead of spending the promised time with Seb, then he had made his choice, he had prioritised her over his only son. He was taking this stance to exert himself and his choice to do what he wanted.

"You still want that divorce? You can have it, all you have to do is go to your mum's and that will seal the deal," I said. "I've had it." I was crying, out of temper and frustration, but mostly because of my disappointment in him and his behaviour.

"Do it then," he shouted back at me, "as if I care? You'll realise what a mistake it will be to divorce me, you have had too much of a good thing going with me. Divorce me, as that would get me out of my depression straight away. Instant cure. You want to know what has caused my depression. coming home to you. I have it all day at work, you have no idea what it's like, I go back to an empty flat, I'm on my own, work, flat, work, flat. I come home on holiday and all you do is nag, nag, nag all the time."

Since he had arrived home, we had actually had a good time together and that is what made the situation so difficult, the ongoing conflicting emotions, the mixed messages, the yo-yo effect. But I was determined I was not going to allow myself to be manipulated anymore. I recognised this familiar game; we had played it too many times. Twist it all so I'm to blame for whatever situation he had got himself into.

"For once you are right" he shouted back, "we can't go on like this and I don't fucking want to go on like this. I asked you for a divorce last year and what have you done about it? Absolutely nothing. You said you would, and you haven't, you're a liar, you live in a fantasy world if you think I still want to be married to you. I've told you before one day I'll get drive into the desert and you'll never see me again. None of you will ever see me again. If that doesn't tell you what I think of all of you then what does?"

"Don't let me stop you," I said. I was aware how immature my response sounded but I was hurt by that last comment: All of you? Who was that? Me, Josh and Seb?

The rant continued: "Let's see how you get on without my money. How are you going to keep up with your friends without my money?"

"What? I pay for holidays, treats, I even sometimes pay for shopping, your money only pays the bills. I even buy the air tickets when we come out to you on holiday. If you earn so much money, why does it seem like we're always broke? We live off a bloody overdraft so really what is the point in you working away this time? Why are we overdrawn? Where does the money you get in Oman go to?"

He responded: "I'm not talking to you about it; I've had enough of you interfering with my life. I'm going to my mother's because that's the only place I feel comfortable. Can you imagine that? I don't even feel comfortable in my own house because of you."

He could not stop himself: "This is my house not yours, when we get divorced it will be you that leaves not me; I'll make sure of that."

He came closer, too close, and jabbed two fingers into my arm.

I retaliated with a comment I knew would rile him, "Really? Well and whose money bought this house'? It certainly wasn't yours."

I had put 75 per cent of the deposit down on the house, comprising the proceeds from the sale of my flat in London and money saved from my FCO job in Lagos. I had been well paid, and the many perks included free housing which enabled me to save what in my 'financial world' was a lot of money. He continued to feel emasculated by that and I knew he had never told his family. He had probably boasted that he had bought the house with minimal or no contribution from me. I wanted to hurt him for putting his mother before Seb, the bastard.

"When that comes out in the divorce, I'll probably get the house anyway." I told him, "So you can go and live with your mother, seeing as you prefer to be with her than us."

His anger was apparent. If this had been an animation a big black cloud would have been looming over him getting bigger and bigger.

"I'll never leave this house' he shouted back at me, "it's mine not yours. Just you wait and see, I will get this house, not you, you won't get one brick of it! You won't get anything of mine. I'll make sure of it."

It was time to get away from him as he wanted to escalate this to justify lashing out at me. I moved towards the kitchen door and turned the handle, but I had been too slow to recognise the threat. He grabbed me by my arm and swung me around violently. My left arm was flung across my chest, he seized my wrist, I tried to pull my hand away, but his grasp got tighter, he pushed my arm down, flush against the door, and he knelt against my right side pushing his weight as hard as he could against me. I tried to push him away with my left hand, but he grabbed my fingers and forced my hand back and my arm up until my hand was on my head; while squeezing my hand too tightly, he somehow grabbed a bunch of hair and pushed my head back against the door; again and again he banged my head hard against the door panel. His face was so close to mine and in an irrational, mad moment I thought he was going to kiss me! His face was bright red, foamy spit had gathered at the side of his mouth and that spit splattered on my face as he told me I "was a fucking bitch."

He turned his body to the left and his weight shifted. With a sudden jerk his left arm was up and his forearm under my chin; he leaned in pushing my head further back down the door. The side of his hand and his thumb were pressing further into my neck, my face was even closer now to his own, almost touching; I had no option but to look straight at him. His eyes were black and piercing, his mouth in a snarl, his neck veins were bulging. Who was this person? I didn't recognise him, not as M, not as my husband. He looked deranged. I knew I had to get him off of me. He was shouting, but I had no idea what he said. I don't think I heard him at the time. I only heard noise.

"Get off me, get off me," I said over and over again, sounding I knew, more desperate each time, and knowing that that desperation fuelled his power against me. He was pushing harder into my neck.

I was petrified of what was going to happen next. It was becoming difficult to breath, I couldn't swallow, panic was rising, I had to do something to get away from him. My right hand, as he shifted his position, was, I realised, free; I formed a fist, raised my arm up and swung it out and punched him hard on the left side of his head. It was enough; he stepped back, probably more from shock than from pain, as he wasn't expecting it. I took advantage and managed to push him away, I got out of the kitchen and ran up the stairs, convinced he was behind me. I slammed the bedroom door and shot the bolt. I listened but I couldn't hear him, it was quiet, I knew he would kick the door in if he wanted to, to get at me. He had done that before. I was shaking and crying and couldn't catch my breath. I had experienced his aggressive behaviour before but nothing on this scale.

I knew the way he had looked at me – had there have been a knife to hand he would have stabbed me, and I'm sure if there had been a gun to hand, he would have shot me, with no thought of the consequences, because in that moment he would have thought himself invincible, his power magnified by the physical abuse he administered. I had never seen him so enraged, so vexed; the hatred towards me had been palpable.

I looked in the mirror, there were red patches on my neck and visible finger marks around my wrist. I sat on the bed telling myself, 'get him out of the house, make sure that Seb is OK, and get rid of him.' I didn't sense that he was behind the door; he wouldn't have been able to contain himself if he was. Slowly I opened it and peered out, the landing was empty, I could hear the radio on downstairs in the kitchen. I put my ear against Seb's door, all quiet. Of course, it could only be about 7.00am.

'Let him go to his mother's, it's the best thing that can happen,' I reassured myself;

with my mobile under my bra strap for easy emergency access I, apprehensively, went back downstairs. The kitchen door was partly open, and there he was, stood behind the ironing board pressing a shirt.

"What are you doing?" I asked.

I should have predicted the sarcastic response: "Ironing my shirts, what does it look like?"

"Why are you doing that now?" I asked, incredulous.

"I'm packing; I am going to my mother's."

He was folding the ironed clothes into neat piles and systematically packing them into his suitcase. Thank goodness. 'Play it cool, be normal' I thought, he would be out of here soon enough. He was eating a piece of toast between ironing, he had deliberately left the butter knife in the marmalade jar, a pet hate of mine, it seemed it wasn't enough that he had tried to throttle me...

He had a routine of leaving his keys and wallet on the kitchen window ledge whenever he came in, regardless of whether he was back from a trip to B&Q or home from abroad, when he would add his passport to the bundle. Yet on this trip home he had failed to put his passport in the usual spot. When I had asked him where his passport was, he had told me it was in his backpack and he would get it, but he hadn't. I was suspicious, what was he hiding? A trip I didn't know about. I had to get to the bottom of it and had to find the passport before he left. In the dining room, in an otherwise empty holdall, were the Christmas presents from Seb and me. It was usual practice to bring an empty bag to fill with shopping to take back, although when I had gone shopping and asked what he needed he had told me 'nothing'. A quick look in his backpack and jacket pockets failed to produce the passport. It was obvious he had hidden it; it had to be in his hire car. I heard him go into the toilet, so I snatched the car keys from the windowsill, pressed the zapper to open the car doors, and quickly replaced the keys.

I watched him take his case into the dining room. 'He must be getting his things together to leave' I thought, 'it's now or never.' I went back out to the hire car; the boot was empty, nothing on the back seats, the door pockets, or in the glove compartment. Sat in the passenger seat, I pulled down the sun visor and saw him approaching in the rear-view mirror. He had his bags and jacket.

"What are you doing?" Before I could answer he ordered me "out!"

He threw his backpack toward the rear seat a little too far to the left, so it knocked me on the side of my head. I told him I wasn't budging until I found his passport and that I knew he had hidden it to conceal a secret trip.

"Have you been away with Tracey then?"

I knew that was not true, but I didn't know what else to say as I was now convinced, he was concealing something. I could have kicked myself for not searching for it earlier and brought myself back to reality. 'Focus, just get him to leave.' the voice in my head was telling me.

"Give me the house keys and I'll get out of the car" I told him.

"Why would I do that?" He looked genuinely puzzled by my request.

"Because when you leave, you're not coming back to this house. If you go, you'll never get back into this house again. I told you that before and I meant it."

He laughed, an authentic sounding laugh, as if he actually thought this was funny.

"I'll be back because it's my house," he replied.

"Give me the keys or I'm not getting out of the car."

He was standing in the driver's open doorway and made as if to throw the house keys over the railway track which ran behind the fence at the end of the drive. He must have realised he might not make the distance, so rather than lose face he put the keys into his pocket. He walked around the front of the car to the passenger side where the door was open, bent down, picked up snow and stones from the rockery and pelted me with both. I was wet, and the stones hurt. I was freezing cold as I was only in my PJs and a pair of flip-flops. I managed to slam the passenger door shut in spite of him pulling against me. I knew I needed to get out, the dynamics had changed again, and I was frightened he would come for me. What did it matter about the house keys? I could change the locks as soon as he had left. Within seconds, I hadn't even noticed he had moved, he appeared in the driver's seat, as I opened my door, he turned the key in the ignition, the engine was on.

"Get Out!" a voice in my head echoed with increasing urgency.

I had one foot on the icy ground and the other in mid-air in the process of stepping out when he started to reverse at speed. I was hanging on to the door handle and my left foot slipped on the ice. I was going to go under the car and as I couldn't stay upright, he would drive over me. The open car door caught on the garden railing; he braked before the door could be snapped off. I hit the ground and sharply rolled away, pulling my legs up towards the railings as he reversed down the driveway at even greater speed. As he turned on to the road the car screeched and sped off. Who knows if he ever looked back?

Momentarily, I couldn't move, despite the cold and the damp, I was incapable of picking myself up, until I suddenly remembered Seb's bedroom window overlooked the driveway.

"Oh, please don't let him have seen this" I spoke out loud.

When I got back in the house there was no sign of him, but I was sure the noise, especially of the car, would have woken him. I pulled my sweatshirt on and leant against the radiator for warmth, I couldn't stop trembling. I knocked on Seb's door and found he was watching TV. I told him dad had gone to grandma's and I wasn't sure when he would be back as we had had an argument. I tried to assess his reaction, whether he had seen or heard anything? He seemed nonplussed by the news and told me he would get up in a minute as he was starving. I couldn't gauge if he had witnessed anything or not, I wasn't going to push it though, I would see what transpired during the day.

I went into the dining room to check that M had taken everything with him so he would have no excuse to come back, but he had left a few things behind. Marzipan fruits were M's favourite sweets and it had become a Christmas tradition that Seb bought him a box every year. From the mess before me it was obvious, he had opened that box, tipped out the contents and trod them deep into the long woolly strands of the rug. His Terry's Chocolate Orange had been unwrapped, squashed underfoot, and smeared over the floorboards. The Morrissey CD Seb had also bought him was broken into several pieces yet had been carefully re-assembled like a jigsaw puzzle on the coffee table, the cover snapped in two. I turned to see Seb behind me. I explained dad had lost his temper with me and it seemed he had smashed whatever was close to hand. I told him how sorry I was, that this was a symptom of dad's depression, that he hadn't meant to do it, he should know how much he had loved his presents. I told him I was sure he would apologise when he came back, while I secretly hoped he would not be back. I told him to watch TV in the front room while I made him breakfast.

On the kitchen worktop I found a pile of bubble wrap and a torn cardboard gift box, while on the draining board there was an empty bottle. I recognised it instantly. Knowing how much M liked unusual whiskies, I had bought him a vintage bottle while in Edinburgh just before Christmas, matured in Jerez barrels for 12 years hence the costly price of £110. Forgetting I had flown up with only hand luggage I had to have it sent by special delivery which added to the cost. After claiming how happy he was with it, he had repackaged it to keep it to savour back in Oman, but it seemed his preference had changed as he had poured it all down the sink. He had found the time and the contemptible inclination to destroy Seb's Christmas gifts to him. I had reached breaking point, as if I needed one; the only way forward was to divorce him. It also confirmed what I already knew: there was something very, very wrong with him.

Three days passed with no word. While I didn't expect my usual wake up message or email, I thought he might have texted to tell us he was OK or maybe gone one better and said sorry. We had never, ever, in 18 years of marriage, gone this long without contacting each other. I didn't know why I worried about him after what happened, why should I care? But I couldn't help myself. There was a history of his aggressive behaviour, but nothing comparable to what had happened on the Saturday. I despised him for what he had done, our relationship had changed now forever; there was no glossing over this with excuses, pleading, apologies, remorse or gifts. There was no way I would ever forget or forgive this time. Making up was in the past and would stay there. No longer would he be able to convince me that it was my fault that an argument had started, that it was due to my behaviour, my wild imagination, my PMT or indeed his low mood which I had made worse by questioning or challenging him.

I had given up counting how many times had I told him that those incidents would chip away at our relationship, chip, chip, chip, until it altered its shape, its strength, its whole matter, until it altered the path that we could take together and indeed this is where we now found ourselves. Left with nothing but a bent and twisted frame, unrecognisable from what our love and marriage had been, it was now empty of all substance. That was it, the end.

So again, why should I care? Was he being non-responsive to spite me; he knew me that well, what buttons to push, that I would still worry about him, regardless of the circumstances under which he had left? Was it his mental health that made him behave like that? Or was he very much in control of his actions and this was an extension of his previous violent behaviour and anger? I genuinely thought at the time he was trying to kill me, and as such I couldn't comprehend how he would have acted that way without an invasive influence: depression? voices? could he be bipolar? An organic diagnosis might also explain his odd behaviour during the last year too, let alone the ironing and meticulous folding of his clothes after trying to strangle me. How would that have appeared on a Crimewatch reconstruction?

I had the option of calling Isabel to find out if he had gone there but I didn't want her to know what he had done, and I didn't want to speak to her anyway. I had just needed to know that he was safe, but nothing was going to stand in my way of applying for the divorce. I had tried calling his UK and Omani mobiles, but both went straight to voicemail. I had emailed with no response. On day four I decided if I hadn't heard from him after my morning clinic, I would have to act. I was exhausted, my whole being was preoccupied with reliving the assault; it was on replay in my head. Meanwhile I tried hard to keep a sense of normality at home. I had told Seb I had a feeling dad had been called back to Muscat again and was obviously still upset over our argument, hence he hadn't been in touch. What else could I tell him?

Chapter 6

There was still no word from him four days later, I was so worried; what if whatever had driven him to harm me might also be the cause of him turning in on himself? If I could find out if he had returned the hire car it would relieve some of my anxiety and give me an idea of what had transpired since he had left home, maybe even confirm that he had gone back to Oman, that he was safe. I decided to call the car hire company at Manchester Airport. I was lucky that a certain lady answered my call that day. It is only now that I appreciate the huge debt of gratitude I owe to her. The information she shared became, one year later, a game changer, and as such transformed the course of our lives forever, but at that time neither of us knew the significance and true value of our conversation.

I explained that my husband had hired a car on 22nd January and was not due to return it to the end of the following week, that we had an argument, that he had stormed out four days ago and had not responded to my efforts to try to reach him. I realised there was limited information given data protection that she could share, so to my shame, I played the depression card. I told her how his history of poor mental health was contributing to my concern and I was very worried he had come to harm; I hoped she could help me? Given the circumstances she would do her best to help, I was thankful. She could tell me she remembered M; she had rented the car out to him and also received it back on Sunday, his trip was cut short as he had been called back to work as a matter of urgency. Even in that situation, I thought to myself he had to try to make himself seem important, as if the woman at the car hire company cared.

"Do you know if he caught his flight?" I asked.

She couldn't be sure, but as the car hire company was off-site, she was able to confirm that he had taken the company shuttle bus back to the main terminal.

"How did he seem?"

She said, "he was chatty."

Indeed, he was. They had spoken about his previous car hire as she had served him then too and had recalled he had been very precise about the vehicle he had requested then: the newest and most luxurious car in their fleet. She had been curious to meet him after receiving his emailed request. That was the reason, she explained, that she had remembered him so well and had thought it odd that this time he had taken the most economical car in the fleet.

"The opposite end of the range from his Christmas hire," she elaborated.

He had explained that away by only having needed the current hire for the round trip to the airport and back as it would save him "messing around with a taxi."

I didn't understand what she was telling me, what Christmas hire? As far as I knew he had never hired from this company before and he was, of course, in Oman at Christmas.

"Are you sure it was him?"

"Yes, no doubt about it, he had definitely hired the BMW at Christmas. Mind you it was registered to a different address then, this time he registered the car to his mother's address, shall I give you that address?"

She was being so helpful.

"Yes please," thinking why would he register it to his mother's address and not ours?

The address she read out was actually our home address; she went on to give me his mother's mobile phone number which was M's UK mobile phone number.

She was in full flow now as she continued: "The address he gave at Christmas was a different one though; it was an address in Bromsgrove. Is that your address?"

"No, that's not me, I'm not in Bromsgrove." I had never heard of Bromsgrove.

"Would you like that address?" She asked.

"Oh yes please," she gave me the address along with the phone number he had provided on that occasion; it was his Omani phone number.

"Are you absolutely sure it was him at Christmas?" I asked, as none of this made any sense, I hoped she would tell me she had made a mistake, how could he have hired a car at Christmas when he was in Oman? I couldn't conceal the surprise in my voice, but it seemed, she hadn't noticed as she went on to share further information which verified it was him: he had used the same Omani bank card to make both bookings which were made via the same email account and his driving licence had been scanned into the system on both occasions; she readily reassured me that there was no doubt. Confused, I thanked her for her help several times over and ended the call.

I was in a daze, I seemed incapable of processing the implications of this newly acquired information against what I knew to be true: He had emailed, we had spoken, he couldn't come at Christmas because he was too depressed, to support that decision he had consulted a Relate counsellor who had agreed he should not travel, but it seemed he had come regardless? Maybe he had arrived and realised he couldn't cope and went to stay with someone in Bromsgrove? But who? I certainly didn't know anyone in Bromsgrove, but it was obvious he did. Trying to avoid the inevitable I ran a question-and-answer session in my head on every possible scenario, for example, had he booked the car in his name for somebody else? No, it was his licence that had been scanned. There was only one thing for it, I had to find out who lived at the Bromsgrove address, although I felt I knew the answer. It would be a female and he was having an affair with her. No wonder he was so resistant to talking to me about Christmas and his depression, what a bastard.

So, I went online to 192.com and readily paid the £19.99 to obtain a full summary of the occupants at that address. I was surprised that a couple and their teenage children were registered as living there, but maybe the husband had moved out? A landline phone number was listed, I had no choice but to call it, I had no idea what I would say if she answered and was hugely relieved when the phone went to answerphone. The recorded message said it was Donna and Mike's phone; it provided direction to send a fax or to leave a message, I assumed if Mike had left the marital home, surely, she would have removed his name from the answer phone? But I desperately needed to confirm that he was not having an affair and to do that I had to keep searching for more information, because that was exactly what it looked like. Mike wasn't on Facebook and a Google search drew a blank. I called my good friend Lucy to update her, she said she would check on LinkedIn and within minutes she called back to report she had found him, he was a director of an international contracts and construction company with offices in Muscat and Birmingham. A quick route planner search showed the Bromsgrove house to be only 25 miles from his office. That's it, I thought, that's the connection, he must know these people from Muscat, but it still didn't explain why he used their address.

The threat of the true circumstance and the real hurt that came with it, loomed large, whatever the reason he had been in England at Christmas. To conceal that had he gone through the pretence of calling us, including on Christmas day on his Omani mobile, he had mailed from his Omani work address, but worst of all, how could he have lied to Seb? I struggled with the idea that he had been in the country and not come home, as surely the one place he would have felt able to be, given his depression, was at home, not at a friend's house or a place to be all alone. But the other pressing question now was about his depression: was that a truth or a lie?

I went down to the beach and to the water's edge; as I walked there, I tried to decipher the truth from all that I had learnt that morning. His no show at Christmas, plus the car hire evidence that he was in the UK, coupled with the mystery woman in Bromsgrove and his aggressive and violent outburst, just the week before. It all had to be linked but I didn't know what to do or how to find out. But what I knew for sure was that our marriage was over; at least I had some direction to follow there. I called and made an appointment with William, my solicitor. I explained that I now planned to move forward with the divorce application, not on the basis of two years separation, which I confessed was not true, but rather on the basis of M's unreasonable behaviour, which unsurprisingly is the commonest grounds for divorce.

To my surprise it was suggested that I re-consider, as such action might displease or vex my husband and in retaliation he might turn off the money tap. Enforcement, if necessary, would be difficult with him being in Oman. But I was prepared to take that chance, as these may prove to be our final dealings with each other. I was determined to act honestly throughout the proceedings, as I hoped he would, but I soon realised how far honesty lay outside the scope of his conscience.

Examples were required to demonstrate he had behaved in such an unreasonable manner that I now found it intolerable to live with him and as a result the marriage had irretrievably broken down; well, that would be easy enough to prove, I thought. I cited his absences from the family home; Seb had seen his father for 31 days in the previous 14 months and that I had also just discovered that he was in England over Christmas and New Year while he had pretended to be in Oman and in doing so, had provided the most clear-cut example of how he had manipulated me. To say I no longer trusted him was an understatement.

I no longer believed his female friendships were platonic either. That notion had sat comfortably with me when I had faith in him, when I believed in him, when I loved him. But I could denounce him now for what I knew him to be, an unfaithful, heartless prevaricator who put himself before his children and wife. For what? Sex? Money? Who knew? But one thing I was sure of: the sooner we were rid of him the better. I had been quoted £2,000 as the cost for the divorce, which I couldn't afford, but I hoped I would be able to persuade M to pay for it.

He had finally got in touch via email to let us know he was back at work in Muscat. Oddly, given all that had transpired prior to his volatile departure, he had resumed his pattern of early morning mails. Had I chosen to encourage him I believe he would have continued to email me throughout the day, as he always did, as if what had happened between us was of no consequence.

Although I resented the idea of it, I knew I needed to keep our relationship as amiable as possible to facilitate the easiest way through this divorce. Also, at that point, I still held out hope that I would be able to encourage him to build on his bond with Seb; however, he still had to explain to his son why he had left him without saying goodbye, but he never did. In fact, that violence filled day was the last time Seb ever saw his father.

By mid-March, the relevant paperwork had been couriered to M in Oman, returned and submitted to Birkenhead County Court, and as a result the Decree Nisi was issued on 17th April 2013. This is the document that confirms that the person seeking a divorce is entitled to bring the marriage to an end once all the legal requirements to obtain the divorce have been met. Even though I had been the one that had applied for the divorce, to know it was now in progress still hit me hard. My stress levels were rising and were exacerbated by what followed.

I knew it was a crazy idea when it was inside my head, and when I had said it out loud it sounded even crazier:

"Vicki, I think my husband has married another woman!"

"What? What are you talking about?" I could hear the incredulity in her voice; I think she thought I had finally lost the plot.

The idea had taken shape during yet another night of fitful sleep. I had woken around 3am and joined that nocturnal group of menopausal and stressed women across the country who occupy those sleepless periods of late night and early morning. To entertain myself I flipped through updates on Facebook and drifted on to my soon to be ex family's pages. My niece Megan had posted a new profile picture of herself, sunbathing poolside, in front of an Arabic facade hotel; in the background I recognised what looked like the distinctive mountains that surround Muscat. I enlarged it and obtained a clearer image of the flag on the hotel rooftop; yes, it was the Omani flag. I wondered why she would be in Muscat. Additional new pictures included one with her mother Stella, in which they were both smartly dressed; Stella had an oversized fascinator perched on the side of her head. I associate such headwear with the races, christenings or weddings and I doubted she had attended either of the former, so I was curious about whom she would know in Muscat who had got married?

Teresa, another of M's sisters, had also added a new profile picture of herself too with her two daughters, Amy and Zoey. All three were also in party dresses, they stood in a lush, tropical garden. I searched for more information; Amy's account was private, but Zoey's page was open. She too had recently changed her profile picture to one of a pool surrounded by large palm trees; the backdrop looked very plush. The link to her Twitter page had several similar photographs, including one of parrots on the balcony of her room.

On 27th March, just three weeks before the Decree Nisi was issued, she had written she "would arrive there tomorrow." Two days later she had tweeted '*Hiya #sunshine #holiday #beach*' and added more palm tree pictures; she asked her followers "how sunny is it there?"

The next day she had tweeted that Louis from the group One Direction was staying at her hotel. A friend had asked if she was "getting ready for the wedding?"

She had replied "Yes I am."

She had posted again later that night and described her embarrassment at her mother's drunken Scottish dancing with even drunker men on the beach.

I questioned why his sisters and nieces would be visiting him in Oman, at Easter, during one of the hottest times of the year and when air fares would be in the higher price bracket, but I had the answer: for a wedding, Zoey had confirmed that.

I had the oddest feeling that I couldn't explain, and I tried to stop myself from going there, but I strongly felt that it was M's wedding, that he had married another woman in Muscat. I had no evidence or means of rationalising such a thought, which I knew was totally illogical, after all M was still married to me! We had been together just three months previously and I had only filed for divorce less than two months prior to his family visiting him. But no matter how hard I tried I couldn't shift that feeling.

I had momentarily floored Vicki with my comment that "I think my husband has married another woman." But she had quickly recovered and offered the explanation that Omani weddings often have several hundred guests and with true Omani hospitality, if it was known that M's family were visiting, given M had been invited, the invitation would have been extended to include them too. I accepted that explanation as it sounded a lot more plausible than mine, but in truth, crazy as it sounded, I was not entirely convinced.

I forwarded the photos to Vicki, and it was a case of instant recognition for Zoey's shots: the Al Bustan Hotel, one of, if not the most, prestigious hotel and certainly the most expensive in the whole of Oman. An average room cost several hundreds of pounds per night; a single glass of champagne was £26. She couldn't recognise Megan's location though; it was too nondescript. I wouldn't have been surprised if M had deliberately invited the five of them out to visit on an all-expenses holiday, he probably provided spending money too, so he could spend a chunk of our money on impressing his family with the added bonus of depleting his assets, and therefore, any share that I might receive. I knew they would not be able to afford a trip like that themselves. Teresa was a single parent and even if Stella could pay, he would not have allowed it, after all this was his ego trip, and he did have a history of throwing money at his family.

The other issue was why Seb had not been invited to join them as it would have been an ideal opportunity for him to see his father; he could have travelled out with them and had company if M had to work. So, I called M to enquire, why his family had been in Muscat at Easter and why Seb had not been asked? He was shocked to hear my voice, but more so by my question, and his response was to emphatically deny the visit. When I told him I had seen photographs his tone altered; he was wavering, and I could sense he didn't know how to play this. Should he be angry and try to shut me down or should he be nice in an attempt to control the situation? He asked again how I knew they had visited and if somebody had told me, as his family had severed all contact with me, I presumed because he had told them of our plans to divorce, I didn't know who the 'somebody' he referred to would be.

When I told him about the Facebook photographs, I heard that familiar sharp intake of breath through gritted teeth, an indicator of mounting anger. The dialogue that follows is again, as I remember it and believe it to be an accurate representation of what took place. He instantly went on the defensive; his voice became louder and he replied with a machine gun rattle response:

"Why shouldn't my family come out, I am not responsible for people choosing to visit Oman or visit me, I'm not going to question why they came, does my family need your permission to visit me?"

If I had responded it would only have fuelled his anger further, so I changed tactics and asked why Stella was wearing a fascinator. He lied when he said he didn't know what a fascinator was and followed the same pattern of the previous response:

"Surely Stella could wear what she wanted?" He told me he was not responsible for what his sister wore and asked, "What are you the clothes police now?"

I cut him short and queried why all the girls looked very dressed up and asked what his explanation for that was. He didn't have one and suggested that they must have been going out somewhere special. He pointed out he wouldn't know as he was not with them 24/7, as he had to work.

"I'm not as nosey as you, wanting to know everything about everyone."

I told him I knew he must have paid for the trip and asked how he justified putting them up at the Al Bustan when Seb and I were living off an overdraft. But apparently, they had not stayed at the Al Bustan, as he had accommodated them all in his apartment, with him, at which point I let the issue go as it was obvious that he was still incapable of giving honest answers.

I asked him why Seb had not been invited to join that trip; he told me that he knew such a request would be pointless as he could preempt my negative response, so rather than upset Seb he had chosen not to ask. So, he was the martyr to the cause, willing to sacrifice time with his son; I could imagine how he would have portrayed that scenario to his sisters. He had not considered asking Seb; if he had wanted to, he could have liaised directly with him without my involvement, nothing had stopped him from doing that other than his own selfishness. I was not economical in my response when I told him what a useless father he was; predictably he put the phone down on me. He had shut down this conversation as he had done throughout our marriage whenever there was an issue he wasn't comfortable with, or if he couldn't think of a good enough excuse to get himself out of a sticky situation.

I checked my emails from the time of the group visit; they were light-hearted, we had exchanged several emails a day and on 26th March he had sent me one with smiley faces. Each of his emails ended with a kiss, as did most of mine in my continued efforts to keep contact as cordial as possible; the content and tone of his emails were very much like the ones before the January incident. I had to play the game as that was what he expected; in the past when we had argued I was always the one who came back, to make it all OK again. Now it was a case of 'don't rock the boat', I certainly didn't trust him, and this incident gave me yet even more reason not to.

On 27th March, I had emailed the Form E which we both had to complete for the divorce settlement and listed the three options we had already discussed concerning the best way forward regarding maintenance and finances and asked:

"If you have time to consider, shall we talk about it on Saturday and you can let me know your preferred option?"

His response ran to two words: "Number 1."

I replied: "OK."

An abrupt change in attitude response; was it the content of the mail or was he too busy preparing for his family to arrive? He had mailed on the 28th to remind me of the poor wi-fi at the flat and erratic internet access on his phone and written:

"So, contact over the weekend might not be the best."

He had clearly planned to limit interaction between us while he was with his family. Family? Little did I know then just who was included in the family that weekend.

Intermittently, the notion that he had married another woman resurfaced from time to time in my mind, especially as he continued to become unnecessarily difficult. But I didn't share it with anyone as I was aware how insane it sounded. But it had found a place in my head where it had taken root, and while it never grew, it never went away either.

Part 2

Chapter 7

The next step in the divorce proceedings was for both of us to complete the Form E, which is a comprehensive form that sets out both parties' financial details including income, capital, and other relevant information evidenced by the previous one year's financial statements, and a schedule of outgoings and expenses also has to be included. There was a lot of work and effort ahead. The information supplied is used to inform an understanding of the financial position of both spouses and should, if completed honestly, enable a fair financial settlement. There is a duty to provide full and frank disclosure on the Form E, as it states, '*proceedings for contempt of court may be brought against a person who makes, or causes to be made, a false statement in a document verified by a statement of truth,*' the latter is signed when you complete your form.

To save legal costs M persuaded me it was in our best interests to complete the initial paperwork ourselves with the required supporting evidence, and after we had exchanged the forms, we could negotiate a mutually agreed financial settlement with legal input kept to the minimum, and therefore, at a more affordable cost. As a gesture of trust and commitment, I insisted that he send six months' worth of bank statements up front, before he had completed the form, and that if he failed to do so I would revert to William's advice which had been to make an application to court for a financial order. This, I believed, would show him that I meant business. As I couldn't trust him, I anticipated that he would fall short of my request.

I kept the knowledge of his covert Christmas activities to myself. My plan was to lull him into a false sense of security in the hope that he would slip up and I would be able to gain more information about the truth, as I would never hear that voluntarily from him. It was only when I was asked questions about M's income that the realisation hit me. I had never seen details of his contract, his salary or the bank accounts in Oman, I had just accepted all that he had told me. But for reasons I could not explain at the time, when he was last home, I had sneaked his wallet and taken photos of his debit and credit cards and been surprised to find a total of seven cards stashed there.

Predictably, the bank statements were not forthcoming as promised. He offered the excuses that the Omani Bank statements did not fit the parameters of his printer and apparently online access to his UK STE Bank was not possible in Oman. Disbelieving, I called the STE bank helpline to corroborate this and was informed that online accessibility was available throughout the Middle East. How gullible did he think I was? My offer to request hard copies from our local bank on his behalf went unanswered, so, as he hadn't actually said no and as I was becoming increasingly frustrated and suspicious by his delaying tactics, wondering what else he needed to conceal other than the Christmas trip, I decided to act.

I went to our local STE bank and explained, to keep the divorce confidential, that M needed one year's worth of account statements as his accountant could only accept hard copies. To circumvent the data protection issue I suggested they send them to the house so I could forward them on. The bank staff knew my husband worked in the Middle East, and I exploited that when I explained I was acting on his behalf as he was currently located in the desert with poor communication. I was far from comfortable in pulling the wool over their eyes, but from now on it was all about us: me, Josh and Seb. I had to play him at his own game or else I knew we would not get anywhere. It was agreed, I would receive them in the post the following week.

Ironically, the very next day, M emailed his downloaded copies without explanation as to how that had been achieved given that there was no online access, and interestingly the Omani Bank statements followed shortly after. That same day, on the way home from work, I received a call advising the hard copies were ready for collection; it felt like Christmas had come all at once! I was nervous, I would be foolish not to prepare for more revelations of dishonesty and cheating. With the large brown envelope in my hand, I rushed back to the car; it took a lot of self-control not to rip it open there and then but prepared for the worst I knew I had to wait. The short drive home, the coffee made, I sat at the kitchen table, "Here goes."

I remained sitting there for some time in a state of shock, it was far worse than I could ever have expected. I knew he was a liar, but this, this was beyond anything I could have anticipated. There in front of me, in black and white, was the evidence of M's trips home without our knowledge, not once, not twice but three times in the past one year. I could not believe what I was seeing, I had had no idea that he had lied to me for so long or why.

But it wasn't just me, it was Josh and Seb too, and goodness knows who else. I had so many questions but now, more than ever, I needed all of my self-control to not tell him what I really thought of him. I could not react no matter how much I wanted to call him and tell him what a lying bastard he was. This needed careful handling, no matter how hurtful these revelations were; I had to keep control.

I collected the online copies that he had mailed from my printer; even at first glance It was obvious that there were discrepancies between the two sets of statements, but how could that be? They would need to be forensically examined; I did not want to miss a thing; fortunately, Lucy offered to help. The next afternoon, in bookkeeper mode and sitting at her regular seat at my kitchen table, Lucy unpacked a notebook, coloured pens and the largest calculator I had ever seen. The drinks were poured, the chocolate digestives opened, and we got to work and began the comparisons. We cross referenced the statements, meticulously added up figures and created a spreadsheet. Our astonishment grew as we realised that to cover his tracks, he had removed all transactions pertaining to his clandestine UK trips and in addition concealed 75 entries and hidden transactions that totalled over £12,000.

He had made payments into two separate accounts in Essi's name in excess of £1,240, possibly to conceal funds? I couldn't be sure. But what was evident was that he had given her £500 at the same time as I had asked him to give Seb £200 to cover costs for food, drinks and spending money for his school trip to Russia, which he had declined to do on the basis that he could not afford it. He had sent only £120 and told me to make up the difference, yet another example of how he favoured Essi, then aged 23, financially over Seb and Josh.

He had made six further payments to his mother in random amounts which totalled over £2,300. I wondered if this had been to pay for the air fares for his sisters and nieces that Easter? To hide the accumulated total between his mother and Essi of over £3,550, he had to delete or alter other transactions to make the statements balance; for example, on the legitimate September 2012 statement a payment of £50.19 was drawn in favour of a hardware store whereas the same entry on the online statement had been altered to read £150.19.

Amongst the altered entries I recognised a legitimate one. I had passed my Diploma course in March and had unexpectedly received a vintage bottle of Lanson's, our wedding champagne, in a beautiful presentation box from M; the card read:

> *Congratulations. Keep this till I come home, and we will drink it together to celebrate your success. I always knew you could do it. Love Maurice.*

I had thought it an odd gesture and an even odder message at the time, but now?

On 26 July M had made a cashpoint withdrawal at a cashpoint in Birmingham, which was two days after he had requested that I loan Stella the Range Rover. I could see that that week he had stayed at hotels in the North West and at a five-star retreat, close to his sister's home. Further entries indicated he had remained in the UK for at least another ten days. So, the Range Rover would not have been returned by the Friday 26 July as he had promised, as it was now obvious it was never intended for Stella's use, but rather for his own use, which explained his anger at my refusal to loan it to her and his comment that he would *have to hire a car.* It was now apparent that Stella was involved in the deception, but why had they conspired together against me? What did it mean? The confusion I felt was overpowering, I could not comprehend that he had deceived us for so long and in such a horrible way. I kept asking myself the same question: why?

I checked our email correspondence from that time:

On 24 July he had written that he was *'angry and fed up'* with me and that the more he thought about it *'the less sense it makes, the only reason I can think of for you to say no to Stella is to get your own back for her not returning the car on time last time, pure vindictiveness. She has got to do a long drive and needs it more than you do, given you are only driving 50 miles. She knows she was wrong last time when she returned it late, why do you have to hold that against her?'*

Well, if she knew she was wrong, why had she never apologised to me or returned the key?

In another email from him on 28 July, 2 days after his actual arrival in the UK, he had described his business trip to a desert site via the town of Nizwa, and wrote he was surprised that it had only taken only a couple of hours, as he had thought it would take longer travelling on dirt roads. While in bed in the desert camp doing a crossword puzzle, according to another email, he had enquired after the weather *'is it still raining?'* yet according to the hard copy bank statement while in that desert bed he had simultaneously spent hundreds of pounds shopping in Gap, Levi's and Selfridges in Birmingham. On 1 August he emailed to tell me he had decided to work from home as he was exhausted after the desert trip, but according to the same bank statement he was in the comfort of a five-star hotel in Manchester at a cost in excess of £100.00 per night.

I had no need to check emails for memory prompts from the Christmas 2012 trip; it was still, unfortunately, all too raw. It transpired that he had actually arrived in England on 19 December, 3 days before I had been due to collect him from the airport. Reflecting on how he had duped us and put us through so much stress and unhappiness at that time was unfathomable. The day he had mailed Seb to explain why he wouldn't be home for

Christmas he was actually shopping once again in a Birmingham branch of Waitrose. He had done a large and expensive shop on New Year's Eve too, but his email on that same date was apologetic as he hadn't been in touch the previous day:

> *I haven't left the flat, I think I have Norovirus. I must have caught it from that one day business trip to Dubai, I'll mail you properly a bit later.*

But it seemed according to his authentic November STE bank statement he had made an actual 'trip' to Dubai within 24 hours of returning to Muscat after Essi's graduation. This was when he had told me he had to return to work the long weekend to make up for the time he had just spent away. He had spent in excess of £700 on a two night stay and a restaurant bill in a five star hotel. I somehow doubted he had indulged in such luxury alone.

The real bank statements listed on-line purchases from a well-known motorbike site just prior to that last visit to our home. Puzzled, I called the company and persuaded them, as my email address was similar to M's, to send me a duplicate receipt. Now I knew why he had kept his holdall empty and why he had to visit his mother that fateful day in January: the motor bike parts he had ordered had been delivered there. There were additional motorbike related purchases evident on the other statements too, yet I never knew for sure that he even had a motorbike, he had also failed to declare it as an asset on his Form E. He had spent in excess of £2000 on additional on-line and in store purchases during the same timeframe that I had been forced to manage the household expenditure by using the overdraft facility on our joint account. He had declined to clear the overdraft of three years standing on the basis that we could not afford it. He had also removed from the same bank statements monthly payments to yet another credit card, but this was one I was unaware he even had, and was one which he also failed to declare on his Form E.

Not knowing what to expect next we moved on to the Omani statements; the layout was unfamiliar to us as the financial transactions were recorded not only by date but also by time to the exact second. This system proved to be useful, as it quickly became apparent that at least four of the monthly statements, in spite of their looking very official, had also been tampered with.

In the May 2012 statement, a payment to a mobile phone provider for 12 Omani Rial was listed twice, 13 days apart but both at exactly the same time, to the second: 06.43.08; another payment listed in the August 2012 statement as having been paid on 11 June was also listed on that same May statement and appeared between entries made on the 15 and 20 May but with the 11 June date. A transfer made on 30 June and listed accordingly on the June statement also appeared on the March statement between the 4th and 9th of March. We identified 11 obvious fraudulent entries that followed this pattern.

I called the Omani Bank and enquired if, as ludicrous as it sounded, it was possible that a payment made in August or June could appear on a statement (in effect before it had even been made) issued one to three months earlier. I required this confirmation as proof of his deception to show William. The bank representative verified what we already knew, "it was impossible."

On the 1st of every month M transferred a fixed amount from this Omani account to his UK bank account where it would appear as a credit on the same day. While this transfer appeared on his July UK statement as a credit, there was no trace of it as a debit on the equivalent month's Omani statement. I decided to check the historical exchange rates on the dates of the transfers and found that they did not correspond with the deposits made into his UK account. 13 of the 16 transfers differed in multiples of £100, the total difference for all transactions was a few pounds less than £2,500 which was how much he had managed to conceal from me in this particular ruse.

The Omani statements showed just four supermarket transactions and not one fuel payment made in more than a year, from what he had declared to be his only Omani bank account, yet I knew he, like me, used his debit cards for such purchases. More thorough investigation was required and as such further anomalies were revealed.

Given his 2 sisters and 3 nieces had visited Muscat for 8 days over Easter in 2013 and according to him had stayed at his apartment, there was a distinct absence of additional expenditure for groceries, entertainment or restaurants, even though he would have undoubtedly flashed our money around to impress them. Earlier that year M had told me he had made efforts to reduce his living costs by exchanging his car for a smaller model and by downgrading the apartment to a one bedroom, which had made me question how he could accommodate five additional adults. Yet these statements showed an increase in both his monthly rent and car hire cost rather than the expected decrease.

The payment for the UK airport hire car from January 2013 was listed. I clearly recalled that the car hire representative had confirmed that M had used the same payment card for both the Christmas 2012 and January 2013 hire, yet there was no record of the December payment. That too had been removed in his efforts to conceal that visit. Lucy then drew my attention to an entry in the October 2012 statement: a cashpoint withdrawal at the nearby designer outlet. I checked the dates; it was the half term holidays and also a five-day public holiday in Oman, so he had been just 20 miles away while we once again were led to believe that he was in Oman. I didn't bother to check my emails this time, I did not want to know.

The alterations to the statements demonstrated how he had sought to increase his outgoings and reduce his income as well as to hide available funds and his trips home, home to the UK, but not to his actual family home. Why would he deliberately deceive us?

I felt very low and had no idea where to go from this point. A friend suggested that to obtain more information I track the IP addresses of his emails. I had to Google IP addresses to find out that it is the unique identifier for every machine that uses the internet. The IP addresses provide the location an email has been sent from. I knew Phil, the owner of the local computer repair shop, from when he had fixed my laptop, so that was where I headed late that afternoon for help. He explained that tracking an IP was an easy process, but I lacked the capacity to perform even the simplest tasks, I was too distressed.

We logged into my Yahoo account and I selected a few innocuous emails for him to demonstrate on and he was right, I probably could have managed to do it, but not in my current preoccupied state. Phil asked me why I was so interested in IP addresses and I explained that I had an errant husband who seemed to be in two places at once. I hoped that the IP addresses would help me pinpoint those locations more precisely and I highlighted the Christmas 2012 emails allegedly sent from Oman and sure enough the IP address proved he had sent them from the Birmingham area.

I then asked Phil to check a couple of emails from M in August 2012 which had puzzled me at the time. As I was about to confirm a family holiday for that month M had withdrawn on the basis that the dates clashed with Ramadan and he would be expected to be in the office full time to cover colleagues' absences, so instead, Seb and I went to visit family and friends in Washington DC. I had noticed, on our regular email exchange during that trip, that the times on his emails appeared odd: they showed a nine and half hours' time difference when the actual difference between DC and Oman was eight hours. M had explained that away as a peculiarity of the routing system, which I accepted at the time, but now, I had to know if it had more significance.

Phil was intrigued, as was I, when the IP address showed those emails had been sent from New Delhi, India. M had told me that, prior to my meeting him, he had worked offshore in India and he swore that he would never return as it had not been a good experience. So why had he been there? Especially when he was meant to be in Oman? A pattern was definitely developing. Instinctively, I knew what I had to do next; uneasily I asked Phil to check the email exchange over Christmas 2011, when Seb and I were in Muscat and M was supposedly in the desert. As he faced the screen, I saw Phil's expression change, he turned to look at me. "Birmingham?" I asked, and slowly he nodded, "Birmingham" he said. I told Phil how significant that finding was. I'd shared with a virtual stranger the most decisive assault on our family my husband had ever committed, or so I presumed.

I had to get out of the shop; I wanted to be alone to process this disturbing turn of events. It was only then that I noticed the time, it was after six, the shop had closed at five, yet Phil had stayed on to help me.

I asked what I owed for his time, but he declined payment, and told me "If I've helped to nab the bastard, then I'm happy."

Phil became the first of many who, on hearing my story over the following years, offered assistance, support and kind words and actions beyond my expectations, all in their endeavours to help me "nab the bastard."

When I got home, I went straight to my bedroom and without a conscious thought took off the ring that I had worn so proudly as an emblem of my unconditional love for my husband, Maurice James Gibney, for the previous 18 years. The same man who had abandoned his 13-year-old son and his wife in Oman at Christmas 2011 to fly 6,000kms back to the UK for no doubt, another woman.

Chapter 8

I was excited to tell William about our discovery of the fake bank statements and the money M had concealed and spent. The Form E stated, '*If you are found to have been deliberately untruthful, criminal proceedings may be brought against you under the Fraud Act 2006.*' I believed we could clearly prove M had purposely set out to deceive both me and crucially the courts, so surely his actions were criminal?

As a result of his premeditated deceit, I presumed that the court would look favourably on my case, but to the contrary, it seemed that it was me who was in trouble, not him. However, I was told that, apparently M would not be penalised for lying or concealing funds or assets, as attempting to hoodwink the courts was so commonplace that the courts did not waste time or funds chasing reprobates such as him. Whereas I on the other hand, had potentially committed a crime in how I had obtained the authentic UK bank statements. I was forbidden to share these statements with either the solicitor or barrister as they could then be implicated as 'my accomplices,' and for their own self-protection they sought advice from The Law Society. A conference was scheduled to discuss the 'sensitive issue' as it was now referred to and to also address the discrepancies on M's Form E. I had also identified additional missing documentation: he had failed to declare additional bank accounts and shares, and extra credit cards, so we needed to prepare a questionnaire to challenge him on these issues .

We met on a hot morning around an old wooden table in William's office. His practice was above an undertaker, the room was stifling, no breeze came through the partially opened, net curtained window. The conference was scheduled to last for three hours: in attendance was my barrister Mr. E chosen by William, William and Lucy who took notes. I don't know what I would have done without Lucy by my side. The majority of the discussion was around the bank statements, both fraudulent and genuine; I was again chastised for how I had obtained the latter. Mr. E repeatedly quoted legal precedents for such incidents which he was incapable of translating into non-legal jargon for Lucy and me to understand, despite our requests to do so. I made notes to Google later.

The case of Immerman V Immerman had set the guidelines for the circumstances in which confidential information used as evidence is obtained by parties, other than through the court process, and which in some cases by acts which might include criminal acts and/or which constitute a civil wrong. It was implied, therefore, that I may well have committed a criminal act by obtaining confidential documents.

Both William and Mr E struggled to understand our clear and precise bank statement spreadsheets in spite of numerous explanations. It seemed their focus was concentrated on my possible criminal behaviour that was reverted back to at every opportunity. The meeting dragged on for five hours through lunchtime, with no offer of a cold drink or even a biscuit, at a cost to me of £300 an hour. When it finally concluded Lucy and I went straight to the nearest bar and ordered a large white wine and the same sized bowl of guilt free chips each. We were hot, exhausted and frustrated, I felt we had made little progress, I was rapidly realising that I was a fool to have thought that being honest and transparent through these discussions would be in my favour.

That night I read the Law Gazette online and felt I had grasped a basic understanding of what was required to ensure I could use the bank statements as evidence, so the situation now seemed more hopeful. I learnt that the Court of Appeal had stated that in exercising the power to allow the evidence or not, the court would be guided by what is '*necessary for disposing fairly of the application for ancillary relief or for saving costs*' and will take into account the importance of the evidence, the conduct of the parties, and any other relevant factors. I felt able to challenge the allegation that I had obtained the genuine statements unlawfully and therefore could not use them, on the basis that, due to M being away so much, I managed all of the housekeeping and bills, and had historically opened M's post and made payments on his behalf. In addition, all of our confidential correspondence such as bank and credit card statements were stored together in an unlocked, shared filing cabinet and so surely, I had not done anything wrong? It was a relief when William cautiously agreed with me.

Our routine first appointment, which is a hearing with the judge where a discussion takes place around any additional information that may be required before the case can proceed to the next stage, was scheduled for the end of July. However, we were informed it had now been moved to 30 October, as M had made an application for postponement as he would be out of the country (which was his permanent state anyway) The court should have sought our agreement to this request but had failed to do so and instead acted on its own volition. The three-month delay concerned me; I worried that he planned to disappear with all our money.

It was agreed that we would make an application to the court for permission to question M about the genuine/fake bank accounts. Without the court's permission to do so, both my counsel and my solicitor may have had to withdraw, so I had no option, I had to do what was required in order to retain them. The application would further increase the costs pertaining to M's fraudulent actions which already weighed heavily on me. I had to look towards obtaining yet another credit card and continuing, for the first time ever in my life, to run up further and considerable debt.

The court mockingly allocated a date for this hearing as 15 August, the date of our eighteenth wedding anniversary. Our application, heard by the district judge, was for us to obtain instructions from the court that would permit us to use specific original documents belonging to the respondent but now in the possession of the applicant to ask questions of the respondent.

Our application had been drafted with the supportive statement as ex-parte, this is when a decision is made by a judge without requiring all of the parties to the dispute to be present at a court hearing. Unexpectedly, the judge insisted we lodge yet a further application to the court to enable the matter to be dealt with it. A week later, via a phone call, we learnt that the district judge had decided we had to make an application on notice, which meant we would have to advise M of our intention to seek the court order, which would clearly undermine the whole purpose of the application. We queried his decision and informed the court that the Solicitors Family Law Association Resolution guide had been used for reference when the application was made and that stated that the application should be made ex-parte. Curiously, this legal point of reference was unknown to the court, who requested a copy of the guide be emailed to them, for information.

Meanwhile, Seb and I had gone on a holiday I could ill afford, but my mindset at the time was 'What the heck; if I'm running up all this debt, let's at least enjoy a tiny part of it,' although our enjoyment was slightly marred by William's frequent emails. As our trip came to an end, we received good news: the district judge had agreed to our request, an order had been issued that allowed us to question M on his fraud and deception.

But it did not seem right that I had had to challenge the courts at my own expense, given that M had acted untruthfully and illegally. However, unbeknown to me at the time, this was just the first of many such issues. We issued a challenging questionnaire to M and, maybe because he felt he now had no other option, M finally appointed a legal team based in Liverpool. This triggered a burst of correspondence between our solicitors as his team tried to catch up with proceedings, although he had failed to share with them his attempts to defraud, so the job fell to William to update them, and I wondered if this was done at my expense.

Without notice M reduced his monthly payments to our joint account by a third, but as we still had the same outgoings and were still overdrawn, I had no clue how I was expected to make ends meet. Contact between him and me had been minimal but in mid-August he had inundated me with numerous emails on the subject of his imminent relocation to the UK. He claimed that his contract had ended and he now expected to return to live with us in the family home. I had responded to inform him how inappropriate that would be, but he had challenged me, and I was scared, especially given his previous aggressive behaviour. I feared he would appear on the doorstep to confront the issue and try to gain entry. Fortunately, William was able to confirm that as we had been legally separated for four months it was not permissible for him to return to the former matrimonial home, (FMH). In response, M told me I had left him with no alternative but to rent a property in the close vicinity of the FMH and that he would spare no expense in finding one equivalent in size to our five bedroomed house, just for himself. This was particularly stressful to hear as we lived in a small town and there would be every possibility of a chance encounter on the street or in a local shop between Seb and his father.

M listed a string of interviews in his quest for employment across the country from Kent to Aberdeen and stated that he would need the Range Rover to drive to Scotland; he would collect it en route from his interview in the south. I had no legal grounds to object or refuse him access, and he would need to take my key as he claimed Stella was out of the country. In spite of his giving me a date on which he would return the car, I suspected I would never see the vehicle again. It was registered in his name, so I needed to obtain proof that he had taken the car in case he accused me of disposing of it. So, on the day he was due to collect it, Josh came to the house and stationed himself in an upstairs window and took pictures of M driving the car away. While this might have seemed extreme, now that I knew just how cunning M could be, I could not take any chances.

Josh noted M had arrived in a local taxi at approximately the same time he used to arrive home from the airport having taken the overnight flight from Oman, he also had tagged luggage with him. M had thrown an empty water bottle over the garden wall, Josh retrieved it, it was an Omani brand. Later that day, I called the taxi company on the pretext that he might have left keys on the seat; they inadvertently confirmed that he had been picked up from Terminal Three, where the Oman Air flights land. It was now apparent he had come straight from the airport and not from an interview 'down south' as he had claimed.

I appealed to M not to move locally and questioned why he would commit to a rental property before he had even got a job, especially if he found work in Aberdeen. He replied that he was free to live wherever he wanted and that was as close to us as possible. I wanted to be prepared so I enlisted the help of a local estate agent acquaintance who made discreet enquiries amongst his colleagues, but it transpired that M was not registered for rental viewings with any agent within a ten-mile radius.

As expected, I received an email to inform me that he had taken legal advice and was under no obligation to return the car. Furthermore, he claimed it had broken down, and was parked in a car park at Manchester airport and would be collected from there by the garage who would do the repairs when the elusive spare parts became available. I didn't believe any of it, especially as his solicitor had confirmed that he had flown back to Oman and that his contract was not due to finish until April 2014. It was blatantly obvious that he had concocted the whole pretence of accommodation and interviews solely to cause me further anguish and to remove the vehicle from my possession.

As the October hearing rapidly approached and we waited for answers to most of our questions including those on the fraudulent bank statements, the pattern of delayed responses became the norm during the ongoing proceedings. On the day of the hearing at Birkenhead Family Court M and I were kept in separate rooms while our legal teams met in the corridor to thrash out financial agreements and discuss issues before going before the judge. For example, it was agreed that I would keep my share of my dad's flat, and he would keep his share of his father's house which he claimed was still in probate, our shares were of equal amounts and so it made sense that they would be excluded from financial negotiations.

The moment came when we were called into court, but unfortunately there was a last-minute delay, so we were held in a large waiting area together. My first glimpse of M in 10 months was a surprising one. He had always prided himself on being a smart dresser and had taken great care over his appearance, but that day he was dressed very differently. I was immediately drawn to his feet encased in patent, pointed toed, lace up shoes. He was so self-conscious about his size 12's he deliberately chose shoes that made his feet look smaller, yet today, it seemed that he had chosen to accentuate their oversize, as they appeared enormous and reminded me of clowns' shoes. He wore a grey shiny suit, crumpled from where he had been sitting for so long, the cloth looked cheap, the trousers were too long. His shirt was white with broad purple stripes, his tie was floral patterned in bright yellow, red and pink, I smiled broadly and was grateful for his fashion faux pas as it empowered me to act.

He sat down and looked directly out of the window, not having looked in my direction once, so I sat opposite him and fixed my glare hard upon his head. After a few minutes he got up and with head still turned, walked away. I was determined to make him look at me. So I walked straight over to him and stood close, facing him; my heart was pounding, but whether it was his clothes, his demeanour, the circumstances in which I had last seen him, or a combination of these things, I simply didn't recognise him as being my Maurice, my husband, it was as if a familiar stranger stood before me, someone who if you passed on the street, you would do a double take and ask yourself if you knew that person.

Under my breath and barely loud enough for him to hear I called him a 'fucking cunt,' the latter a word I had never said out loud before, and he heard me. He called across the room to his solicitor Amanda, a petite young woman who came running over with folders in hand. He politely asked her, and this dialogue is written as I remember it:

"Can you remove this person please? She is being abusive and intimidating me."

"You need to move away from my client now," this female, probably half my age rudely ordered me, "Move away right now."

I stood my ground and asked her, "Did you hear me being abusive? Do you see me intimidating him?"

Her response was, "If you don't move away now, I will get your solicitor."

Was this a threat? I told her to go ahead and fetch William, so she hurriedly left the room and the door banged behind her. Through the glass partition I could see her shaking her head, animated in conversation with William. The security guard in the corner sat watching, nonplussed, I am sure he was used to much worse than us.

M whispered to me "You fucking bitch. You'll get what's coming to you, wait and see. You won't win, I'll fuck you right over."

William came rushing in, bypassing the security guard's request to check his bag, M's solicitor followed hot on his heels.

"Yvonne, you shouldn't be talking to Mr Gibney, come with me."

"No William, not yet. I want to ask him as he hasn't asked me, or bothered to instruct her," my forefinger directed at his solicitor, "about access, about his son, about Sebastian. Does he want to see him?"

"Do you?" I turned and asked M directly.

The security guard and others sat waiting for their cases to be called; M answered me in a deliberately loud voice:

"This is what I have to put up with, can you see that now? I told you she is crazy, she isn't making any sense, can you take her away." As if I was some lunatic who needed to be put in a straitjacket and packed off for ECT.

But I too could play to the crowd, so I turned and addressed both William and

Amanda.

"I have asked the father of my son, who by the way hasn't seen or made any effort to contact him since January, whether while he was here, did he want to see him? If that is the action of a crazy woman, then yes, I'll walk away, as it's obvious he is not interested in seeing his son, which is probably for the best as what sort of father is he?"

I immediately turned my back on him and walked away, as I did, I caught the eye of a woman across the room, she smiled at me and nodded. I understood, she was showing her support, I smiled back at her in gratitude.

Within a few minutes we were called into court. He sat on the opposite side of the room where, again, he stared out of the window while I focused on the district judge and tried to engage as best I could. The outcome was, as expected, that the opposition needed to provide the outstanding information and what we had agreed so far between both parties was signed off by the judge. I was relieved, it had been a long day but less traumatic than I had anticipated.

At home that evening Seb asked me, "How was it? Did dad ask about me?"

I told him it had all gone as expected and that as we were deliberately kept apart, I had not had the opportunity to talk to "dad." What else could I have possibly said to my boy?

On a Sunday morning three weeks later in mid-November, Vicki called. She began the conversation with the ominous statement:

"You know I am a good friend and that's why I'm going to tell you what happened last night."

I knew instantly she had seen M with a woman, and I was right. She and Sam, along with their friends Sarah and Ali, whom I had met during the Omani Christmas visit, had gone for a drink the night before at the Sports Bar at the Intercontinental hotel. On arrival, they had instantly spotted M seated on a bar stool at the end of the bar next to a woman. Conscious of what they had seen, she told me they had scurried to a corner table and taken up a vantage point to observe him. Vicki had ducked into the smoking room where, concealed by the tinted windows, she had sat a few feet away from them, virtually chain-smoking while she observed them together.

Vicki described the woman as bottle blonde, late 40's, wearing a simple white top and black pants with a muffin top. She suspected that this woman was a work colleague as there had been no laughter or physical contact between them, but rather what she perceived to be just boring conversation, citing the behaviour between M and me as a comparison: always touching each other, flirtatious laughter and banter. She told me that onlookers never doubted that we were a "very together" couple whereas there seemed to be a distance between him and the blonde.

The year before, on their arrival in Muscat, Vicki and Sam had made plans to meet up with M on several occasions, but he had cried off and failed to turn up at the last planned meeting, so they had eventually stopped calling him. An hour or so into the evening Sam had laughed; he had the most distinctive laugh, once heard never forgotten. It had caused M to momentarily glance over his shoulder and, after recognising 'the laugh,' he had nodded to their group. A few minutes later Sam had got up to go to the toilet and M had followed, they had met each other in the lobby. As old golfing buddies they discussed the Muscat courses and the recent rise in membership fees. As Sarah joined them on her return from the toilet, she heard M say to Sam:

"What happens in Muscat stays in Muscat aye Sam?"

I will always love Sam for his reply: "No, I don't think it does Maurice."

Sarah said hello as the blonde joined the group and introduced herself as Suzanne. I had grilled Vicki, I asked her what accent she had, I wanted to know every word of their conversation, could she be the woman from Bromsgrove? But according to Sarah, she had a neutral accent and they had parted company immediately after her introduction. There was nothing more to go on other than Vicki's assurance that there was definitely no romantic connection between them. M and his friend had stayed on at the bar for a further hour after the impromptu meeting and had left without saying goodbye.

That same morning, after Vicki's call, I had emailed M and said that if he was involved with another woman I would rather he tell me, as I didn't want any surprises at the forthcoming Financial Direction Resolution (FDR) hearing. He denied any involvement with anyone, let alone the woman he had been spotted out with and told me that if Vicki had paid attention, she would have seen that he was out with a group of colleagues, of whom she was part. Vicki was adamant that they were alone, I knew he was lying, but given Vicki's descriptive report, I was sceptical that she was a romantic connection. I didn't care if he was romantically involved with another woman, but I was fearful that a new partner might exert an influence that might not be favourable to us in relation to the financial settlement.

The one question Vicki and I have since asked ourselves time and time again is why she didn't go over to say hello to M and to introduce herself to his friend, as she would have definitely done that in any other circumstance? Who knows what might have happened if she had, how might that have changed everything?

The FDR hearing was scheduled for 18 February 2014. The purpose of this hearing was to facilitate the financial settlement between both parties and reach an overall agreement. As such, there was an ever-increasing amount of paperwork to complete and there were several areas of contention to be dealt with. M had submitted a letter dated 18

December 2012 as supporting evidence with his Form E, which indicated that I proposed to file for divorce on the basis that we had lived apart for two years and he stated therefore that we had separated in 2011 not 2013. One of the questions on M's questionnaire of me requested that I confirm the date we had separated and that I supply reasons and evidence as to why I relied on the date. Mr E concluded that the date according to M, was the date of our separation, contrary to my statement that we had separated in January 2013. I explained why I had first instructed William at that time, but astonishingly my own counsel was disbelieving, and emphasised that I should consider my position very carefully. And that I needed to be cautious in reference to dates and to ensure that honesty and truthfulness were of primary importance. It appeared they believed M over me. This attitude was offensive and imbalanced given that I was their client and the honest party. I wondered if M's team reminded him of the importance of telling the truth, which would inevitably remain unheeded if they did.

I wrote my statement; I could easily supply the required proof both photographic and documentary. I included copies of wedding anniversary and Valentine's day cards and details of birthday celebrations and gifts, in addition to a chronology of events that clearly proved we were still together as a married couple until 2013. I also provided dates of romantic breaks away together, my trips to Oman in 2011 and his trips home on leave from Oman during 2012. In explanation of the letter, I wrote the following in my statement:

> I deeply regret ever being untruthful on my initial presentation to my solicitor and I am doubtful that I would have ever continued to go along with it, even if the situation had occurred where I needed to. I am naturally a very honest person, and it is this trait that Maurice had taken advantage of as I would never question his motivation which I now know was rooted in deceit. While in the latter half of 2012 the topic of divorce had been discussed but at no point was a decision made to separate. In December 2012, I had acted unilaterally when I contacted my solicitor and misrepresented the situation to appease my husband's state of mind as at that time, I believed this action would contribute to diffusing his depressive state and enable his scheduled arrival home for Christmas, which was my priority. However, I now believe he was not depressed, but rather implied it as a deliberate act to set in motion a rationale for his justification for not returning to the family home that Christmas, as he had an alternative itinerary. On reflection and with hindsight, I now realise I was coerced into this deception to underpin Maurice's conviction to himself and to convince others that we were separated at a much earlier date, to

justify his unreasonable and secretive behaviour since January 2011, given that, that behaviour would have been deemed highly inappropriate within the normal values and standards of a marriage.

Meanwhile, back in Muscat, Vicki had checked out the residential address M had put on the Form E, she had driven through the area which she knew well, checked maps and made local enquiries to no avail, she confidently reported that the address did not exist. Yet when they had met him at the Intercontinental Hotel a few weeks earlier he had told Sam he was still living in the same apartment where I had stayed with him. Why would he lie about his address?

I was keen to apply for a costs order against M to recover costs incurred in obtaining the court's approval to use the real bank statements, but I was advised that the application would be costly in itself and had limited chance of success on the basis that M had not breached a court order but had rather ONLY deliberately lied and defrauded. My legal bill was now over £17,000, I was beside myself with worry, I was accumulating more and more debt. What made the situation worse was that I strongly suspected M was deliberately being obstructive and instructing his solicitors with irrelevant demands that increased my costs and would probably delay proceedings.

William insisted I revise some of my responses to M's questionnaire on the basis that they were too long and inappropriate; I suggested I should have been advised on how to complete this questionnaire in the first place. I felt it was very important to my case that my narrative remained as I wanted in order to demonstrate how I was manipulated by M in reference to the December 2012 divorce application and why I changed my position to grounds of unreasonable behaviour. It was also important to me that my narratives demonstrated how this was his modus operandi and had been throughout the latter years of our marriage, and now the divorce process. He had little, if any, regard for Sebastian's and my well-being. This simply reinforced my belief that he would not comply with the court's maintenance order and that if, as I suspected, he would continue to live overseas, it would probably not be possible for any such order to be enforced.

In early January, a trail of correspondence was received requesting I produce further 'Immerman documents,' on the basis that M was unable to answer certain questions on our questionnaire without them. However, they did not specify what documents they referred to. We wrote back twice requesting clarification, but his solicitors only responded with threats to obtain a court order with costs against me, to force me to produce these documents, but I had no idea what they were asking for. I told William this was a ridiculous situation and instructed him to stop responding at the cost of £150 a letter, as the onus was on M's side to list the documents they referred to. Two weeks after their initial request we were informed they wanted M's passports, details of all flights including boarding passes and other travel from 2008 to 2013, irrespective of the relevant timeframe for the Form E as this questionnaire covered the dates from 2012 to 2013; they also asked for M's laptop.

The only items that remained at the FMH were a passport that expired in 2006 and a broken laptop from around the same time. There were numerous boarding pass stubs and old airline tickets, not one relevant to the divorce timeline; even William agreed that the documents would not enhance his answers in any way, but I duly dropped them off regardless. Another demand followed for M's current laptop which M claimed he had left behind, in January a year earlier. This was accompanied by the inevitable threat yet again of a court order with costs if I failed to comply. I felt, if left to his own devices, my solicitor would have entered into yet more protracted dialogue on this redundant issue, so I insisted he send one letter only to tell them M had obviously taken his laptop with him, and instructed that if this explanation was challenged, to call their bluff and let them seek a court order. However, we never heard from them again on this issue. It was apparent, well to me anyway, if not to my legal team, that these requests were further delaying tactics and would be used to support an application to delay the FDR hearing.

M had emailed that same week: his plan was to return to the UK at the end of the tax year when his contract ended. I knew he would seek to postpone the FDR till after that date, a shrewd tactic as his unemployed status would impact on us negatively regarding the financial outcome and maintenance support. He also told me that some of his responses to my questionnaire would be hurtful and distressing, I didn't know what he meant by that and chose not to ask him to elaborate, as I didn't need any additional stressors. I was off sick from work with stress related illness, yet there was a limit to how much time I could have off and while my work colleague, Chris, had been amazingly supportive, there was a limit to how much I could lean on friends for, and I had certainly been very needy during the preceding months. I felt so overwhelmed and just wanted it all to be over.

Chapter 9

It was two weeks before the Financial Dispute Resolution (FDR) hearing; I felt wrecked emotionally and physically. I had lost confidence in my legal team, they lacked the dynamism I needed to secure the best deal; after all, the outcome of this hearing would determine our future financial security. We were approaching the final hurdle and I was not confident that we would walk away from this with the best result for me and the boys. I had long since lost faith in the family law court as I struggled to understand why M had not been penalised, it all seemed so unfair. I had foolishly held the expectation that the law was just and abided by the rules, but that was not the case.

The responses to our questionnaire from M were long overdue and had, yet again, exceeded specified deadlines. William was still chasing up outstanding paperwork; each letter increased my bill and therefore my debt. I knew M would relish the distress that the ever-increasing legal bills and debt would cause me, which would serve to cause him to delay even further. While my legal documentation was complete, there were still outstanding questions that needed to be answered and it seemed now was the time to tie up the loose ends. Firstly, there were the Birds in Bromsgrove; the UK bank statements fiasco and the IP addresses indicated that he spent considerable time in the Birmingham area, so who were these people and what was the connection? How did they fit into his clandestine activities, into his double life?

From one of my many ring binders I extracted the original 192.com printout containing their details. On auto pilot I picked up my mobile, withheld my number and then tapped out theirs. Once again, the conversation is written here from memory and is as close to the original conversation as I remember it. The phone was answered by a man and off the top of my head I began:

"Hello, I am calling from ***** car hire, Manchester airport. I am trying to contact Mr Maurice Gibney who hired a car from us last Christmas. I appreciate that it was some time ago, but he registered the car to this address."

"That's right but he doesn't live here," the man said, "he lives in Oman."

"Yes, I'm aware of that." I had no idea where any of this was coming from, but it flowed.

"I have tried to contact him on his Omani email and phone, but I haven't had a response. The problem is that the car he drove at that time has been impounded by the police due to an incident which," I stressed "Mr Gibney had no part in. It's just that the police have asked us to provide the details of everybody who has hired that car. Out of courtesy I wanted to let Mr Gibney know that I had passed his details on to the police."

"Well, as I said, he doesn't live here, he just stays every time he comes back from Oman."

Every time he comes back from Oman.? I had two-way traffic in my head: listening in one lane and simultaneously thinking of what to say in the other, the voice in lane one asked myself what he meant? Why would he stay with him? Again, what's the connection?

Little did I know that I was about to get the answer to that question, and that that answer would literally shatter my world and that I would never be able to make it whole again.

"And are you expecting him back anytime soon?" I asked.

"No, he won't be back for a few months," he replied.

Well, he doesn't know he is coming back for the FDR hearing then. Keep up the pretence, the voice in lane one was saying.

"Can I just check I have the correct contact details for him please?"

I recited his Omani email address and phone number; I held on for a moment while he checked and confirmed they were correct as I knew they would be, it was merely an attempt to keep him on the phone.

"One last question, if you don't mind. I will write to Mr Gibney again and I will say I have spoken to you. Given data protection, may I ask your name and your relationship to him?"

I had no idea what made me ask that last question as I knew his name; he was Mike Bird and I knew, or I thought I did, that he was connected to my husband through work.

He replied: "Sure, my name is Mike Bird and I'm his brother-in-law."

"Brother-in-law?" I repeated it as the same words brother-in-law resounded inside my head.

"OK, so you are Mike Bird, and you are Mr Gibney's brother-in-law?" He confirmed that was correct. I thanked him and put down the phone.

I didn't understand what had just transpired, as the conversation made no sense. Why would he say he was M's brother-in-law? What did that mean exactly? That M had been living with his sister for so long that they considered him to be a brother-in-law? But he couldn't have been living with her that long, we had only separated a year before, and in any case, he would've said my sister's boyfriend or partner.

The thought that had taken root seven months earlier began to grow: had he married somebody else in Muscat? No, impossible I told myself, no that's not what he implied, it's not what he meant, how could it be. We were still married. I rang Lucy, she was used to my calling with garbled messages, I asked her to come over as soon as she could. While I was waiting, I called my brother Jeff and without disclosing what had just happened I asked him how he would refer to a boyfriend of mine if I had been living with him, for maybe a year?

He gave the predicted reply "As your boyfriend."

"How about brother-in-law?"

"No, it's only brother-in-law when you're married. It might be partner I suppose after a few years, but why are you asking?"

I told him I would fill him in later and that I had to go. I wasn't yet ready to repeat the conversation I had just had, not to anybody but Lucy, who arrived within half an hour.

"What is it?" she asked, concerned. "What has he done now?"

I told her. Sitting at the kitchen table I relayed almost word-for-word the conversation I had just had. She was dumbfounded.

Something wasn't right and it didn't make any sense. It's crazy that he said that he was his brother-in-law because that would mean he had married his sister or whoever she is?

I decided to call back from the landline so that my number was visible, and I would tell Mike Bird who I was and ask him why he had told me he was M's brother-in-law. Lucy was armed with a notebook and pen, she would record the conversation as I repeated it, to ensure we had an accurate record, I had a feeling that I knew what he was going to tell me, and I so feared, I might not remember the conversation, but it was imperative that I did. The following dialogue is extracted from those written notes as well as the conversation as I recall it.

I stood in the middle of the kitchen, anxious, fearful of what I was about to hear, my finger was trembling as I pressed the number for the second time, my throat was dry, my chest felt tight, and I could feel a panic attack looming. "Take control, take control" I repeated softly to myself.

A woman answered, I guessed she was Donna Bird. I introduced myself.

"Hello, my name is Yve Gibney and I'm calling you because I received a call from *****
car hire, Manchester airport, earlier on about a car hired by Maurice Gibney registered to
your address."

She interrupted "Yes they called here too, they spoke to my husband."

I was conscious of Lucy taking notes, so I tried to speak slowly in spite of wanting to
blurt out whatever I needed to say.

"Yes, I know they spoke to your husband," I said, "that's part of the reason why I am
calling. The lady from the car hire company said she had spoken to your husband and
he had referred to himself as Maurice's brother-in-law. I was curious, so I hope you don't
mind me calling. I want to know why your husband would say he was Maurice's brother-
in-law."

"Well, he is Maurice's brother-in-law, she said matter-of-factly. Maurice is married to
my sister."

I repeated: "Maurice is married to your sister?"

This time not necessarily for Lucy's benefit, it was my way of confirming that I had
actually heard what she had just said.

She said it again "Maurice is married to my sister."

I repeated for the second time "Maurice is married to your sister" my heart began to
pound so hard it felt as if it would burst out of my chest, my left hand which held the
phone began to shake so violently I had to place my right hand over it to stop the phone
banging against my ear, but even then, the base tapped the side of my face repeatedly.
Lucy stared at me; she certainly wasn't writing anything down now, her mouth was partly
open, her features looked frozen. I knew she wanted to say something, but the words
weren't coming out.

Donna must have thought this a very odd conversation, she continued "but Maurice
doesn't have a sister called Yve."

"I never said I was his sister," I somehow managed to respond.

"You said Maurice was married to your sister, but I never said I was his sister."

She asked the million-dollar question: "So who are you then."

And the priceless answer followed: "Who am I? I am his wife."

I could sense her disbelief through the phone, she didn't know what to say and I
certainly knew how that felt. I repeated it, almost as if I had to verify it to myself as much
as to Donna.

"I'm his wife, I am his wife."

My whole body was shaking now. Lucy had started to write again but had still not said
anything. Donna began to flounder, telling me that she didn't normally take phone calls

like this, or give out information. She told me she didn't know what to say. Somehow, I took control of the situation. In a futile effort to try to turn this situation into the horrible misunderstanding I knew it was not, I asked:

"Are we talking about the same Maurice Gibney?" I knew that we were.

"Does he come from Liverpool? Is he balding, 6 foot and works in Muscat for an Omani company as a contracts' manager?"

I desperately wanted her to acknowledge that against all the odds this was a case of mistaken identity, but I knew she wouldn't be able to do that, it was pointless. It was him; it was my husband and he had married her sister. Her voice quivered as she confirmed that it certainly sounded like the same Maurice Gibney. She was audibly distressed and told me she had to go, she repeated that she doesn't normally give out information on the phone.

She told me she "didn't know what to say."

I sensed she was about to put down the phone, I begged her not to:

"Please don't go, we need to talk. I know this is a shock, it's a shock for me too."

I needed to carry on the conversation. I needed to find out more. But she repeated that she had to go.

"Look me up on 192.com," I told her. I gave her my full name and my address; she would see that Maurice was still registered as living here, in my panic I was clasping at straws.

"You have my phone number, please call me back."

"I don't have one of those phones." I didn't know what she meant.

I told her to dial 1471 to get my number. "Look me up in the phone book,' I'm listed; there are no other Gibney's in the phone book."

Forgetting amidst the horror of the moment that she wouldn't have my local telephone directory. I told her that this was not a joke, it was very real, and she had to call me back, we couldn't just leave it. She promised she would call back in 20 minutes.

I sat at the table and repeated the conversation to Lucy. We both knew now that we had to acknowledge, bizarre though it seemed, that it was true, that my lying dog of a husband had somehow married somebody else: Donna's sister, but we didn't have a name. I have limited recall of the next 30 minutes; my head was spinning, and my heart continued to pound, my fingers tingled, my throat felt like it was closing, I was experiencing a full-blown panic attack, it was hardly any wonder. Lucy and I recited the conversation over and over, we couldn't get our heads around it; we could not grasp what we had been told, let alone think about the implications of it. I did not understand how this had happened, or when it happened or why.

Who was my husband? Other than being, it seemed, the husband of somebody else as well as me. I didn't know what to do, this was one life encounter I had not been prepared for. We realised at this point that more than half an hour had passed. I doubted Donna would call back, so I called her; Mike answered. He sounded emotional as if he were holding back tears, he was polite and quietly told me:

"We can't talk to you now, we're sorry, we are very, very sorry, but we can't talk to you now. Thank you for calling."

I wasn't surprised he sounded so upset. I did not know where I had found the inner strength to externally appear to hold it together, I was in a numbed state of shock.

Not knowing what to do next, Lucy suggested I visit Isabel who, if she knew anything about this craziness, was sure to tell me the truth. She had not been in touch since I had started divorce proceedings, we missed her as she used to visit regularly. but she had failed to reply to voicemails, I accepted that was her choice although I never understood her motivation: I wasn't divorcing her.

I wasn't capable of making the journey on my own, so I picked up Josh on the way. Isabel had recently moved and now lived close to Teresa in Liverpool. Her bungalow was opposite the cemetery where M's father's ashes were buried, although I doubt she ever went to visit that grave. It was a cold, dark and wet evening, we had never visited this house and Josh kept losing the signal on Google maps for directions and we got lost; it took us some time before we eventually found her road. We parked outside and apprehensively knocked on the door. Isabel, while surprised to see us, made no effort to invite us in.

"Hello Isabel, I hope you don't mind us coming to see you, we won't stay long, it's just that I've had some news about Maurice, and I need to talk to you about it."

My opening gambit was unrehearsed, and I think she interpreted it as bad news about M. Maybe, subconsciously I had worded it like that in an attempt to gain entry. It worked; she opened the door wider and after another slight hesitation reluctantly let us in.

We stood in the centre of her plainly furnished front room, we were definitely not welcome visitors, we were not even invited to sit down. I explained that the news I had heard earlier that day about M that seriously perturbed me, and that as my mother-in-law of 19 years I trusted her to give me an honest answer. I stressed too that I had nowhere else to go, no-one else to ask.

She looked distinctly uncomfortable but made no effort to respond, she just stood looking at me, waiting for me to say more. I hadn't forward planned or thought of a script, I just spoke from my heart. I explained I had a conversation with someone that morning who had told me that M had got married to her sister in Muscat.

"Was it true?" I asked.

The look on her face gave it away. The question was unexpected; it was apparent that she did not want to answer it, so she simply chose not to. Instead, she told me she didn't know why I was asking that question. Looking increasingly awkward she walked behind the sofa, I had the impression she was trying to hide from us.

"Who did you talk to?" she asked.

"Some people from Bromsgrove, Donna and Mike Bird."

She leant over the sofa and began straightening the antimacassars, she wouldn't look at me, but tried very hard not to reveal by her body language that she even recognised the names as she continued smoothing out imaginary creases from the lace edged cloth.

I continued to question her and I remember this conversation distinctly because I replayed it numerous times in my head for a long time afterwards. "The girls were in Oman last year, is that when he got married?"

"Well, I don't know why you're asking me that question, I wouldn't know the answer to that" she replied.

"Of course, you would," I smiled, "you're his mother! You would know if he had got married again."

She repeated herself, "I don't know why you're asking me that."

I tried a different tactic: "You share a car with Teresa so I'm sure you would know when she went on holiday and where she went to."

"They have never been to Oman as far as I know."

But we all knew that was a lie.

"I have seen photographs of them in Oman, Isabel. Maurice told me they had visited."

With her back to us she picked up the sofa cushions and pretended to rearrange them, by lifting them up and replacing them in the same position; she would not look at either of us.

Josh moved closer to her and looked directly at her, at which point she exclaimed: "Josh! I didn't recognise you."

Placing a cushion back on to the sofa she told him to sit down, bringing a fleeting second of normality to the proceedings.

She asked how he was, "Good thanks grandma" said her grandson who had just learnt that his stepfather, her son, had married someone else while still married to his mother.

"How about you? Have you been keeping well?" Josh enquired in an effort to bring some normality to a bizarre situation.

She did not answer him, she was busy back behind the sofa plucking imaginary dust from the green velour. I remained standing. I took in the room, looking for wedding photographs, there was none but then she was never one for having framed photos on display. I steered the conversation back on track:

"Isabel please just tell me the truth. I know the girls were in Oman last year and so do you. Was that when he got married?"

I was feeling shaky and began to feel lightheaded, I needed to sit down, so in spite of not being invited to do so, I sat, perched on the edge of the armchair. She did not want us there; her unwillingness to engage or to answer questions, the tension in the room, was palpable.

"Why have you come here? Asking me all these questions? Causing trouble."

I reiterated that I just wanted to know the truth: I had a simple question that needed answering "had he married somebody else?"

"Please, just tell me the truth, it's a simple yes or no answer, has Maurice married someone else?" I pleaded with her for a response.

"You are just trying to cause trouble, coming here asking questions that I don't know the answers to."

If the answer were no, she would have said no, but she couldn't say yes either, she had to be covering for him, I had had enough. Maybe I could shock her into responding.

"Isabel, we are still married," I announced, "We are in the very final stages of divorce; we go to court in less than two weeks, but you need to know we are still married." That's why I'm here Isabel because I don't understand what is going on."

While she had evaded eye contact throughout the conversation, she wasted no time in stepping forward and looking me straight in the face, agitated, she repeated herself:

"Why are you causing all this trouble? What is wrong with you?"

The realisation dawned; she thought we were divorced; she knew he had 'remarried.'

"Isabel you need to hear the truth; we are not divorced; we are still married."

She stamped the short distance to the front door and in an attempt at a dramatic gesture opened the door wide. Josh and I were still seated, but began to get up, anticipating what was coming.

"Get out, get out and don't ever come back. I never want to see you again."

Josh said goodbye, but she did not reply. Within seconds we were out of the door and it slammed shut loudly behind us. We turned to look at each other, I knew what Josh was about to say.

"Mum she knows the truth: he has got married to someone else."

I felt my heart break as I wiped away the first of many thousands of tears, "I know, Josh, I know."

Chapter 10

Still reeling from the shock of the day before and all it entailed, I emailed an update to William. I knew he now considered me a difficult client. I felt unsupported and felt that the firm was not handling my case as effectively as they could do, so I had become increasingly forthright in requesting a more proactive approach as I felt they pandered to the opposition's unreasonable demands. By doing so, they had enabled them to have control over a situation that we should have controlled, particularly as we knew that we could not trust his submissions. I wondered what William and Mr E would make of this latest development.

That Sunday morning as Seb and I were standing in the hallway saying bye to Josh, the house phone rang; Seb picked it up and instantly looked alarmed.

"This is Seb," he said.

I thought it was a call from my father's nursing home with bad news, I whispered to him "Is it pop?" he shook his head and mouthed at me:

"It's dad." "Yes, she's here, I'll pass you over." he said into the receiver before passing me the handset.

It was M, who straight to the point, albeit politely, asked why I had gone to his mother's house the night before. I replied by telling him that he knew why we had gone to his mother's house, as surely that was the reason for his call. He insisted he did not know and asked me again, I repeated my answer. He was riled, he wanted information that he was not going to get, he sounded more aggressive. predictably, as he was not getting his own way. He asked again, why I had gone to visit his mother, this time I remained silent.

"Going there and behaving like a crazy woman, demanding to be let in?" he made no attempt to contain his anger.

I told him he knew that wasn't true. He continued to accuse me of pushing her aside and forcing our way into her house.

"Well, Maurice, all I can say, again, is that it is not true. Ask yourself why I would do that?"

"You tell me? Why would you shout at her and bully her and force your way in? That's the only reason you took Josh with you, to intimidate her!"

I laughed out loud. "Do you know how ridiculous you sound? That I would take her grandson along to intimidate her?"

I knew my responses were winding him up, but I didn't care, in fact I enjoyed it, I was safe, he couldn't touch me, he was on another continent.

"Why did you ask her all those questions?" I didn't answer.

"She thinks you need help, so do I, there is something very wrong with you."

I told him to stop exaggerating and that if he had something to say he should just say it and stop avoiding the real issue. It was his turn not to answer. He was aware of the reason I had gone to his mother's and I guessed was worried, he would want to know exactly how much I knew; well, I could play the game and I could play it well, better than him as I, for the first time in years, had the advantage. So, I continued,

"If you know what questions I asked then you know why I was there."

I was not going to give him anything, I was going to make him say it, I was going to make him bring up the 'marriage' and if he didn't there was no way I was going to.

"You know why I went so what is it that you're really ringing for?"

"I don't know why you went to my mother's; she didn't know why you went, that's why I'm calling."

I told him that his mother would have relayed exactly what I had said, that was the reason she had called him and that, in turn, was why he was calling me now; I reminded him we had not spoken in months. I sensed he was unnerved; he would need to placate his mother, probably the Birds and no doubt me, but that was certainly not going to happen.

I took it to the next level: "Who is Donna and Mike Bird to you?"

"I have no idea who they are, I don't know who you're talking about" he lied.

I laughed; a deliberate theatrical sounding laugh as I pictured his furious face.

"You are seriously telling me you do not know who Mike Bird and his wife Donna Bird are? Is that right?"

I deliberately made no reference to the 'brother-in-law' quote.

"I've never heard of them, who are they?" he asked audaciously.

I asked him to hang on, I brought Josh to the phone as a witness to his denial.

"One more time, do you know Donna and Mike Bird who live in Bromsgrove?"

"Never heard of them, never been to Bromsgrove, don't even know where it is."
Josh shook his head in disbelief.

"Well. it seems they know you very well." He was not going to admit the connection.

"So, is that it? Anything else I can help you with?" I asked with feigned indifference.

"I told you, I know you went round to my mother's house last night to cause trouble and upset her 'cause that's the evil bitch that you are and I'm telling you not to", his voice was quivering with rage.

Telling me! How dare he! In no uncertain terms I told him he had no right to tell me where I could go or what I could do and how pathetic he was as we both knew he was lying. I took advantage of the situation to tell him what a shameful father he was, that he had not called Seb or Josh in a year and had not even asked to speak to them let alone asked after them. I swore at him, because I knew I could, my accent became increasingly cockney the more I raged, I could easily have won a part in EastEnders, words not usually in my vocabulary slipped off my tongue with natural ease. For a brief moment I had the upper hand, the first time in many years, and I was able to vent, to vent all my bottled-up anger against him without fear of any physical repercussion. Why did he stay on the phone, why was he still talking to me? Because he had a secret and he needed to know how much I knew about that dirty little secret, otherwise he would have put the phone down on me the first time I had answered him back.

Randomly he told me he had a local girlfriend, that she had a son but there were problems which is why he didn't want to discuss it with me, even though I hadn't asked him to. But I knew that too was a lie because he would never date an Arabic woman, as he lacked a respect for Arabic culture. However, he needed to hurt me, and he thought by telling me that he had contact with another woman's son, but not his own, he would achieve that; and indeed, it would have done had I believed it to be true.

By calling in the first place and by tolerating my insults, he had further confirmed my suspicions. The phone call had lasted 41 minutes at which point I told him I was bored with this conversation and promptly cut him off. Initially it had felt good to have got one up on him, until I thought about the implications of what had just taken place. How ironic, he was talking about a girlfriend while I knew about a secret bride.

Seb relayed the brief conversation he had shared with M who had opened with a "Hello."

Seb had replied "hello."

M had asked who he was and that was when he had answered, "It's Seb."

M had responded "This is your father," then laughed maniacally, and continued "that's if you still have a father? Is your mother there?"

M had not recognised his own son's voice, just as his own father had not recognised him a few years earlier, at his hospital bedside. That was the last time Seb ever spoke to his father.

Later that day I went online and searched how to marry as an expat in Oman. Marriages can only take place if, as a Muslim, you marry under Sharia law. Non – Muslims can marry in a church, or as a foreign resident at your own Embassy, if permissible to do so. An Iraqi and therefore Arabic speaking friend who goes by the name of Swiss Cottage Hussein called the two churches in Muscat for me, but there was no record of M's name in their marriage registers. Hussein was told that they married very few expats and that all marriages must be registered with the notary, whom he made numerous attempts to contact, but the phone remained unanswered.

Two days later I mailed William the following email:

> As Mr and Mrs Bird have not contacted you or me, would it be appropriate to write to them asking them to confirm the information they gave me during our conversation and for you to confirm that I am still married to Maurice? As I am sure you appreciate this situation is exceedingly difficult for me and although I am sure it is true that he has married I still seek confirmation.

The request was addressed later that week at our already scheduled pre FDR hearing conference. It was acknowledged that as M was still married if a marriage in Oman had taken place it would not be legally recognised. I shared my belief that if he had married, I doubted that he planned to return to the UK and that I would therefore never get to the bottom of his financial affairs and the suspected concealment of our money. The response to my email was that under no circumstances was I to try to contact the Birds. To this day I deeply regret having listened to this advice. I had wanted to go to Bromsgrove to confront them in person and if I had I am sure I could have prevented the years of anguish and pain that the boys and I endured as a result of M's behaviour.

Chapter 11

This was the penultimate weekend before the final divorce hearing (FDR). I was nervous about the outcome from a financial perspective but weighing even more heavily than that was the overwhelming anxiety of moving on after the divorce. Not in relation to M, although I was dreading seeing him at the hearing, but more so about how I was going to repair the damage already done to my boys. I felt so insecure: the judge might rule that the family home be sold, I was in huge financial debt and I was struggling psychologically. I also doubted whether I would be able to summon up the mental and physical strength needed to deal with all these issues, although I knew I had to. Yet it wasn't about me, it was about Josh and Seb whose father had left home a year ago without ever saying goodbye. I despised M: for his deceitfulness, his manipulation, his failure as a husband and father; the list was endless, but more than anything, I despised him for the harm that he had caused to the children.

I went to bed knowing I was in for a restless night. I fell asleep about 1am and woke a few hours later; I tried to read but couldn't concentrate. I reverted to my failsafe to while away the night-time hours: Facebook. I looked again at his family's pages, were there any last-minute posts? Any photos? Any possible clues to back up the conversation with the Birds? Nothing. I looked again at Donna Bird's page, still no clues to the 'so called marriage.' I eventually dozed off.

I woke suddenly, having heard a voice in my head: 'Try Fifi, try Fifi' I must've been dreaming. My iPad was still lying next to me open on Donna Bird's page, something clicked, her daughter Fiona, maybe she is called Fifi? There she was, easy to find now I knew where to look. Instinct told me this was the link I had been looking for, that Ms Fifi Bird was going to come through for me, as surely most young women would post wedding photographs? I trawled through every one of her posts, conversations about netball, match results and successes, nights out with friends, new dresses: she seemed like an average, nice, young woman. So where was what I was looking for, not that I knew what that was. A post that was dated 24 November read *'Happy Birthday to the best aunty ever Suzanne Prudhoe.'*

'Umm, who's she?' I thought, at this point more out of curiosity than any inkling that I had found my needle in the haystack, my tab hovered over her name. I clicked and was instantly linked to her Facebook page.

At that very moment, during that second of a transition between Facebook pages, my mind was tired and empty of thought. But that was the very last time that I had that freedom: of thought, of identity, and of a belief in truth, faith and love and marriage. I had no idea that such a simple act of opening a Facebook page would be the transformative event that it was, something that would upset the balance of our lives with such impact that nothing would ever be the same again.

Her page opened on to her profile picture, I could not comprehend what I was looking at. A photograph of a woman dressed in a white, floral patterned dress with a matching bolero jacket, blonde hair in a chignon with a small tiara in the centre. She held a bouquet of white roses and was looking up adoringly into the eyes of a man, who looked just like my husband. His hand was around her waist and he was looking back at her with an expression on his face that I didn't recognise. I don't know how long I stared at that photograph, I had no concept of time or it seemed reality. I cannot recall what was going through my head, the man in the photo looked so much like M, but at the same time I couldn't recognise him as being him. However, one of my first thoughts that I recall now, which seems absurd given the context, was thinking 'well if that is him, has he dyed his eyebrows? They look much darker.'

The photo was marked at the base with the logo *'Fabulous Life Photography.'* Who was this? Had he modelled with this woman for a photographer? That past week since speaking to the Birds I had searched for proof of a 'wedding' and here it was in front of my eyes, but it was so incredible that, at that juncture, I didn't, I couldn't, believe it to be true! I could not grasp the actuality of it all. I needed someone to tell me it really was M, I didn't know if it was, because how could it be? He was my husband, not hers.

It was around 6am, I knew Jo would be awake. I texted: "Can I call, something has happened?"

"Call me" she replied.

What followed was a conversation that very few wives will ever have in the lifetime of their marriage, fortunately.

"What's happened?" Jo asked.

"I've found a picture on Facebook" I explained how I had followed the link and described what I had found. Tears were welling up because I knew the answer to the question I was about to ask, but I needed her to say it, just like then, as I had said it out loud, I knew it was real.

"Have a look Jo, tell me if it's him."

I waited while she logged on. She gave me a running commentary as she opened Suzanne Prudhoe's page:

"Oh my god, Yve, it's him!" Confirmed!

There was my husband looking like the bridegroom on the Facebook page of a total stranger and who looked like he had most definitely married.

"Yve, there's a photographer's website link on the bottom of the picture, I'm going to have a look at it, promise you won't, let me do this."

"OK Jo" I sobbed down the phone.

"I'll call you straight back once I've checked it out," she said.

While I waited, I stared at the picture, taking in every detail. He always wore a white, short sleeve, round neck vest under his shirts as he sweated a lot, even in winter. I enlarged the picture and noticed the rim of a vest just under his shirt collar. There was no doubt now, that vest had confirmed it for me; without that I might have let myself, momentarily, think that Jo was wrong in her identification of him.

Jo called back: "Yve, it's a real wedding, a big affair on the beach, it looks like it must be Muscat, there's palm trees, it's sunny and it looks really hot. There's lots of photos on the website, pictures of guests, the dining tables, people dancing, and there's an elderly woman walking him down the aisle, I think it's his mum."

I could hear the incredulity in her voice, she too could not believe what she was looking at.

"You best look at it Yve, he has done it, he really has married someone else, I'm so, so sorry."

I opened the link; I don't think I had ever been so shocked in all of my life by what I saw there:

There was my mother-in-law walking arm-in-arm with M down the aisle, which was a Persian style patterned red carpet laid over the sand and which acted as a divider between two blocks of rows of white, cloth covered chairs. Isabel, the woman who had told me only one week before that she "wouldn't know" if her daughters had been to Oman the previous year, my mother-in-law of 19 years who had thrown me and Josh out of her house for "coming around causing trouble," was there with my husband, her son, at his wedding. She had given him away to another woman while she must have known he was still married to me.

I noted what he was wearing: a beige lightweight suit that was far too long in the leg, the hem of the trousers bunched up over his black shoes. Black shoes? My impeccable dresser of a husband, who wore Thomas Pink shirts, highly polished shoes, trousers with a sharp crease was wearing an ill-fitting, crumpled suit with mismatched shoes. He looked fatter and his legs seemed shorter than I remembered.

Isabel was dressed casually in a style more suited to a cafe lunch date with a friend. She was wearing a blue and black floral dress, a black cardigan and sensible shoes, hardly wedding attire, let alone suitable for the heat of an Omani spring. Her hair was an odd orange colour and cut markedly short, I knew her to have brown hair, worn in a less severe style. I recognised the Birds sitting in the front row to the right of the aisle. Initially I didn't recognise anyone else in that picture, but then in the corner of the front left row I noticed Megan, in the familiar long pink dress from her Facebook post the previous year, her face partially hidden by large shades. She had her phone poised ready to photograph her uncle and grandmother walking down the aisle when they came into view.

I felt oddly detached from what I was seeing. There were many, many more wedding photographs on the website which had been uploaded on 11 June 2013 and entitled 'Beach Wedding.' The photographer had written: 'I really enjoyed photographing this intimate wedding in the Al Bustan hotel. Such a beautiful location, nice people, and great ambience. Congrats Mrs. & Mr. P.'

The first batch of photographs were of the top table set for the wedding meal and laid with a central white rose and candle arrangement. Tables were named by countries rather than numbers, the top table was Oman, another Norway, name place-cards had a small heart printed on them. The two-tiered wedding cake was featured, each layer encircled by silver ribbon and bedecked with white roses. Other photographs showed the bridal bouquet: 20 white roses edged with gypsophila, another was of her wedding dress hung on a pink padded coat hanger, alongside her shoes, beaded evening bag and the tiara. They had married under a canopy on the beach between palms in what looked like an exceptionally beautiful setting.

On the top table were two vintage style brown paper luggage labels, embossed with a flourishing penmanship: 'The Bride Suzanne and The Groom Maurice.' Each label dated 30th March 2013. I hadn't thought about the date at all, when had this happened? March 30th, 2013, eight weeks after he had left the family home. But that couldn't be right as it would mean I had slept in the same bed and loved this man only two months before he had married someone else.

On returning from work, the day he had arrived home for the very last time, I had found him dozing in bed, within minutes he had made love to me. He had told me how his depression had become all-consuming and how much he knew he had hurt me that past year; how he had regretted not having been home that Christmas and how sorry he was for the upset he had caused. He had held me close and whispered in my ear how he had missed me and how much he loved me, and I had believed him.

Yet all that time, he knew he was about to enter into a marriage with another woman just two months down the line. I felt sick. I retched and retched over the toilet until I vomited, but it was no release. I wanted to scream, as loud as I could: 'You bastard, you rotten, twisted bastard.' My head was spinning, I had a thousand questions, and the most intensive, all-encompassing feeling of absolute betrayal was enveloping me. It held me tight, I felt I was suffocating, there was a weight on my chest that prevented me from trying to take the deep measured breaths I needed to control the panic. My heart pumped so fast I thought it would burst into pieces.

How long had this relationship been going on for? It looked like a wedding that had needed some planning. I spoke to Jo again. She had gone back to Suzanne Prudhoe's Facebook page and told me they had got engaged on 3 May 2012, I stumbled further into a zone of total disbelief. It was just not possible. Seb and I had been out in Oman just five months previously. He had been home on leave numerous times since then, we had slept together, gone out for dinners, walks, held hands, bought each other gifts, spoke to each other virtually every day, texted, emailed, and he had sent me flowers. I was so, so confused. I did not know how this could have happened.

A selection of comments from Suzanne Prudhoe's Facebook page on the engagement read:

Kim: 'OMG need details...... and congratulations.'

Kara: 'Congratulations. Great news xx'

Marie: 'Oman – what a great move'

Sally: 'Hey Suzanne, lovely news – that is what Facebook is really for – details, photos, ring?'

Muriel: 'WOW congratulations Sue, can't wait to hear more about it... Am so happy for you'

Anne: 'Congratulations, and who's the lucky guy?'

Lieke: 'Hey Congrats! Mail me and tell me more!'

Katya: 'Congrats Suz. Fab news – tho clearly a few details needed.'

Fifi Bird: 'ahhhh I'm so excited can't wait to see youuuuu!'

Suzanne Prudhoe had written on May 4th: 'Many thanks to you all. Cheers. xxxx'

The year before my friend Christos had suggested that, given his change in behaviour, he might be having an affair, but I had dismissed the idea and told him that anyone with that level of depression would be incapable of managing his emotions let alone the deceit. How wrong was I? It was much, much more than an affair, it was a whole other life, a whole other marriage.

I called Lucy, I was so distraught I could barely talk but managed to update her, I had to repeat myself several times though as she couldn't believe what I was telling her. She wanted to see for herself and would call me back. As it was close to the FDR hearing and after what had occurred the weekend before, Josh, in his self-appointed role of protector had come to stay. I woke him, and together we turned on the computer in the spare room, I brought up the pictures and asked him what could he see? Did it look like a wedding? He hugged me and told me he had no words. I understood.

We scrolled through all of the photos; there were plenty of group pictures of several women with the bride, but we did not recognise anyone. A heart wrenching close up of M putting a white metal wedding band on her finger was especially difficult to look at. Josh was visibly shocked when he saw his Grandma escorting M to the ceremony, another shot of them both showed them laughing, they looked very happy. Lucy called back; my dear friend had been on this journey with me from the beginning. She had listened and advised during our long walks on the beach the previous summer. I told her everything and she probably thought she had heard it all, until now. She asked me if I had seen Stella in the photos and I told her I had.

Stella was sitting close to Fifi Bird, her black and white dress topped with the 'Fascinator.' that same Fascinator I had seen on Megan's posts 11 months earlier, which had given me 'that feeling.'

"And Essi?"

"No Essi's not there." I reminded her Essi was in Australia.

"She's there" Lucy insisted, "enlarge the picture of the couple sitting together."

I did as she suggested and there was Essi, in a strapless purple dress, bare legs crossed, her hair swept over one shoulder, a beaming smile on her face, nestled in the arm of a young man that I presumed to be her boyfriend Daniel. It was inconceivable to me that she was there. I felt my throat tightening then my chest, again, I couldn't breathe, I couldn't speak. Josh ran for the Rescue Remedy; when he came back, he found me lying on the floor, I had fainted. In the distance I could hear the panic in Josh's voice as he called my name:

"Mum, mum, are you alright? Mum, mum."

He helped me sit up and squirted Rescue Remedy on my tongue and gave me a few sips of water. My world, my family, all that was familiar was now lost, I no longer had any control.

I had been in email contact with Essi just the week before this disturbing event. She had been backpacking with a friend in Australia since late 2012, to earn money to keep travelling, and had taken a job as a hotel receptionist somewhere in the outback. We had been discussing her idea of going back to university to do a master's and her recent interest in environmental factors, prompted by her travels. She was contemplating becoming a vegan and suggested we didn't tell dad yet 'as you know what a meat-eater, he is,' She wrote about her boyfriend Daniel, a graduate from a middle-class family in Leeds. I had joked that I was disappointed as I had hoped he was heavily pierced and tattooed, and we had laughed together as we knew how that would have upset M if he was.

She had shared her forthcoming plans: the following week she would return to Sydney, reunite with her friend who had been working there as a waitress, their boyfriends would join them, and they planned to hire a camper van to drive to Alice Springs. She told me she would be off-line for a while, and I told her I looked forward to hearing all about the next part of her trip. We had shared our news, plans and her secrets to be kept from dad, but the one thing she didn't share with me was that, before they hired that van in Sydney, she would fly 11,700 kilometres to Muscat, to meet Daniel and to be bridesmaid at her father's wedding, wearing matching purple gowns with Fifi Bird. That next part of her trip was also a secret, but this time between her and her dad.

How had any of this madness happened? I just did not understand. How had he married another woman almost one year ago and while we were still married. He was still married to me even then as I sat there in that moment, transfixed by his wedding photographs. None of it made any sense, why was his family there, why was our daughter there? I then had an insane thought: maybe something had happened to me, did I have some sort of crazy amnesia or memory problem, had I forgotten I was already divorced from him? I asked Josh to tell me the truth, was I going crazy? What he told me rang true and brought me back to the harsh reality of the situation.

"Mum, you are not mad, or crazy, or have anything wrong with you, it's him. It's always been him. Maurice and Grandma and all of them, I'm sorry to say including Essi, they have done this, who knows what story he told them all? He has done it, mum, he has married that sister of the Birds just as you said, no wonder grandma lied about it. It's real mum, this is who Maurice is. Please don't think any of this has anything to do with you. This is another of Maurice's games that has gone too far this time, I despise him mum for what he has done to you. For who he is. You've got to stay strong now mum, for Seb and your sake, you've got to stay strong."

At the time I was so consumed by the shockwave of this revelation that I didn't think to question Josh on what he meant by this being one of M's games or appreciate why Josh had for the first time told me he despised M. It was not until some months later that Josh was able to tell me about the harmful experiences: the emotional and psychological abuse and the bullying he had endured throughout his childhood and teenage years, and that the perpetrator was M. He was still healing and acknowledged that his bouts of anxiety and low mood were the long-lasting effects of the trauma he had suffered at the hands of his stepfather.

The dialogue around this issue belongs to Josh and so I have not elaborated any further here other than to say it has its place in this memoir and it is important that I acknowledge Josh as a survivor of M's coercive behaviour and control.

I questioned how I did not suspect that there was another woman in Muscat, if that was where he had met her? The photos I had seen the previous year of his sisters and nieces in Muscat, Stella with her bloody stupid fascinator, all of them dressed for a wedding, I had said that very same thing to M and in response he had denied that they had even visited. Oh, my goodness, the penny had suddenly dropped – I had actually spoken to him about his own wedding!

I had started the divorce process just two months before this bogus marriage. What had he told them all that had made them think it was acceptable to travel to Oman, to get dressed up and bear witness to him marrying another woman while he was still married to me? Did they know we were still married, but supported him regardless? No, they couldn't have, they wouldn't have, why would they? Or had they?

But what about Essi? She had gone out to Oman twice in 2012, in the January just after Seb and I had left and then again for three weeks in the November en route to Australia. At that time, he and his fiancée had been engaged for seven months so surely Essi must have met Suzanne Prudhoe then, if not before in the January?

I had last seen Essi in August 2012 when we had met for lunch in London, it was really good to catch up, but the mood changed when I told her I was concerned about M's behaviour and was worried he was working too hard. She told me she had been trying to reach him, but he wasn't answering her texts or emails, at that time we had both believed he was in Muscat, but he wasn't, he was here in the UK. I had elaborated on my concerns and somehow, I don't know why, it had led me to tell her how I knew that over the years M had caused her lie to me, to not tell me about gifts or money he had given her. I told her it was important to me that she knew I would never have begrudged her anything, it was more an idiosyncrasy of his, that he had to have secrets. It was at that point that Essi had started to cry. I had rarely seen her cry, not even as a young child, I felt so guilty and instantly apologised. But she assured me it was nothing I had said that upset her, it was something else that she couldn't talk to me about, as she had promised someone she wouldn't. We had hugged and I had ended up crying too.

I didn't see her again and sadly, I have not seen her since. She cancelled several planned farewell meet ups with me, Josh and Seb, and in the end left for Australia without saying goodbye to any of us. I returned her farewell gifts to Fat Face and TK Maxx. On the final last-minute cancelled occasion, Seb and I ate all of her farewell cake between us. I think I now understood her distress that day in London and her reluctance to meet again. But how did he get away with it? What had been said to make the engagement and wedding normal and acceptable to the girl I considered my daughter? Nothing, nothing was what it seemed anymore.

Equally as big a question was who was the bride? Miss Suzanne Prudhoe, the woman who had apparently married my husband? I Googled her and found out she taught at the PDO school in Muscat. She was listed as a new member of staff in the school newsletter, having arrived for the September 2011 term. The Bromsgrove connection was now evident, her biography detailed she had taught primary school there for four years before she moved to SE Asia to teach. She had also taught in the UAE and Europe but to the best of my knowledge, any trips M had made to any of those destinations did not coincide with her being there prior to Oman which meant they must have probably met in Muscat. But when? I had been in Muscat for our wedding anniversary in August that year, he had been home briefly that September during Ramadan and then for two weeks in the October, when he had been offered the Netherlands job that ultimately fell through. If he had met her at that time why was he so keen to leave Oman? Was it maybe a fling that had gotten out of hand? A casual extra-marital affair that he could take or leave, exactly as it seemed he had planned to do.

While I have never had much confidence in my appearance, his future bride looked plain and matronly in comparison in the school newsletter picture. She was dressed in a floral blouse and plain, loose pants, she wore no make-up and had lacklustre long, mousey hair, she lacked a sense of 'oomph.' I asked myself and others the question 'How he could have looked across the room or bar or wherever it was that they had met and thought I lust after that woman so much I am happy to sacrifice and deceive my wife and children to have her.'

I went back through my texts from the month of their engagement, May 2012. He was scheduled to travel back home on his return from a business trip to Australia; but due to work demands his plans changed at the last minute, he had flown straight back to Oman instead and came home a week later than originally planned.

On 17 May 2012 before he had boarded his return flight at Sydney, he had texted to tell me he could not wait to see me, how much he missed me, how desperate he was to be with me – and that was just 14 days after he had taken Suzanne Prudhoe to be his fiancée. I realised at that point, back in time, that Suzanne Prudhoe, his new fiancée, and I, his wife, were unified in his absolute disrespect for both of us.

On 29th May 2012, when he left from Manchester airport after his trip home, his text read:

> *All boarded, thanks for a lovely time. I know things have not been easy with me being away so much and do I appreciate your patience and understanding.' I will miss you. X*

I had replied:

> *It was lovely having you home, we felt more connected than since you left last time. All seemed just lovely and normal. Let's hold on to that, hopefully you'll be home again soon, or we can rendezvous half-way but not if that means the middle of the sea!*

He texted me on landing.

> *I'm home, waiting for a taxi, then on my way X*

With hindsight this message was probably meant for Suzanne Prudhoe but not knowing any better at the time it did not seem amiss.

> *OK. Long day for you. Well hope you sleep ok even if you don't have me to snuggle up to' x*

> *No won't be the same. Will miss you more than you will miss me. (He had always said that, that he missed me and loved me more than I loved him). Nearing flat so will say good night and will mail in the morning. X*

> *OK sleep tight will wait for your mail. X*

I continued my Google search and found that Suzanne Prudhoe was the secretary of a local Muscat sub aqua diving club. Was that the reason Essi had enrolled in her diving course back in January 2012? Had diving become the 'new family' hobby? That would mean that Essi had met Suzanne Prudhoe, within just three weeks of her father abandoning Seb and I at Christmas in Muscat. I could not comprehend any of this.

I checked Suzanne Prudhoe's Facebook home page again and found yet another significant photograph: The Taj Mahal. I now knew why Phil had identified the batch of emails with the New Delhi IP addresses. In those emails M had described his anger at having to stay in Oman due to work pressures instead of joining Seb and I on our 2012 family summer holiday. But it was now clear that once more he had lied about his whereabouts and circumstances and chose to holiday with his 'fiancée' instead of his wife and son. To think, I had actually felt sorry for him going without a holiday!

Jo called back, she too had returned to the Facebook page. She asked if I had noticed that not one of the engagement celebratory posts mentioned Maurice's name, in fact, most posts asked for more information, as if no one knew the identity of her mysterious fiancee.. There was one exception though, Jay had written: *This isn't news is it? Confused a tad….. anyway remember where we are for accommodation in Dubai.'* She was confused? Really? Had they been engaged for a while then and delayed the announcement?

I reverted to the PDO newsletter again but there was no other information to be had. But I did note the term timetable, autumn term finished the day that Seb and I had flown into Muscat, Christmas 2011. I instantly recalled how M had parked so far away from the terminal and that he hadn't been in the arrivals hall to meet us. One mystery solved! He must have seen off Suzanne Prudhoe who would have taken our inbound flight home for Christmas, on that last day of term. I could just imagine how he would have told her he would miss her, but that they would only be apart a couple of days. Just enough time for him to dump his wife and son in the apartment and then to abandon them, in favour of her, for the Christmas holidays.

I called Vicki with the latest but unexpected update, in a state of shock she logged into Facebook and instantly recognised the wedding venue: The Beach Pavilion at the Al Bustan hotel; she had been there for lunch just a few weeks earlier. It was the most expensive hotel in the country, no wonder Louis from One Direction had stayed there, as Zoey had written in her tweet last March.

I asked Vicki if the bride was the same woman she had seen him with in the hotel bar? After close scrutiny she confirmed it was, she had lost weight and was made up, but, yes, it was definitely her. Of course, it was, she had introduced herself to Sam and Sarah as Suzanne, but not as his wife of nine months, his newlywed bride. But as Vicki reminded me, there had been no signs of romance or flirting, they hadn't even laughed together. Knowing what we know now, how had he sat in full sight of Vicki and Sam who knew we were still married with his so-called new 'wife'?

What if Vicki had gone over to them, how would he have handled it? No doubt he would have fronted it out, such was the audaciousness of the man. How could he have been so bold? And what about her, what was she playing at? Did she know he was still married to me? And if so, what was he to her, what was his worth that she would risk a spurious and bigamous marriage for? As for him, what would he gain from marrying her that would make committing bigamy a reasonable price to pay to possess it? There, I had finally said it, BIGAMY: I was married to a bigamist and to all intents and purposes so was she.

Chapter 12

I had mailed William to bring him up to speed with this bewildering turn of events. Perhaps, now, he and Mr E would appreciate why I had repeatedly raised concerns that M was not to be trusted. That I had suspected he was hiding funds and had withheld details of at least one other bank account, and specifically an Omani savings account. I had proof of my suspicions: an email sent by M shortly after his arrival in Oman, in which he had confirmed he had successfully opened a savings account as a necessity, as getting a bank card and cheque book with a current account would take much longer; he explained he would need the cheque book because rent was paid by batches of 6 post-dated monthly cheques. We had raised this issue in our second questionnaire of him, which should have been completed months ago, but was only returned within days of this latest shocking discovery, as if I didn't have enough to contend with already.

M's responses to some of the questions on the questionnaire took us no further forward, as he had denied having the savings account and claimed it had been closed once the current account had been activated. My gut feeling was that he was lying, as I was convinced that he would have used it to stash money, and even more so now, but what could I do? Nothing, according to William.

The first question on that second questionnaire referred to the altered entries on the UK bank account statements, which meant that some entries differed considerably from what he stated to be the true online copies of all transactions on his account. We had provided examples and referred in particular to the online copies of statements which did not show certain expenditure by him, namely his secret visits to the UK. We requested clarity and asked him to confirm that the online copies were, in part, false and, if so, to explain how that had come about. We also asked for an explanation of the disparity between the original and online copies.

His reply to that single question stretched to three A4 pages.

He confirmed that the statements referred to and prepared by him were indeed partly false and did not reflect the true transactions as detailed in the original bank statements that I had produced. He also admitted that the disparity between the statements occurred as a result of his having filtered and adjusted the online internet copies in an attempt to conceal transactions made while he was in the UK. He confessed that this had been a deliberate act on his part, and that he acknowledged his actions as misplaced and irresponsible and suggested that the reasons for his behaviour may go some way to explaining his actions, and the reason that he cited for his unlawful behaviour was ME.

He wrote that he had tried to conceal visits to the UK, as the time he had spent there exceeded the expatriate allowance of 90 days to maintain his tax-free status and elaborated that this was through no fault of his own. But rather, the trips were work related, he had come to the UK to source materials not available in Oman. In a further attempt to justify his bank statement alterations he claimed without supplying any evidence to support his outlandish accusation that I had made threats and intended to cause him considerable financial problems and distress by my plans to provide such information to Her Majesty's Revenue and Customs (HMRC). I did not know what he meant by financial problems and distress, but was outraged that he had attempted to project the blame on me for his own deceitful behaviour. He expressed a fear of the court proceedings as the tone of our questions, according to him, included or suggested a threat that if he did not submit to my demands that I would report him to HMRC. Such action, he continued, could potentially have had serious and possible legal consequences for him as a criminal record would seriously affect his earning capacity and he sought my immediate agreement that I would not report him to HMRC. He cited his fear of a malicious pre-emptive strike from myself as the reason for his delayed response to our questionnaire. I had absolutely no idea what he was talking about, this was the first I had heard of any such thing, I was amazed that he had been permitted by his legal team to make such defamatory allegations against me without providing any proof.

M stated that he had had no intention of trying to mislead the court as to his financial status. Yet this was exactly what he had done: he had deceived the courts and in order to disengage himself from the responsibility of his actions he had confirmed his history and intent of continuing to deceive HMRC and then attempted to blame me as the cause for his deceitful behaviour. The irony of his fear of a criminal record was not lost on me, as his relationship with his future 'bigamous' wife was the reason he had concealed his visits in the first place, and he was now no doubt going to get a criminal record in relation to having committed bigamy.

My solicitor had sought confirmation from me that I had not threatened M in this manner. I was not happy with his attitude, but it was also an odd question given that he was the one who had drafted the same questions M referred to as being threatening and demanding. We subsequently wrote to M's solicitor that there was no evidence to support the accusation made, and they, as I anticipated, did not issue a response. What angered me the most though, was that M's statement would go on file at the court, and whoever read it had no way of knowing that the content was not true; thus he succeeded in undermining my integrity to the court, which I knew was his ultimate intention, as well as trying to save his own skin.

He had already used the personal attack tactic in response to our first questionnaire back in October. In that he had focussed on the dispute over the separation date to discredit me; his version of our separation history was that we had separated by mutual agreement in January 2011. He asserted that our marriage had been in difficulty for some years before that date, due to a combination of his working away and my long history of what he claimed was 'unreasonable and explosive behaviour' towards him. I had, according to him, acknowledged my behaviour as unacceptable but had refused to seek help in spite of his encouragement to do so. He had dared to claim that this same behaviour had negatively impacted on my relationship with Josh and that the disputes between us were so troublesome they would necessitate him returning to the UK from France to resolve them. In his opinion my intolerable behaviour was due to the menopause, which was responsible for further irrational behaviour which included my changing the locks on the family home preventing him access when he came home on leave, despite us apparently trying hard to work through our marriage difficulties at that time.

According to M, I had continued to be increasingly hostile toward him in spite of his alleged considerable efforts to support me, and that had led us reluctantly to come to the conclusion that we had to separate. Together, he claimed, we had chosen to keep it a secret from the whole family including the children as no one, not even myself, knew that we had separated!

Once more, he had succeeded in damaging my reputation on the court record. It would now be documented that not only was I malicious and threatening but was also a hormonally imbalanced, menopausal, erratic bitch by the sound of it. Yet again, there was no available option, no recourse, for me to dispute his spiteful accusations, nor was he under any obligation to supply evidence for his denigration of me.

It was apparent to me that, in spite of his written confession of criminal activities, I was the one who was being portrayed as the aggressor and he, it seemed, as the 'poor victim.' Why was I surprised by that? Such were his powers of manipulation which it seemed had even tricked the court too.

Returning to the second questionnaire we had also queried payments to a credit card that had appeared on bank statements but had not been declared on the Form E. The explanation offered was that the card was used solely by one of M's brothers who had supplied a signed statement to that effect. To support this explanation a complicated re-payment system had been described which was easily disputed as he claimed that I had deducted repayments from monies owed to his brother for work he had done on our house, in order to pay off the credit card debt. I called that particular brother to ask for an explanation and why he had lied about the credit card use, and that I had taken money away from him. His response was that he had no idea what I was talking about. It seemed that all these claims and counterclaims were happening at the very last minute, just before the FDR. M had timed it just right; I believed his tactic was to prevent us from challenging his submissions due to a lack of time remaining in which to do so.

The revised Omani Bank statements arrived just six working days before the FDR. They were presented in a different format but as true counter copies and were complete with an official bank stamp on each sheet. The only other difference from the previous statements was that the anomalies were absent. However, I questioned the monthly rent payment deductions as surely, he was living with his 'wife,' who as an expat employee of PDO would have rent free accommodation included in her contract?

I recalled that Vicki had not been able to find the address he had used on the Form E; the address was obviously false and had been added to conceal the true location of his residence. In spite of this set of statements looking authentic, I doubted that they were, but without proof we were not in a position to confront him even if there had been time to do so.

His team were pressing for an adjournment, to postpone the FDR without, as far as I could surmise, justification. I strongly resisted. I suspected M would not return to the UK, especially now he had 'married'; he and his double life seemed settled in Oman, and the threat of a police investigation for what I believed to be bigamy would surely deter his return even more. For some time I had had a constant, nagging fear that M would default on maintenance payments, and while he remained outside of the UK jurisdiction, enforcement of a court order for payment would not be possible. I had raised this fear several times with my legal team but had been shut down, regardless of his established pattern of dishonesty and my opinion of his blatant disrespect for the courts and for family law.

At the same time as the allegations made against me and the questionnaire response, we also had to address the issue of bigamy. I felt an odd numbness during this time, I was beginning to crumble, I certainly wasn't as strong mentally as I had been prior to discovering his 'marriage.' I say strong, but it was all relative; I feared I was on a downwards trajectory and that I would never be able to climb back up again. Friends could not believe it when I had told them what had happened, but I could, because who he, my husband, really was, had never been clearer to me. I was finally, or so I thought, finally seeing M for the Machiavellian character that he is, but how naive was I in my underestimation of him?

A new chain of correspondence commenced between the solicitors on the suspected bigamy topic on 10 February. The content and style of the following are in keeping with the original letters which, for legal reasons, cannot be reproduced here:

> *We are under the impression that your client has taken part in a marriage ceremony on 30th March 2013 with Miss Suzanne Prudhoe in Muscat, Oman. This date is 3 weeks prior to the authorisation of the Decree Nisi.*

> *We invite you to comment and to confirm if the marriage ceremony has taken place by return given that the FDR hearing is in eight days.*

We wondered if now we had lit the touchpaper whether we would trigger an explosion or merely a flicker; we could not predict the response. Their reply and our subsequent response were exchanged 4 days later, the absurdity was that they were both sent on Valentine's Day upset me.

> *Reply: With reference to your recent correspondence in which your client alleges that a marriage ceremony has taken place in Muscat between our client and Miss Suzanne Prudhoe, this is untrue. We ask that your client provides the evidence to support her claim.*

> *Response: We acknowledge your response and the denial that your client has taken part in a wedding ceremony in Muscat. We have therefore enclosed a selection of wedding photographs. One photograph clearly shows wedding labels or table place settings with the groom 'Maurice' and the bride 'Suzanne' written on them with the dates of 30th of March 2013 written under the names.*

Three days later, and just one day before the FDR hearing we still awaited a reply. So, with the hope of progressing matters Josh enlarged one of the photographs, and I passed it to William as further evidence; we wrote again. We made reference to the Valentine's Day letter and attached a further selection of wedding photographs taken from the photographer's website. The enlarged photograph image was that of Suzanne's vows, typed on a sheet of white paper and held in her right hand. The vows are reproduced in the original format as below:

> *Maurice today I confirm my promise to take you to be my husband, to have and to hold from this day forth, to give you encouragement, strength and ..... in all we do. To love and to cherish you, to always be by your side, in good times and in bad . I offer you my support, understanding and love. Wherever in the world we go, whatever challenges we face, we will face them together. I promise that I will walk with you through all of our tomorrows hand in hand. This is my promise to you ....*

In spite of our asking once more for their comments, needless to say, this letter too, went unanswered.

I had also provided my legal team with copies of comments on the wedding lifted from Suzanne Prudhoe's Facebook page, but even if we also sent those, I doubted we would have elicited an appropriate response, his side seemed resolute in their avoidance of the subject.

Some real examples of the comments are:

Abigail: *'Congratulations to you, all the very best wishes to the newlywed couple.'*

Lou: *'Lovely photo and lovely wedding too.'*

Sharon: *'Wishing you a great future ahead.'*

Bill: *'Looking fabulous guys, congrats.'*

Debbie: *'Congratulations Suzanne, about time!'*

I read and re-read every single message on her page, I pondered on the *'about time'* comment but had nowhere to go with it. I checked out the profiles of everyone who had posted in an effort to piece together their story: my husband and his new wife's story, but I only succeeded in tormenting myself even more. By now I was barely sleeping, every time I closed my eyes, I saw that profile picture; copious amounts of wine drunk every night was not helping either, as it made me even more emotional and distressed. His betrayal cut so very, very deep, his infidelity, his licentious behaviour, the immorality and his deliberate disregard for his children, the persistent lying, the list was infinite.

I knew even then it was a wound that would never heal, not for me or for Josh or for

Seb. No doubt with time it would scab over, but inevitably that scab would break down or be picked at many, many times and it would leave a permanent scar that would never fade.

I was immensely relieved when Jo arrived to be with me for the FDR hearing. We had been good friends since we had met at college aged 16. Together, we had backpacked across Europe, the States and parts of Africa and had some amazing adventures and narrow escapes; she was exactly who I needed to be with me on that day. The desire to lean hard on someone, to be able to let my guard down even for just a moment was all consuming. I could not, I would not, have coped alone without such a trusted friend by my side.

February 18th, 2014

On arrival at court, we were sat in a conference room. M was with his team, the solicitor Amanda and his barrister Ms F, in another room further along the same corridor. We would not meet until we were summoned to court much later that morning. A lengthy discussion took place focussed on the bigamy/remarriage and in particular how it was anticipated the court would deal with the bigamy. It was agreed that in all probability the offence of bigamy was 'extra-terrestrial,' which I later learnt meant in legal terms that it had occurred outside of the UK's jurisdiction and as such, meant that the judge would not report the matter as a criminal offence. I was bitterly disappointed, I had naturally presumed that judges worked to a code of ethics that meant they had a duty to at least report a known or suspected criminal act to the police for investigation, but it seemed that that was not the case. In fact, I was told, later that day, that the judge had implied that if I suspected M had committed bigamy, I could report it to the police if I saw fit to do so. How could that be right? That the onus fell to me to report him and not to those whom I understood to be in positions of authority to uphold the law and to ensure that justice is done.

It was acknowledged during the meeting that M had misrepresented the UK bank statements to conceal his visits to the UK primarily to cover up his extra-marital relationship and whereabouts and not just for tax evasion purposes. I was frustrated further when I was informed that no action would be taken by this court in relation to either the fraudulent bank statements or the history of tax evasion.

I reiterated my suspicions of the hidden bank accounts in Oman, which I now believed must also include at the very least a joint account held with Suzanne Prudhoe. The cost of the wedding must have been extortionate given the location and the lavish celebrations; how had that been paid for as there was no evidence of such expenditure on bank or credit card statements?

But it was emphasised to me yet again, that the court would make its findings on the assets already known and not what they might have been, how I wished M were as honest and forthcoming as me, it would have been so much simpler. I was reminded and rather brutally I thought, that if I were unhappy with this then the case would have to go off to a final hearing, but the first available date was not until September. I had already been advised that the cost for such a hearing would be a minimum of an additional £30,000. My bill, by January 2014 had already reached £19,000. It was also estimated that my final bill would be around £36,000, the equivalent of 20 months' salary for me. This estimation was based on the difficulties of my case and in particular the additional costs incurred by M's failure to provide full disclosure, his untruthfulness and the bigamous marriage which all added up to the fact that to conclude my case the cost would now exceed all previous estimates.

I had asked if the judge would inquire about the wedding and was advised he would not. But again, if I chose to go to a final hearing then the wedding situation would be useful and of an advantage to me. How on earth could I have contemplated spending a minimum of another £30,000 that I did not have to gamble on whether or not M might appear or choose to abscond from the whole proceedings. The fear of further debt was too much to handle, the existing debt weighed heavily enough and was well established already as part of my pattern of constant worrying.

Between discussion on the final settlement: the division of finances, maintenance and the management of the former matrimonial home (FMH) Mr E and William met with M's team to thrash out these issues, in the hope that we would go before the judge in total agreement, but that was not going to happen. The first point was the issue of the wedding: I was told when my team reported back to me that M's legal team had refused to be drawn on the issue. They had made their position clear that it was not a marriage ceremony but merely a commitment ceremony. It had also been denied that their client had been cohabiting. While it seemed there had been some discussion about who had paid for the wedding, M's legal team had insisted that they would not engage with any further debate on the issue. There was no impetus or insistence to pursue the argument any further from my side and so that basically was that. My pleas to confront his barrister with the *lovely wedding* Facebook posts, the additional wedding photographs, the vows, the photographer's comments of *the beautiful beach wedding* and to ask her to justify her comment of it being a ceremony of commitment when everyone in attendance including even the bride, believed they had celebrated a wedding fell on deaf ears, their position was clear. As was that of Mr E and William who were not willing to oppose or argue in spite of their client, me, insisting that they did.

At that point, I wished I could open the door and walk away from the lot of them as the realisation dawned, they didn't care or care enough about me, my family, my case. They would not do anything to rock the boat with a colleague. They had made it clear that we needed to press on, the judge would not be happy if we weren't ready to go before him when he called us. That was what was most important to them all. I wanted to scream at them "Fuck the lot of you." No one cared, no one cared.

At that moment I had insight into that elitist, self-serving bias and culture of this aspect of family law representatives. I felt it was all about them, and who they exchanged small talk with in chambers or booked for future hearings or met at legal social functions, it wasn't about clients like me. They were all complicit in their indifference to see justice done that day, justice for me and Josh and Seb, by not pursuing the issue of his 'marriage' or of his fraud or his contempt of court or his act of perjury.

The question of the FMH was up for discussion. M wanted the house to be put up for sale immediately and the profits from that sale split 50/50, which hardly seemed fair given his declared salary was 300% higher than mine as was his future earning potential and, importantly too, I had Seb to consider. M had 'generously' so I was told, submitted details of potential houses for us to consider in the area, all located near the council dump, the maliciousness of those recommendations was apparent to Jo and me, even if it wasn't to anyone else.

Seb had been unwell since M's departure the previous January. His GP, his counsellor and his consultant had all written to say stability was key to his recovery, he needed to stay in his family home. Copies of the letters had been received by M's solicitors. Yet they still vehemently argued the issue in the discussions between the rooms and resisted our request that we were permitted to stay in the FMH even when we finally got to appear before the judge.

Our case was just another case for the district judge who, as predicted, made no reference whatsoever to M's failure to provide full and frank disclosure or to any penalty for not doing so, but thankfully, he did take welcome action on the FMH dispute. He asked Ms F if she had seen the letters he had before him regarding Seb's ill-health and she replied in the affirmative, he then took the opportunity, in a scolding tone, to remind those present that 'the child's welfare is paramount in family law.' In an almost theatrical gesture, he opened a huge book of law and as the relevant section hit his bench with a thud, he read the pertinent part aloud. I felt this interlude had quite made his day whereas Ms F's embarrassment and, I guessed, anger at the judge's reprimand was palpable across the courtroom. I am sure my team sympathised with her and would have told her so given the opportunity. However, a senior barrister present in court did tell me after the proceedings that he never seen such a blatant disregard for a child's wellbeing by any parent as he had seen in court that day from M, which given his years at the bar was saying something.

M avoided looking at me. He was sitting on the opposite side of the courtroom, but we were no more than 6 meters away from each other. The room was windowless, and he stared over his right shoulder at the wall. I looked directly at the judge; I have no idea if he even noticed me. M's appearance was more subdued than our last court encounter, he was dressed in a plain grey suit and white shirt.

The judge ordered that we could stay in the FMH until Seb finished his secondary education which would in effect be until the end of the final term at school or college. I was hugely relieved. That we could stay in our home for the next three years would give us that much needed sense of security which was more important to me at that point than anything else. Whereas for M, it had been about scoring the points against me, winning the game, he certainly didn't need the money from a sale as he was now living in a joint expat income household, and he also didn't need to find somewhere to live either. Could he not see that by trying to hurt me he was also hurting Seb? But maybe he could and just didn't care.

We then returned to our respective rooms, there were still a few points to be finalised. Mr E suggested the profits from the eventual sale of the FMH should be 55 percent in my favour 45 percent to M; this was considered, I was advised to be reasonable. Prior to the hearing I had proposed that I should get awarded the house in its entirety to safeguard our future, my argument being grounded in my belief that there was a real risk of M disappearing or choosing not to pay maintenance with no chance of enforcement, coupled with his dishonesty and the suspected bigamy. But I was told that was ridiculous and that the other side would never agree. The option was raised again of going to a final hearing, where I would have a greater chance of increasing my share. I did not know how clearer I could have been, so once more I had to emphasise that a final hearing was outside of my scope of expenditure and as such could not ever be considered. Therefore, I had to push for the maximum share today, this was my only chance.

Time was ticking by, at this point it was already mid-afternoon and it was apparent both legal teams wanted the proceedings to conclude as soon as possible. We would have to go back before the judge one more time for him to agree to the final order, but to do that, we needed to agree on the remaining issues. I was grateful for Jo's support and being there with me as she agreed I should push for more than the 45/55 percent split. Everyone else was frustrated with me and my insistence on a larger share; the consensus was that the opposition would not budge.

I decided to call M's bluff. I saw it as the only way to bring the matter to a close. I instructed Mr E to return to negotiations with a final offer 35/65 percent split in my favour and to make it clear that this was the final offer and if it were not agreed we would proceed to a final hearing. I had to really force this issue as I was told if I had no intention of going to a final hearing it was wrong to say that I would. But I wasn't bluffing a hand in a friendly game of poker, this was serious, there were tens of thousands of pounds at stake and that was what I was playing for. I banked on M's reluctance to remain married to me for at least another seven months until the final hearing, and he would also have to consider the negative impact the potential bigamy charge might have on the outcome. Reluctantly my team took that proposal forward and his team agreed to it. Of course, I instantly regretted not asking for an 80/20 share, but it was what it was, and I was a lot happier with that outcome than I had been with the figure they were pushing me to accept.

We went back in before the judge who agreed this as the final part of the order. Our teams now needed to write up a rough copy of the order for us both to sign and for the judge to authorise, and then proceedings would be done. An official version would be distributed at a later date.

Jo was not allowed in court so had remained alone in our conference room. At this point I decided to stay in the waiting area which was now empty except for the receptionist and the security guard. Mr E, William and Ms F stood outside; I could see them through the glass doors. The solicitor Amanda came back into the waiting area and took a seat, I could only guess that M was also alone in his conference room.

While I waited Chris called to see how I had got on. Instantly I knew what I had to do, I whispered to him that I was just going to talk, but it was for someone else's benefit. Then in a deliberately louder than necessary voice, I told Chris that I had spoken to my senior police friend at Scotland Yard, which was actually true, and he would try to pull some strings to get information from the British Embassy in Muscat to see if they had actually married there, as if not, maybe the ceremony of commitment at the hotel was just that. His solicitor Amanda was trying her best not to look at me, but I could see, she was hanging on to my every word. I continued to tell Chris how the advice had been to report M to the police, and that I planned to do that the following day.

Amanda jumped up and scuttled off to join the group on the other side of the door. There was an overwhelming sense of deja vu, having stood in that same waiting area last time at court, when she had run off to fetch William to remove me from M's presence. Who was in control now, Miss solicitor? In an instant, William was straight through that door as I said bye to Chris. He asked who I had been speaking to. "One of my closest friends" I innocently replied, and told him he had called to check in on me, to make sure I was OK. I asked him why he was asking.

Amanda had repeated to them what I had said about reporting M to the police. William asked if it were true, if it was what I intended to do?

"Why would I have said it to William if it wasn't?"

On hearing my plans, Ms F, he told me, had said I was not to do that and that he should tell me so. By 'not doing that,' I presumed they meant not to report him to the police for the crime that we all so strongly suspected he had committed. She had said that if I did, he might well lose his job, which would mean he wouldn't be able to work in the world of finance handling contracts worth millions of dollars. A criminal record would prevent him from this kind of work; especially if it were known that he had doctored financial statements. If that were the case it was highly likely my maintenance payments would be jeopardised. How stupid did she think I was? The threat of him not paying maintenance was real enough whether or not I reported him. Most importantly, though, if M's legal team genuinely believed he had only taken part in a ceremony of commitment why were they so bothered by my plan to report him, especially given their insistence that he was innocent of our allegation of bigamy?

Did they really think that I would allow him to get away with a crime? Not only a crime in law but a crime against marriage, a crime against morality, a crime committed against his own family, against his own children.

William asked me again if I really intended to do it. When I told him I most definitely did, I saw what I believed to be a flicker of a smile; I seriously thought he wanted me to. Within minutes we were called back into court and then suddenly it was all over. Jo and I drove straight home, picked up Seb and went for pizza accompanied by the inevitable large glass of wine.

I felt an immense sense of relief that this part was over, but the next part was yet to begin, and I had no idea what it would bring. I had lost all faith in the family law courts and hoped that the criminal courts would find M guilty as we knew he was and that he would be punished accordingly. Not only for the crime he had committed in law but also for the pain and torment, the hurt and the betrayal, and for the harm he had done to those that he professed to have loved and held dear.

Part 3

Chapter 13

While the Facebook evidence and that fateful conversation with the Manns were strong indicators of his guilt, it was the Facebook photo of Stella wearing the fascinator the year before that had first made me suspect that, as crazy as it sounded, he had indeed married someone else. I was absolutely determined to report him for bigamy, so the following day Jo and I drove to the local police station, only to find it closed. We went to the next nearest police station but that too had been closed for some time. Jo's flight home was booked for early that afternoon. I didn't want her to leave; reluctantly, I dropped her off at Manchester airport. I was indebted to her for her support and could have done with her being with me as I made my way alone to the third police station. I hadn't prepared anything to say other than that I had come to report my husband for bigamy. The desk sergeant was baffled and asked me to elaborate, to explain what I meant by bigamy. In my effort to clarify I told her that a local district judge had advised that if I suspected my husband of being a bigamist, I should report him to the police, if I felt the inclination to do so, and as I did, here I was. She now looked even more puzzled but asked me to take a seat and wait.

After a short while I was called into an interview room where a young officer wasted no time in telling me that he had no idea how to handle a bigamy allegation. I wasn't surprised as I knew from my own research how rare bigamy cases are. I provided the officer with a brief history along with all the supporting evidence and he took copies. After a consultation with his supervising officer, he took my statement which he wrote and I signed once I had agreed to the content. I was told that, following a review of all of the information, a member of CID would be in touch. I spent a couple of hours in that room, relaying the series of discoveries including M's attempts to conceal his duplicitous lifestyle and his physical attempts to harm me. I told him that my husband remained in denial that he had committed the crime of which I now accused him. While the officer tried hard to remain professional his surprise at the revelations was apparent.

In countries where monogamy is the normal practice, such as the UK, if a person gets married whilst still being legally married to another partner, they will have committed bigamy, and can be prosecuted under the Offences Against the Person Act of 1861, Article 57:

> Whosoever, being married, shall marry any other person during the life of the former husband or wife, whether the second marriage shall have taken place in England or Ireland or elsewhere, shall be guilty of felony, and being convicted thereof shall be liable to be kept in penal servitude for any term not exceeding seven years.

Dr David Cox, criminal justice historian provided a historical perspective in the Plymouth Law and Criminal Justice Review (2012):

> Bigamy was first classified as a felony in the Bigamy Act 1603 and was as such a capital offence until the passing of the 1861 Offences Against the Person Act, when the maximum penalty was reduced to seven years' imprisonment. As such, for over 250 years bigamy was therefore theoretically punishable by death by hanging, but in practice an offender could usually (though not always successfully) claim Benefit of Clergy which was an exemption from prosecution awarded to clergymen, thereby reducing the sentence to branding on the thumb.

> Before men and women could divorce on equal terms and without blame being apportioned, bigamy was seen as one way in which men, or less usually, women could evade an unhappy and sometimes dangerous marriage and begin afresh. There was a total of over 22,000 offences recorded bigamy offences in the period 1850-1950, when the rates of conviction fluctuated greatly, especially in times of war and the immediate post-war aftermaths.

> Today, Bigamy is an uncommon crime, no longer regarded as a major threat to the institution of marriage or familial stability, as divorce laws have made it much easier for couples to legally separate, and co-habitation outside marriage is much more common than in pre-World War II England and Wales.

Between April 2015 and March 2020, there were a total of 363 cases of bigamy recorded by the police in England and Wales.

If a bigamous marriage was entered into abroad, under some circumstances it might be recognised in the UK for legal purposes but that did not apply to this case. In Oman, male nationals marrying under Sharia law can marry up to four wives, but only if they can afford to do so. As M was a British citizen and not eligible to marry under Sharia Law, he was prohibited from taking more than one wife. According to the Getting Married Abroad section on the GOV.UK website: *'If a marriage or civil partnership followed the correct process in the country where you got married then it will be recognised in the UK.'* So, if they had actually married according to Omani law, they had fulfilled the criteria for M to be charged with bigamy.

As I walked back to my car, I felt a huge sense of relief. I was comfortable with my actions, I had done the right thing regardless of the outcome or the consequences. I would just have to be patient now and wait for the police to contact me. I updated William, not that he would have any part to play in a potential criminal case, but because I thought it polite and fitting to do so.

Within a week of the FDR hearing, I was forwarded a letter from M's solicitor who had invited me to apply for the Decree Absolute within seven days. Using what was now a familiar tactic, they said that if I failed to act as requested, they intended to make the application themselves and would apply for a court order for me to pay the incurred fees in doing so. Yet as the applicant I had a 12-month window from the date of the Decree Nisi to apply for the Decree Absolute, so in theory I had until mid-April to make the application. I was puzzled by the urgency of their demand and could only think it related to the bigamy issue; maybe he thought it would all go away once we were legally divorced, but that was never going to happen. Apparently, it was unusual to apply such pressure but as there was no reason why the Decree should not be made absolute, I was advised I should do what was requested of me. So, once again, I had no choice but to agree to their demand. What difference did it make now anyway, I told myself, as I had already made the complaint to the police? So, the Decree Absolute was issued on the 10 March 2014, and our marriage was subsequently dissolved, in the same month, but one year after, he had married or had his ceremony of commitment (depending on who you believed) with Suzanne Prudhoe in Oman.

I pondered on this issue and decided to write to Suzanne Prudhoe, as I could not believe she would have 'married' him if she had known he was still married to me. She had the right to know the truth of the situation and given that I doubted anyone else would tell her, the responsibility fell to me. I tried hard to write a factual and unemotional letter; I did not want the content to be misinterpreted. Copies of the actual correspondence are as follows:

22nd February 2014

Dear Suzanne

I am writing to you in this format due to the gravity of the content.

My name is Yvonne (Yve) Gibney and I am married to Maurice, albeit we are going through the process of divorce. On February 18th, 2014 both Maurice and I attended an FDR hearing at Birkenhead Matrimonial Courts, once the court orders agreed at this hearing are issued, I will be able to apply for a Decree Absolute. Until the Decree Absolute is issued, we remain legally married. You have therefore, entered into a bigamous marriage with my husband.

As a consequence of the FDR hearing this has been reported as a crime to the police and other relevant authorities in the UK and in Oman. I understand that this case has been taken up by CID in the UK.

All of the attached documents which will confirm the situation for you are taken from our divorce legal paperwork, and all of these documents are held on file with my solicitor, Maurice's solicitor and the Birkenhead matrimonial courts.

If you wish you may contact William my solicitor who will provide any information you require on telephone number or email, both provided.

Alternatively, if you feel able to contact me my details are mobile phone number, landline number, email, all provided.

I understand this is difficult for you to read as it is for me to write but believe you need to know the truth.

Regards

I enclosed a list of the attachments with an explanation of the content of each as follows.

1) Copy of the Decree Nisi issued on 17 April 2013.

2) My statement of case which confirmed I had petitioned for divorce against Maurice on grounds of unreasonable behaviour and which contained examples of that behaviour.

3) My reply to M's request for further information with explanations in reference to the disputed date of separation. This included my counterclaim and the evidence I had supplied to support the dates I claimed we had separated and petitioned for divorce.

4) My position statement for the FDR compiled by my barrister and submitted at the FDR to the judge on 18th February 2014. I explained what the FDR hearing entailed and included documents that contained both relevant and not so relevant information but in its entirety for completeness and transparency.

5) I also sent copies of the Immerman application which referred to my having original copies of the bank and credit card statements that Maurice had altered and falsified as part of his Form E submission. I described how in the 130 entries he had removed were all transactions related to his three trips to the UK during 2012 to 2013 that I had been unaware of, 'these were trips I now believe he took with you.'

6) The Conduct document which referred to my 'discovering photographs of the ceremony of marriage between you and Maurice on 8 February 2014.' Note line 4, my barrister writes 'entered into a bigamous marriage ceremony with a person named Suzanne Prudhoe in Muscat.'

7) The letters from my solicitor dated 12 February 2014 on the subject of the ceremony of marriage.

8) The three letters from my solicitor dated 14/02/14. Self-explanatory content which acknowledges Maurice's denial of taking part in a ceremony of marriage in Muscat on 30/03/13.

9) For your information, at the FDR Maurice continued to deny he had taken part in a ceremony of marriage on the aforementioned date and location and stated it was a ceremony of commitment and not a wedding.

I had the package couriered to her school in Muscat and marked as confidential, for her attention only. I received a text notification it had been received and signed for, thirty minutes later my landline rang from a withheld number. There was inaudible whispering at the other end, I said hello several times and asked who it was even though I knew who it was, but there was no reply, and the call was abruptly terminated. That was the only contact made as a result of that letter, she never reached out to me in any other way, nor did she make contact with William.

I felt sorry for her and thought of her as a victim albeit in another way as it seemed she was manipulated and controlled by M. How tight a rein did he hold her with, if he could persuade her that the legal documents I had sent were false? Inevitably, he would have made up even more lies to convince her that I was unbalanced, envious, malicious or who knew what? He would say or do whatever it took to keep her believing in him, regardless of the conflicting evidence I had provided and which she, no doubt, interpreted according to what she wanted to believe the most. Her failure to act, even in secret, showed how successful he was in his absolute control of her, and sadly, I doubt she even realised it but rather interpreted it as an example of his love for her.

I knew I had to write to Essi too, and I found that letter very difficult to write. I was writing out of concern not only for her, but for Seb and Josh too; they were and would continue to be affected by the fallout of M's unscrupulous behaviour in so many ways. I struggled to understand how M could have deliberately sabotaged the relationship between his daughter, me and her brothers, a strategy that appeared to be meticulously planned to harm all three of our children, purely in order to achieve his own selfish ends. If I ever needed proof of his sociopathic tendencies this unconscionable behaviour was it, his willingness to destroy the happiness and love between siblings, possibly forever, although, I hoped that would not be the case. But that bond of love and respect they had for each other was not retrievable, it would never be the same again, he had made sure of that.

In addition, as if that were not enough, he had chosen to use Essi to support his lies, as her physical presence as bridesmaid at his sham wedding was the irrefutable proof of his status as a divorcee. How would she ever come to terms with or accept his actions or be reconciled with his manipulation and exploitation of her, as his daughter, and how he had used her attendance at that wedding to endorse his right to marry. Surely, if your daughter knew you were still married to her step mum of 19 years, she would hardly agree to be your bridesmaid. Or would she?

I couriered the package to the address I had been given for Essi in Australia.

Dear Essi

I am writing to you in this format due to the gravity of the content. I believe I now understand why I have not heard from you since my last email, the content of which must have in part, conflicted with information that Maurice had told you regarding the divorce process. Firstly, you need to understand that Maurice and I are not yet divorced, we are legally separated and have been since April 17th, 2013 but NOT divorced. We attended an FDR hearing as part of the divorce process on 18/02/14 at Birkenhead Court. All of the attached documents which will clarify the situation for you are taken from our divorce legal paperwork, and copies of all of these documents are held on file with my solicitor, Maurice's solicitor and the Birkenhead Matrimonial Courts. I will refer to these further on with explanation to their content.

Throughout the divorce process Maurice has made malicious and untrue statements about me and in particular about my mental health status during the period 2008-2010 and claimed we had agreed to separate on 04/01/11, and to keep it 'secret' to protect Sebastian. This is untrue. I can only conclude that Maurice must have told you and the rest of his family the same story as this would justify why he would have been free to marry Suzanne. I do not believe for a moment you would have been compliant in attending his 'wedding' if this were not the case. I am unable to describe to you the depth of emotional distress and shock I experienced when by a series of circumstances 2 weeks ago I saw their wedding photo on Suzanne's facebook page and subsequently the photographs on the photographer's website. This was exacerbated by the photo of you, as I believe as bridesmaid, and of Isabel walking Maurice 'down the aisle.'

A week earlier when I first received information on a possible wedding, I had visited Isabel with Josh for confirmation, she denied the marriage and that any members of the family had ever visited Muscat. As you know Seb is under the care of a psychiatrist and a counsellor, I have attached a copy of the letter his therapist Ms H submitted to the court as evidence. Note line 4 of the second paragraph which refers to 'Seb's parents are in the process of going through a divorce at the moment.' Ms H is now aware of Maurice's 'marriage' and has advised me of the importance of being honest with Seb about the situation.

I am sure you can appreciate Essi how difficult this will be for him and will inevitably compound his feelings of abandonment and rejection by his father, but I have no option but to act on the therapist's advice. I therefore need to ask you, if you feel able to do so, to share with me 'the story' – I'm sorry I do not know how to describe the information Maurice would have given you, that led you to believe that we were already divorced and that he was therefore free to marry again. I need to know this so I can relay it to Seb to enable him to understand why in particular his sister, and his grandma and his aunts and cousins all attended his father's 'wedding,' while his father was still married, and to be more precise not even legally separated from his mother.

I understand this must be very difficult for you to read but quite simply you also need to know the truth. I discovered the 'wedding' photos on 08/02/14 and on 12/02/14 my solicitor wrote to Maurice's solicitor asking him to confirm he had taken part in a 'ceremony of marriage.' He denied it and asked for evidence. The solicitor sent a selection of 'wedding' photographs including an enlarged photograph of Suzanne's vows which read 'Maurice today I confirm my promise to take you to be my husband, to have and to hold from this day forth...' We received no comments.

On 18/02/14 at the court, Maurice stated it was a 'Ceremony of Commitment' and again denied marriage. As we were attending a matrimonial court ironically it was out of the judge's remit to deal with it as bigamy is a crime. It has now been reported as such to the police. There are copious amounts of paperwork that I could share with you Essi, but I have attached the minimal amount required to confirm the truth of this situation. If you wish you can call or email my solicitor, details attached, he will provide any information you require. Josh is fully aware of the situation and will help you to understand, he will always be there for you as will I. It is important to me that you know that.

Thinking of you

I also sent an explanatory note with the paperwork that I had attached which included the same information I had sent to Suzanne Prudhoe plus the letter from Seb's therapist which contained the recommendation that I tell Seb about his father's bigamous marriage as referred to in my letter.

I thought I knew Essi so well. I anticipated it would be hurtful for her to acknowledge the truth of the situation, but I was banking on her being the weak link in M's chain of deceit and that she would do the right thing and provide the information I had asked for. But I have never received the response I had hoped for, in fact, to date I am still to receive a response. I have not heard from her since March 2013. While that break in my heart has never healed, I remain hopeful that one day maybe it will start to, and she will come back to our family.

March 1st, 2014

My friend Celeste was visiting from America and while on our sightseeing tour of Liverpool I received a call from CID to schedule a visit for that afternoon. So, we returned earlier than planned to meet with the two detectives, one female and one male, and sat together around my kitchen table for an hour and a half. If they tried to conceal their shock at M's behaviour, they didn't do too good a job. DC Sharpe, the senior detective, told us he had never heard of a case such as this in his 20 years on the force. I was really pleased that the officers not only believed me but had an immediate grasp of M's modus operandi as they proposed that M must have built up a pretence over time and lied extensively to his family to maintain his double life. At their request I identified family members from the wedding photos; they were shocked when I elucidated on the lead up to Essi being at the wedding as bridesmaid.

I explained my rationale for having written to both Essi and Suzanne Prudhoe and showed them copies of the correspondence I had sent. They recommended, and I agreed, that now the crime was officially being investigated I should not contact her or the Birds again. They speculated that the details of my original call to the Birds must have been relayed to M and that he had concocted a story about me, maybe that I was a stalker. They agreed with me that, as Donna Bird did not recognise my name or respond to my claim that I was his wife, it was apparent she knew nothing about me. They asked for M's contact details, they intended to make contact with him only after they had spoken to the Birds, which would be their first line of enquiry. Celeste expressed concern that as M had lied throughout, there was no reason to believe he would not continue to lie in his responses to them too; to my relief they told us they expected him to do just that. Isabel was not high on their list of witnesses but after I had told them about her response to my question "has he married in Muscat?" and her "I wouldn't know" answer she would progress up the list, which would be useful as I felt sure she would not lie to the police.

It was a wonderful feeling to know that the police planned to actively pursue him, I knew this would not be a priority case for them compared to other crimes they had to manage but that didn't matter to me. Now I had met the investigating officers I trusted them implicitly. I was filled with hope that the whole thing would be dealt with appropriately and, most importantly, that he would be punished for his crimes against us.

By concealing money from us M had in effect stolen from his own family, that it was a deliberate act was difficult to accept as was all the betrayal and deceit. My frustration was compounded by the courts failure to act, given that he had broken the law. But I was not prepared to let him get away with it if I could help it. I also questioned why I should have to pay for his concealment, not only financially but with increased levels of stress and emotional ill health. So, I set about re-examining all of the bank and card statements and, as I suspected, there were no entries that I could relate to the wedding expenditure such as: the white metal wedding rings, the engagement ring, the cost of the venue, catering, flowers, bridal wear, the list was endless, as I guessed the cost was too. If his Omani statements were authentic, as he had claimed they were, then their affair and subsequent marriage had undeniably been paid for with money concealed in undeclared accounts. He would also have paid the airfares for all of his family, including Essi's return flight from Australia, and undoubtedly paid for her boyfriend's flight too, as it would have been important to him that he appeared as the generous and wealthy father of the girlfriend. I researched the costs and estimated the airfares at around £5,000. His relatives had flown from the UK on KLM, I knew that as I had seen a Tweet of Teresa's expressing her frustration at their luggage having been mislaid in Amsterdam airport.

I wondered if they had enjoyed a honeymoon – was it the trip they took to Cape Town in summer 2013 while once again he had pretended to be in Oman? I had checked the IP addresses from emails received from there which, like the hidden 2012 trip to India, had odd timings which had raised my suspicions. Unsurprisingly, there had been no financial references to either of these trips on his credit card or bank statements either.

Coincidentally, a short time later, my friend Rosie had stayed at the same hotel I had identified through the Cape Town IP address as she had emailed me from there as an exercise to confirm it was the same location. In yet another coincidence, I actually recognised the hotel from a family holiday we had taken when Seb was just a toddler. We had all stayed in a hotel on the very same street on the Cape Town waterfront. I doubted he had pointed that out to Suzanne Prudhoe though.

I thought, rather naively, that if I could prove his failure to provide full and frank disclosure then I might be able to recoup some of my legal costs. I also thought that maybe if I could prove he had cheated me out of more money than he had declared on his Form E, I could get my divorce settlement set aside and re-evaluated. But there was at that time, unbelievably, no legal recourse available to me to do so. I raised the issue with my legal team and was advised that, as the suspected bigamy was mentioned at the FDR, as was the issue of M having rectified the submitted fraudulent bank documents, I would have no case anyway. But even if I had a case and there was a route to follow there would be the question of how to fund more legal expenses? I had exhausted all possible lines of credit and could not have coped with the stress of yet more debt hanging over me.

But in spite of all of that, I was not prepared to give up trying as I felt very let down by the system of family law. I could not understand how in a divorce case if one party flagrantly breaks the law and then admits to the criminality of their actions in writing then no penalty is applied or even considered. The fact that the court ignored M's admission of fraud and deception without applying the charge of contempt of court as stated on the Form E was incomprehensible to me, and equally as perturbing. It was clearly indicative of how they managed such cases. This allows the perpetrators, who I am sure, even without supporting evidence, are mostly men, to act disrespectfully towards the law and the legal process of divorce. More importantly, the courts lack of action causes them to act as enablers, allowing the lawbreakers to steal from their partners and children, which inevitably leads in most cases to financial hardship and distress. I was going to try my best not to let him get away with it and I hoped that if he were sentenced for bigamy it would help my cause. But to achieve that I needed to start gathering more information and evidence wherever I could.

Chapter 14

As a child growing up, I had wanted to be a journalist, but as my passion to travel grew my ambitions changed to being an air hostess or a long-distance lorry driver as they both represented ways of traveling. In reality, before training as a nurse and in order to fund trips, I worked as a barmaid, a cleaner, a waitress, a shop assistant, a Christmas postie, and even a dancer, but one profession I had never considered was detective. I surprised myself, though, once I started my detective work and realised just how good I was! At the beginning of the evidence gathering I reached out to the women friends I had made on my various postings and travels around the world for help with research and information. We joked we had become the international arm of Alexander McCall Smith's Ladies Detective Agency, the doors of which did not close until four years later in April 2018, having successfully achieved their purpose.

March 2014

As part of my plan, I would have to obtain the costs of the wedding, and to do that I contacted the Al Bustan hotel to enquire about wedding packages for a date the following year. Not the ones advertised on their website but specifically one just like the Gibney/ Prudhoe wedding which I pretended I had been a guest at. I had to smile at my own creativity, as I would have been a very unwelcome guest!

I spoke to the wedding planner; she uploaded and shared the details of the wedding and then followed up with emailed confirmation of options and costs, as well as links to recommended wedding suppliers, such as florists. I felt a twinge of guilt at deceiving her as she had been so helpful but as I was not going to obtain the information any other way, I had to do it. She confirmed that 50 guests had attended the celebrations and based on the historical conversion rate at the time, I was able to work out the approximate costs in sterling of the 'ceremony of commitment' or 'wedding.'

They had married under a cabana having walked down the red carpet, with guests seated either side exactly as I had seen in the photographs. The ceremony was followed by a champagne reception with canapes and the entertainment was provided by a harpist. A harpist? WTF! M listened to Morrisey and Oasis, I doubted he even knew what sound a harp made.

Dinner was selected from the set menus and there had been a free bar serving alcohol and soft drinks. I could see from the photographs that there was an absence of guests of Arabic appearance so I guessed that their wedding menu choice would have been the one with the most familiar foods, rather than the alternative Arabic or Asian menus. The starter contained a Mezza with a variety of salads, there was also a vermicelli chicken soup, and a selection of breads. There were eight options for the main courses that included lamb, two types of fish, beef and chicken with various vegetable and rice accompaniments. The dessert selection sounded particularly tempting, (I have a bit of a sweet tooth): coffee opera cake, vanilla crème caramel, strawberry cheesecake, Umm Ali (a delicious Arabic bread pudding), chocolate mousse with candied orange and fruit salad with rose petals. Let's not forget the wedding cake too.

A DJ provided the music for the post-dinner festivities. Photographs of the happy couple dancing had been posted on the photographer's website and I wondered why in the heat of the night (average night-time temperature for March is 25C/77F), and after at least a few drinks M was still wearing his jacket, buttoned up on the dance floor.

The approximate costs as I worked them out to be were as follows:

Beach pavilion venue: £10,652

Cabana: £602

Red carpet: £110

Champagne: £140 per bottle x 20 for champagne reception and wedding toast = £2,800

Finger food for the reception: £1,155

Harpist: £520 for a 45-minute set

Alcohol/soft drinks at a rate of £32 per person per hour, given that there were 50 guests for a possible eight hours, the cost (not including champagne) was £256 per person, the total cost was £12,800.

Wedding cake: £190

Dinner, four-course meal (based on cutlery at place settings) £93.48 per person, the total meal cost was £4674.

Linen napkin hire: £44

Discotheque: £1,750

Flowers: the quote was based on wedding photographs: £740

Executive suite for two nights for the bride and groom: £1810

Rooms for family x seven based on standard B&B rate: £190 per night x seven nights: £9310

Flights: £5,000

Visas for family: £320

The total cost per head for all foods and drinks worked out at a staggering £432.38 per person.

I was unable to obtain confirmation of a pre-wedding dinner, but I was sure there had been one, and why not, as this was certainly a no expenses spared wedding. I was sure it was an all-expenses paid holiday for his whole family too. There would have been additional expenditure, such as the photographer, hair and makeup, bridesmaid's dresses, airport transfers, tours and family entertainment and meals. Not knowing these costs, I was unable to include them in the total of known wedding expenditure, which was an exorbitant amount of £51,332, and which equated to two and a half times my annual salary.

As the celebrations took place before we were even legally separated, the money he spent belonged to me just as much as it did to him. So, in effect, I had helped pay for a very large share of the bigamous wedding celebrations. There was no doubt that I had contributed my half of the cost of Suzanne Prudhoe's engagement ring and very probably her wedding ring too. How about that? It felt like I had been played in a bizarre game of double jeopardy. I was sickened by the exorbitant amount of money squandered by M in his role as puppet master, purely to enable him to pull the strings of those he supposedly loved and cared about to dance so ecstatically to his wedding tune.

There were questions that still needed to be answered, most importantly why did a ceremony of commitment have the appearance of a wedding. The Facebook messages from guests and well-wishers reflected that too, as not one message referred to a ceremony of commitment. As I had never heard of this type of ceremony before, I researched it online. I learnt that it provides an opportunity for couples to express their love and commitment to each other, rings can be exchanged, but there was no mention of an engagement prior to the ceremony. It is not a legal ceremony and is normally led by a celebrant, but there was no celebrant listed online in the whole of Oman. There was an arm barely visible in one of the cabana photos that must have belonged to the person who had married them, but who was that?

The section of Suzanne Prudhoe's vows that Josh had enlarged, and we had sent in evidence to M's solicitor had read: *'I confirm that I take you to be my husband'* and that phrase niggled me because why would you *'confirm?'* Surely the wording of vows was that you take him to be, unless of course you have already taken him to be your husband. I was so bothered by it that I checked the actual definition of the word 'confirm' in the Oxford Dictionary, it read *'to establish the truth or correctness of (something previously believed or suspected to be the case).'* That raised my suspicions further, had they already married elsewhere and was this really a ceremony of commitment? He had been most adamant that it was, but I reminded myself that he could not be believed. Was I overreacting by hanging on to a single word? No, because instinctively it felt right to do so and I had followed my instincts throughout this whole shabby process. I was not going to stop now.

There was also the matter of options for marrying in Oman as a non-Muslim foreigner. We knew, thanks to Hussein, that they had not married in church. An idea began to take shape – had they been married at the British Embassy and then had the commitment ceremony? That would explain the odd wording of her vows and the wedding comments.

I couldn't help myself, I had to call the British Embassy in Oman to enquire how I could find out who might have married there in the past year. I was asked to email my request. I tried hard to wait quietly for a response, but I was too impatient, as I was hopeful that my suspicions would be confirmed. Instead, I called back the following week and was told my request had been reviewed but that due to data protection the information could not be shared. I read between the lines though as I thought I had detected in the administrative officer's intonation that there was actually information to be shared.

As I was not eligible to apply for the data release, I needed to find someone who could do it. Maybe if I raised the bigamy issue the data protection act could by bypassed? I needed a way in, to be able to discuss this further. A trusted friend from my FCO days still worked at a British Embassy overseas and provided the phone number of the Oman desk at the FCO in London. Each country, worldwide, has at least one designated officer in London who handles generic issues related to that particular country at that country's 'desk.' I felt I was off to a good start as the desk officer was Nigeran, we had a chat about Lagos and then feeling comfortable I broached the subject and she kindly told me she would look into it. This time I knew I had to wait until I was called back, as I had been far too cheeky in the first place by approaching her for assistance. I was appreciative but disappointed by her response, that the data protection act could not be circumvented but as the information was potentially part of an active police case, she suggested that the police should contact the embassy directly. Seemingly there would be a lot of paperwork to be completed but if the information requested was available, the police would be provided with the documentation. Although she did stress, it may take some time to process in Oman. So, reluctantly, as I had so wanted to be the one to discover the truth, I passed the information on to the detectives and considered my next move.

April 2014

I was back at work and trying to re-establish some sense of normality to our family life. My emotions were all over the place, it was difficult enough coming to terms with my marriage being over and that I was now a divorcee, but it was the circumstances that had brought me to this point which I struggled with, and it was a long way from being over.

I was in the process of evicting M's brother from my rental property as he was in serious rent arrears; an imminent court case was looming which would enable me to evict him. I was dreading any contact with his family. Brian's supporters had made threatening and abusive phone calls to me; I was so intimidated by them I had reported them to the police. I suspected that M had a hand in causing this situation to be more unpleasant than it already was.

I was also, very reluctantly, having to correspond with M on the issue of his personal possessions. He had been given two months from the date of the FDR to collect his belongings which included his clothes, a lifetime of personal effects, sound system and an old Jaguar car that he had been working on. But the two months had passed without any attempt at collection. But wanting his possessions gone, I extended the timeframe and even suggested a member of his family make contact and collect his more personal belongings, while he organised a removal company to pack up and remove the bulk of the items, which I thought, given what had taken place, was a generous gesture.

He insisted though that he had left behind at the house expensive pieces of jewellery, including a watch worth £3000, but he had most definitely done no such thing. Why would he leave such items behind if he knew he was never coming back? Interestingly, he had failed to declare any of these items, which had a total value of approximately £5,000, on his Form E, which stipulated any personal item above £500 to be listed as an asset. But that did not stop him from reporting me to the local police for theft; however, they did not pursue his allegation as it was a divorce-related issue.

Based on previous experience, I anticipated a letter threatening to take me to court would soon appear, and I was right. It alleged I had been obstructive and prevented him from collecting his belongings, in spite of my having done as much as possible to expedite and facilitate the process. They also accused me of having his 'high value items' in my possession and that if I did not comply with their demands within seven days their client would pursue me for criminal damages and planned to return the matter to court and implied, I would be responsible for costs and referred to 'consequences.' I instructed William not to answer the letter, I had had enough of their threats and he had no proof to support his allegations, as they were not true.

In a later email, M requested I send him the family photos that were stored on the home computer, I responded by asking for clarification of what 'family' he referred to? These are the actual emails sent.

I asked, *Why would you want photos of me, Josh and Seb, when we mean nothing to you? You discarded us at the very first step on your journey of duplicity that you now reside in so comfortably.'* He did not repeat this request again.

In earlier correspondence in late March and then again in April, I had requested the following from M:

> *Please supply me with the information that you gave to Jessica and your mother which made them believe you were free to marry Suzanne on 30 March 2013 and attend the wedding at our expense. While I note you never made or acknowledged any reference to this wedding to me, this is about Sebastian and my having to tell him about the situation on the advice of his therapist.*

I had already sent him copies of Seb's health records attached to the original request which he had ignored.

> *The implications of your failure to respond is despicable as has been your behaviour to Seb, Josh and me throughout this whole process. You have thought of no one other than yourself, your actions clearly demonstrate just what you will do to satisfy your financial greed and your need to control. I understand that in spite of her knowing the truth about your relationship and your wedding, Suzanne has stayed with you. You chose well Maurice, in being able to identify a woman who will be willing to accept living a life of deceit and be content with it, and who is happy in being complicit in the hurt and pain caused to Sebastian.*

I did what I could to assist the police and sent them the email correspondence between myself and the wedding planner which confirmed the details of their 'wedding reception' in the hotel booking records. This, I was told, provided the additional proof required to inform M that they now had enough evidence to arrest him on suspicion of bigamy, which he had denied in earlier correspondence with the CID detectives. Once again, he had insisted it was a private ceremony of commitment.

My friends in Oman had confirmed that all expatriate residents were issued with an electronic residents' card which contained all of their personal data including marital status. The cards are registered to the central police database. I also forwarded this information to the DC's; if they could apply for his particulars it should provide the definitive proof they needed.

The investigation was progressing, I had been told that a member of Suzanne Prudhoe's family had become distressed during a telephone conversation with one of the detectives when asked about the wedding ceremony. The police had followed up on the abandoned call with a letter requesting confirmation of her attendance at the wedding, the response was still outstanding.

Most importantly, an interview date had been set for early May for M to attend the police station where he would be formally spoken to in relation to the matter of bigamy. At last, some progress. I wondered how he would try to wangle his way out of this one. I would have loved to have known what was going on in his head at that time, what he was planning to say and do, if he was prepared to produce false documents to the police as he did in the divorce case, and how confident he might have felt about the police interview. I wondered if he had really thought I would go through with reporting him. He knew me well enough to know that once I set about a project, I would be 100 percent committed to it regardless of how challenging the cause may be. But I do believe he underestimated me on this issue, just as he did when he believed he would succeed at keeping the bigamous wedding a secret from me.

I was instructed not to have any further contact with M, now an interview date had been set. This meant I had to pass the responsibility for his possessions over to William, which would of course cost me, but I could justify it to see him charged. While part of me eagerly awaited the next update from the detectives, the other part of me battled with my anxieties. As the date approached for M to be in the country, I became increasingly fearful. I had shared with the DC's M's history of volatile and unpredictable behaviour and violence towards me and was told to call 999 immediately if he should arrive at the FMH. I was hopeful that he would be charged after the interview, but I knew that, inevitably, he would project the blame for his situation on to me just as he had blamed me rather than take responsibility for his illegal actions during the divorce process. I expected a retaliation so, as an extra precaution, I had additional locks put on the front door and on all the downstairs windows. it was an old house and M knew where the house was the most vulnerable if he wanted to break in.

I needed a distraction, so focussed on obtaining more information; I looked to the photographer who referred to the *'beautiful beach wedding,'* who might prove useful; Josh volunteered to email her. Following my example, he claimed he was planning his wedding at the Al Bustan later in the year and enquired if she were available to be his wedding photographer, as he was impressed by the *'Mr and Mrs P wedding'* photos featured on her website. She declined and explained that weddings were no longer part of her portfolio but did tell him that the Al Bustan was *'a beautiful location to get married.'* Her statement caused further confusion as I thought they couldn't have got married at the hotel. Unfortunately, this also meant we were not able to obtain her costs which had been part of our motivation for contacting her. I never did discover why she referred to them as Mr and Mrs P as opposed to Mr and Mrs G.

May 2014

It was a happy day when I heard that CID had finally had the opportunity to interview M and I appreciated their sharing with me some of the details of that interview. The statement I had given at the police station had been read to him and he had apparently picked it apart and used the opportunity to tell the detectives that I was a very bitter woman, and it was that bitterness that had driven me to make the allegation of bigamy. He had accused me of sending hate mail to both Suzanne Prudhoe's family and his own family, which was not true. He had told the police that the celebration at the Al Bustan was only a ceremony of commitment and not a 'proper wedding' but did agree that it had looked like a proper wedding.

The interview had lasted several hours, and I was told it seemed to go around in circles until M was informed that 'his family' (not us of course) would be questioned as witnesses. This, I understood, had been the turning point: he had become more co-operative and open in his responses but had also requested a break to recompose himself, as he had become distressed at the thought of 'his family' being involved. When the interview recommenced, it was concluded that M had more or less admitted to a marriage in Oman, but that he might have been unaware an offence had been committed. It was agreed that he would supply proof of the marriage, and that if it transpired it was not a legal wedding the case against him maybe amended to one of attempted bigamy, as opposed to actual bigamy.

At the time I remember wishing I could have been a fly on the wall, and in a way that wish did come true. In 2018 during another court case against M I had the opportunity to listen to that actual police interview. My initial apprehension at hearing his voice again for the first time in four years had been unnecessary as I had actually ended up laughing out loud at some of M's responses to the questions asked. Especially as he was talking to two very experienced detectives who no doubt would have seen straight through him. An example, which I had been told about after his interview and had gone some way to lightening my mood at the time, was that when asked if the hotel had been under the impression it was a wedding, he had suggested that they might have thought it was a fancy-dress private party! What bride would be happy knowing that her husband had referred to their wedding as a fancy-dress party?

M had been informed that this was an ongoing investigation and therefore he would be expected to maintain regular contact with CID and be re-interviewed on his return to the UK in July, 2 months later, or earlier if required; this was part of his bail condition. He was advised that I must not be contacted, either by himself or any agent acting on his behalf; not being one to miss a chance to denigrate me, he had assured the detectives that he would not contact me as I would only make up lies about him if he did.

I will never know what went on his head, or who he really was. While I had trusted and loved him unconditionally, he had schemed and plotted against me with his unfaithfulness and duplicitous lifestyle which eventually culminated in his ultimate betrayal. Through the years of deceitfulness, the divorce proceedings and the bigamy trial, he had systematically conspired to destroy our family emotionally and financially. I could not understand how he could have done any of it and simultaneously continued to maintain an impression of normality to all concerned including his bigamous wife.

Chapter 15

June 2014

The police contacted me to request a copy of M's statement to the family courts in which he had admitted to the fraudulent documentation submissions and his reason for doing so, along with the supporting evidence. It was to be submitted to the CPS in the hope that he could be charged with perjury, and of course I was more than happy to oblige.

July 30th, 2014

Although it had also been agreed at that interview that M would forward a copy of his ceremony of commitment or wedding certificate to the police at the earliest opportunity on returning to Oman, he was still to produce it. When chased he had used the by now all too familiar phrase of 'I was in the desert' as an excuse for his poor communication. That expression is now firmly established amongst my friends as an excuse for tardiness and failure to complete a task on time.

It was a busy time, as on 31st July we were both due back at Birkenhead family court, a hearing had been scheduled to amend a section of the divorce settlement. At the FDR hearing in February, it had been agreed and written into the Final Order that I could remortgage the house for an additional £60,000 without my ex-husband's agreement or involvement. I needed the additional funds to enable me to pay off my legal bill and the multitude of other debts that I had incurred during that past year. However, due to a clerical error, the word 'further' or some such similar word had been omitted when the Final Order had been typed up. As the existing mortgage was £58,000 it meant, as the order stood, that I could only re-mortgage for £2000 and not the £60,000 that I needed. This error could be amended under the 'slip rule,' which is a process by which the court may correct an accidental slip or omission in a judgment or order. The district judge agreed to the amendment, and to validate it both parties had to sign in agreement.

In the same Final Order, it was also specified that M had two months to collect his personal possessions from the FMH, and that he had to provide me with 28 days' notice of his intention to do so. I had tried my best to facilitate this but without success, as M had insisted that he would pick and choose the items he would collect, namely the TV and sound system, which had been allocated to him, but not his clothes or his un-roadworthy Jaguar that took up most of the garage space.

I could have predicted this turn of events as some personal items were date specific such as family photos, CDs, DVDs and magazines bought in the latter years of our marriage and as such would have been inconsistent with his alleged date of our separation. I considered, given the circumstances, that his behaviour was unreasonable. I was not prepared to store his personal possessions until he saw fit to collect them, if he ever would.

But, in spite of the judge's request to do so, M had refused to sign the slip order and took the chance to assert his 'authority' and applied his own condition to his signing and in doing so held me to ransom. His solicitors stipulated he would only sign if I extended the timeframe for the collection of his personal possessions by a further three months. I had no option but to agree as I was in a desperate financial position. I had already paid the costs related to the current mortgage application and would forfeit that if he did not sign as soon as possible. Once again, I was at a loss to understand how it could be considered acceptable that M could not only refuse the district judge's request but in addition apply his own terms for his signature? Let's not forget, I was also paying not only for the privilege of rectifying the solicitor's error in not ensuring the original order was accurate in the wording of its content, but also for M to take back control over the re-mortgaging of the house, and the collection of his possessions contrary to the original Final Order.

Being on tenterhooks waiting for confirmation that he had been charged and my very genuine fear of seeing him again across the negotiation table in the court sent my stress levels further out of control. My brother Jeff called to offer support; I mooted the idea that M, leaving it to the last possible moment, would probably check in with the police after our morning court hearing the following day. But as Jeff did not expect him to accept the charge he doubted he was even in the country. The following day was the last day of Eid-El-Fitri, the celebrations which marked the end of Ramadan. If M were in the UK, I would expect him to return imminently to Oman as normal working routines would resume at the end of the holidays.

Unbeknown to me, following our conversation, Jeff called the Birds' home under the guise of being an old friend of M's. He must have sounded plausible as he described a pleasant woman who had told him to call back in an hour as "Maurice had nipped out to the shops."

That knowledge fuelled another disturbed night, as I now knew for sure I would have to face him in court. But I needn't have worried as he did not attend the hearing. His divorce barrister Ms F explained her client's absence was due to his being on an assignment in the desert in Oman, thus creating the image of a wonderfully romantic and daring man. I burst that bubble when I explained to our respective legal teams and the Judge that that actually wasn't true and that I could confirm that a relative had spoken to Ms Prudhoe the previous day who had confirmed her client was indeed in the country and staying at the Bromsgrove address. Ms F retaliated with the comment that she would act on information received from her client, and her client only, and that she had absolutely no reason to doubt him.

So, I expanded further and told them that that very morning, I had emailed the CID detectives who were investigating her client for bigamy to tell them that he was in the country. I took the opportunity to alert them all to the fact that if he failed to report to CID that very day, he would be in breach of his bail conditions and as a result would be placed on the Police National Computer as a 'wanted person.' Maybe Ms F might now rethink her reasons not to doubt him? I relished the idea of him being arrested at the airport at passport control or even better as he was trying to board his flight, that was my own private fantasy in which I could feel his shame. But at that moment, when I said it, I wanted to remind them all of the character of the person they were dealing with, and that once again, he had mis-represented himself to the court. But it proved to be to no avail, as the judge said that his appearance was of no consequence and his presence could be excused.

Yet I had not been offered the option of non-attendance. I'd had to request a day's leave at short notice and suffer the embarrassment of the explanation to support my request to my manager. That M had stipulated conditions for signing the slip order and declined the Judge's request was not questioned but merely accepted. Once again, he was not held to account for his manipulation and control of the court system or most importantly how that impacted on me. How was the system so flawed and inequitable?

But I tried to find a positive and that was that I would now be able to re-mortgage as planned and also that hopefully we would soon be rid of his possessions, so no part of him or sense of his presence would remain in our family home. I was now more determined than ever to do what I could to ensure he received just punishment for his crime. To achieve that I needed to start gathering more information and evidence wherever I could.

It had taken me a lot of time and online research to finally accept that the family law legal representatives had no responsibility, other than perhaps morally, to report suspected crimes, such as bigamy. I still struggled to accept that he would not be charged with contempt of court or perjury for the falsification of the bank statements during the divorce process.

August 1st, 2014

I made no effort whatsoever that day to keep the smile off my face. M had not responded to the emailed or phone communication sent by CID to remind M of his bail conditions. As he had failed to report back for charging and as a result breached his bail conditions, he had been placed on the Police National Computer and was now a wanted man.

August 4th, 2014

I received a call while at work from CID to request copies of our marriage certificate and the Decree Absolute; these were needed to accompany the evidence being sent to the CPS, as M was about to be charged with bigamy. He had finally presented himself to be charged. Excitedly, and holding back tears of relief, I passed the request to William's PA and asked her to send copies asap to DC Doyle. However, my excitement was short lived, as the DC warned me to be prepared, because M might get off with a caution; a colleague had advised her that this was a possibility. I couldn't believe it ! Was he really going to get off with a caution, especially after breaching his bail conditions? What did that say about the crime or the worth associated with the institution of marriage or respect for family and the damage he had caused to our lives? Clearly that crimes against the family were not considered serious enough to warrant anything more than a caution. I was beside myself, had we come this far for him to receive a pathetic slap on the wrists and told not to do it again. A caution for a crime that can carry a seven-year sentence, surely not.

As soon as I could I left work. I was a mere five-minute drive away from the police station where he was being held, it seemed, waiting to have the policeman's finger wagged in his face as he collected his 'caution' reprimand. My colleague Chris advised me not to go, and while I had always welcomed her input and valuable support throughout, I was on a mission, and nothing would stop me. I parked up outside the entrance; I didn't know why I was there, I just had to be. After an hour or so I had calmed down; I pulled away still looking in my rear mirror in case he should appear. I drove to the beach, but sat in the car, distressed. The DC called shortly after to confirm that he had been charged, only with bigamy, but he had been charged and the case would go to court; there was no mention of a caution. I breathed the biggest sigh of relief. He WAS going to court after all. I wasted no time in messaging my friends and my support network with the good news, but I could not lose the niggling feeling that, somehow, he would 'get' me for reporting the bigamy in the first place. He would most definitely have put his personal safety net of revenge in place somewhere along the line.

Mid-August

I recalled my conversations some months earlier with the British Embassy consular staff who had mentioned a 'certificate of no impediment to marry.' My inner detective came to the fore, I needed to know what that was and if it was of any significance. The GOV.UK *'getting married abroad'* website provides a drop-down list of countries from which I selected Oman and learnt that in order to have enabled the bigamous wedding M would have had to sign an affidavit that confirmed he was free to marry, and this was what had been referred to as *'the Certificate of No Impediment to Marry.'* I downloaded a copy and have included it here to demonstrate that the form was not a simple one, it could not have been filled out in error or by accident but as a deliberate attempt to deceive. The guidance given was to complete this affidavit by typing in personal details and that it should be signed in the presence of a consular officer once the document had been checked.

AFFIDAVIT OF MARITAL STATUS

I,   make oath and say as follows:

The following is information about myself:

Surname, All forenames, (as shown on passport), Male/Female, Date of Birth, Place of Birth, Usual Address, Occupation

All forenames and surname of Father, All forenames and surname of Mother, Mother's maiden name,

British passport number, Date and place of issue of passport,

Marital Status

If divorced, date and place of issue of decree absolute

If widowed, date and place of death of previous spouse

I am not under 18 years of age or [I am under 18 years of age but the consent of the persons whose consent to the marriage is required by law has been obtained] or [I am under 18 years of age but there is no person whose consent to the marriage is required by law]

A marriage is proposed to be solemnised between me and (name) of (usual address)

a   (nationality) National at   (church, mosque, temple) on (Date)

I am free to enter into this proposed marriage and believe that there is not any impediment by reason of kindred or alliance, or other lawful hindrance, to this proposed marriage.

Sworn at the British Embassy, Muscat

This   day of   2013

(Signature of deponent)

Before me,

British Embassy, P O Box 185 Postal Code 116, Muscat, Sultanate of Oman

I had read the guidance, also on the GOV.UK website, on perjury as contained in the Perjury act Section 3a and b:

(1) If any person—

(a) for the purpose of procuring a marriage, or a certificate or licence for marriage, knowingly and wilfully makes a false oath, or makes or signs a false declaration, notice or certificate required under any Act of Parliament for the time being in force

relating to marriage; or

(b) knowingly and wilfully makes, or knowingly and wilfully causes to be made, for the purpose of being inserted in any register of marriage, a false statement as to any particular required by law to be known and registered relating to any marriage.

So, my opinion, for what it was worth, was that by swearing an oath and making a false declaration M had committed perjury. I decided to write to the Crown Prosecution Service (CPS) to ask why, in addition to the bigamy charge, he had not been charged with perjury; this was also in part fuelled by his previous history of, and admission to, having altered the bank statements with his Form E submissions. This is the actual letter, which in hindsight, is probably too long-winded and contains a few errors in my relating the course of events, but at the time it represented my feelings and what I believed to be a true record of events.

September 10th, 2014

Dear Madam or Sir,

I write regarding my former husband, Maurice Gibney, and the current charge of Bigamy against him. He was charged on 4th August 2014, and this case is to be heard in Birkenhead Magistrates Court on 17th September 2014. I write because it is my belief and understanding that, in the process of committing this offense, he also committed perjury as defined by the Perjury Act of 1911, section 3 and b. I hereby request that this charge, and the resultant charges of contempt of court and fraud, be investigated and levied against him.

The facts of this case, as I understand them, are these:

On a date known to yourselves, but not disclosed to me, said Maurice Gibney did knowingly and falsely declare himself free to marry, whilst in the British Embassy in Muscat, Oman. This false declaration caused the Embassy to falsely issue a Certificate of No Impediment to Marry. This certificate is a requirement of the Omani Government for UK Nationals to enter into marriage whilst resident in Oman. This also put the British Embassy and its officials in the position of unlawfully conducting and subsequently registering this marriage, which they did on the basis of Maurice

Gibney's knowingly false and perjurious declaration. The bigamous and unlawful marriage took place on 30th March 2013 at the Al Bustan Hotel, Muscat, Oman and was officiated over by a UK-based consular officer.

At the time he made his declaration at the Embassy, Maurice Gibney was fully aware of the fact that he was not free to marry under UK or Omani Law. At this point in time, he still gave me every impression that he was fully committed to our marriage, although in previous months we had discussed separation. He had visited and stayed in the family home as my husband and as father to our son as recently as late January 2013, at which point no legal action had taken place to initiate divorce proceedings. It was not until 21st February 2013 that I even filed a petition for divorce. The legal requirement for a minimum 3 week posting of Intent to Marry at the Embassy strongly suggests that his false declaration took place before the petition to divorce was even filed. In fact, the bigamous marriage of Maurice Gibney to Suzanne Prudhoe took place before even the Decree Nisi was issued on 17th April 2013, and almost a year before Maurice Gibney was divorced and free to marry in the eyes of the law, on the issue date of the Decree Absolute on 10th March 2014.

Of particular relevance to the degree of forethought with which this perjurious declaration, and its sequelae of bigamy, fraud and contempt of court, was committed is the fact that the bigamous wedding on 30th March 2013 was particularly lavish and would have required significant forethought and a long-term intention to deceive. Through Social Media and the subsequent admission of his family members, we know that numerous UK based family attended this wedding. Furthermore, the exclusivity and stature of the wedding venue would have necessitated significant advance notice to book an event on what was the Easter weekend of 2013.

The committing of the offense of perjury, on the occasion of the false declaration at the Embassy and subsequently, also affected our divorce proceedings which were carried out by both the Court and myself in ignorance that this bigamous marriage had taken place. In the course of the divorce proceedings, Maurice Gibney declared on the Form E that he was not currently cohabiting, nor had he any intent of marrying in the near future. This was patently a falsehood, as was everything else which he declared on the Form E, including the nature and whereabouts of his assets and possessions. He signed this, stating its veracity, in full knowledge that he was committing fraud and in contempt of court as is clearly stated above the signature area.

Prior to the FDR hearing on 18th February 2014, Maurice Gibney was given the opportunity to revise this statement, both in court and through correspondence between our respective counsels. On 14th February 2014, almost a full year after the bigamous marriage, he still denied in writing that he had participated in the ceremony of marriage, which we now know took place eleven months previous. He denied this in the face of photographic and written evidence to the contrary and showed neither remorse nor contrition. He has continued to treat both myself and his now 16-year-old son with nothing but contempt and scorn, damaging both our welfare and psychological well-being.

In conclusion, I respectfully request that the CPS investigate the allegations with a view to additional charges to Maurice Gibney, who has knowingly acted with a flagrant disregard to the word of the law, the authority of the Courts and any sense of moral conduct.

Yours sincerely

The first hearing was one week later. The reply I received to this letter arrived some time afterwards and informed me that the responsibility for charges against a person lies with the police, not the CPS. I continued to correspond with the CPS on this issue and other complaints related to the final bigamy hearing well into 2015 without a satisfactory resolution.

September 16th, 2014

I had followed up on my letter with a call to the CPS. During the conversation it had been suggested that the case may be settled the very next day in court; I was totally unprepared for that, I had not even been asked to submit my Victim Personal Statement, and I had been assured by the police that the case would be referred to the crown court. As the DC's were unavailable, I called William, I was upset and needed reassurance that that was not going to happen. William told me, and later confirmed with a criminal barrister friend of his, that bigamy was on indictment only: offences which can or must be tried in the Crown Court are known as 'indictable offences.' He also said that a date for crown court appearance should be set tomorrow in court and that if he were going to plead guilty then he could indicate his plea tomorrow. I appreciated William's efforts, but I should have known it would come at a price: £88. However, it was worth it to feel more confident as I was becoming increasingly anxious anyway without this added pressure.

Wirral Magistrates Court was built in 1887 and as Lucy and I climbed the wide stone stairs it seemed it had not changed since that time. We were directed to sit on one of the many rows of old wooden benches in a large waiting area. On the wall in a glass fronted framed cabinet the court listings for the day were posted: M's name was there alongside the charge of bigamy; I took a photo. Yet in spite of seeing it in black and white, and having waited eight months for this day to come, it still seemed unreal to me, there was a feeling of uncertainty as I had no way of predicting what would happen next. I was also about to see M for the first time since the divorce hearing which unnerved me, I couldn't anticipate how I would react either. I also had a feeling that it would be wrong for me to presume that this long-awaited day was actually the beginning of the end. And unfortunately, I was right.

We had not been briefed on what to expect, so the two of us sat there and waited, but I became inpatient, where was M? He wasn't in the waiting area with us, maybe he wasn't coming? I asked a court usher to point out M's solicitor to us, and it wasn't long before the usher caught my attention and tipped his head towards an approaching man whose appearance and swagger told us exactly how self-important he believed himself to be.

I approached him, and said, "Good Morning" and extended my hand as I introduced myself.

I asked if I could take his card, and he told me "No, I could not," he made no effort to take my extended hand, but rather turned and walked away without another word. I could only presume it was a pathetic attempt to intimidate me. What had I done to him that he should have been so rude to me? Other than to be the victim of the crime committed by the perpetrator he was defending. However, the usher kindly told me his name, Mr Q and gave the details of his chambers, and proceeded to tell me that he was regarded as one of the best criminal lawyers in Liverpool. Apparently, he only took on the most serious cases. No doubt the best didn't come cheap I thought. Lucky M, he was in a position to pay, but he was guilty regardless, and no amount of money spent could change that.

I explained to the usher that I was nervous about having to face M and asked if he could please request that he sits at the other end of the room, away from us, when he arrives. But I was told, he was already here, sat in his own private room, and no doubt consulting with his lawyer. He reassured me not to worry, he would stay there until he was called into court, so he wouldn't be sat in the public area with the victims or with those that couldn't afford such expensive briefs.

I noted a flurry of activity out of the corner of my eye; there was our DC, a welcome sight, and as I would shortly learn, also the bearer of very welcome news. He was standing talking to another man who, unbeknown to me at the time, was my CPS lawyer; M's Mr Q joined them. Something was happening, there was animated chat and Mr Q did not look pleased; the DC looked over and smiled at me. Lucy and I got up and tried to appear casual as we approached the group, we stood just close enough to be in earshot, but our efforts were poorly timed as it was just as the trio broke up, although we did catch Mr Q say,

"Well, that's a game changer," as he hurried away across the waiting area and down the corridor.

"What does that mean?" I asked Lucy.

DC Sharpe explained that some new evidence had come to light and was on its way from the British Embassy in Oman; while it could not be shared with me at that time, I should know that it was very important to the case. During the discussion that followed it was revealed that M had submitted a fraudulent Decree Absolute to prove he was divorced and therefore free to marry Suzanne Prudhoe. I also learnt that M planned to plead not guilty and would request to be tried at Crown Court, although it was suggested that he would probably now change his plea as his lawyer had been made aware of the pending arrival of the proof of his crime. So, would he be charged with fraud too, as well as bigamy, I asked albeit too eagerly? Possibly, but the CPS might consider the fraud to be part of the bigamy charge, because it enabled him to commit the bigamy.

The CPS lawyer said the case, if it proceeded to Crown Court, would be high-profile and would attract a lot of media interest, the thought of which instantly upset me and detracted from the good news they had just shared. I didn't want my personal and professional life compromised by M's nefarious crime being splashed all over the front pages, and how would that affect Seb and Josh who were already suffering as a result of M's disgraceful behaviour? I had never considered or thought about press interest.

I noticed that M's Mr Big Shot looked vexed, he was talking intently into his phone, while pacing a small area by the courtroom entrance. I wondered what was happening. And what was M thinking? Tucked away along a corridor somewhere, I was convinced he must have lied to his lawyer and not told him about the fake Decree Absolute.

Someone in our group, and I don't remember who, said "we had the equivalent of the murder weapon, but now we have his fingerprints." Oh, how I wished they could tell me more.

It was now 10.45am, we had been there since 9.00am. The usher told us my case, or rather M's case, was complicated so we might be called sooner to get it over and done with or later, as it might take longer than other cases, so we were none the wiser. I did a quick sweep of the building, I wanted to find his hiding place, to see him before he came into court, but I had no luck and walked back to Lucy only to spot an agitated Mr Q on his phone again, his whole demeanour had changed, he no longer seemed so cocky. He looked directly at me, but I might as well have been invisible, I now understood the expression 'he looked right through me as if I weren't there' as that was exactly what he did.

At 11.09 M was called into court. Lucy and I were already seated in the cramped area at the back of the courtroom which was smaller than I had expected. He walked in, looking directly ahead and clasping a bottle of water. He stood before the magistrate who asked him his name and address after having curtly told him to put his water bottle down and then to speak up. He gave a local address that neither of us recognised, I guessed it must have belonged to his brother Brian. He remained standing there in silence while an adjournment was requested because new evidence had come to light. Mr Q requested the next hearing be heard in his client's absence as he could not be expected to return to the UK from Oman again in such a short period of time. The date given for the next hearing was the following week, and so it was adjourned until September 24th, 2014 and M was given unconditional bail. He left the court immediately after the decision, he had not entered a plea, I didn't know why as it was black and white, he was guilty.

We were baffled, nothing had really happened other than he had been given permission to not bother to return for the next hearing as it seemed it was too inconvenient for him. How was this acceptable? He was a criminal and yet the court were bowing to his requests. If he couldn't come back, he should stay and return after the second hearing. I was furious, maybe I was directing my anger that I should have felt toward him at the system instead. But I couldn't believe it, why shouldn't he have to appear the following week? Would the court have allowed a single parent with childcare issues the same consideration? Or if he worked in Scotland as a labourer? Or as a waiter in France? Did he get priority treatment because he had money, a good job, a smart appearance and an expensive legal representative?

The CPS lawyer explained that the following week's hearing would be to discuss sentencing, but I didn't understand that as he had not yet pleaded guilty. I could attend if I wanted to, I had every intention of doing so, Lucy would accompany me. He told us M was still in the building, talking to his lawyer. I asked Lucy if she minded waiting in the lobby with me, as I was determined to talk to him or at him, I didn't care. How dare he have put us in this position, caused all three of us the harm and heartbreak of the past year. This might be my only opportunity to say what I wanted to say, I had no idea what that was, I was just so filled with loathing for him, further fuelled by the court's indulgent attitude towards him. We sat on yet another hard bench by the entrance, there was only one way in and out so we wouldn't miss him. I doubted that he expected us to lie in wait.

I turned to see him nonchalantly descending the stairs, in a smart light grey suit; his face froze as he saw me, he looked pale for someone who lived in the Middle East. I was up off that bench in an instant, I was stood next to him, he moved forward out of the large metal doors, I was by his side, with him every step of the way to the station which was only a few minutes' walk away.

I asked him why he had done it? Why had he lied? Why had he married another woman? These were questions I had to ask, I never expected a response, I certainly didn't get one, not even the slightest flicker. His expression remained fixed, he looked straight ahead. I told him to look at me, but he wouldn't. I was on his left side, I wanted to see his wedding ring, a thin white metal band, probably platinum. He held a train ticket folded in half in his hand, I couldn't see his destination; he was also holding a Mont Blanc key ring, with a car key attached. Who other than someone who wants to flaunt their wealth has a Mont blanc keyring?

It was a sunny day, and I was wearing sunglasses that concealed the hate in my eyes, but I'm sure he felt it exuding from my every pore. I was so wound up. I swore at him, I told him what a bastard he was, how I hoped he would go to jail and be punished for what he had done. I told him how one day he would regret losing us, losing his sons.

He walked faster, I walked faster, in what seemed like seconds we were at the station, the ticket collector noticed us as soon as we entered, it was no wonder as I was having a one-sided dialogue, he approached and asked if I was OK. As M leaned forward to press the button for the lift, I told the ticket collector we had come from the court, and that this bastard, with a finger pointed at M, was a bigamist who had abandoned his sons to marry another woman while he was still married to me. And continuing to give the ticket collector more of an answer than I guessed he had bargained for, I told him that M had never said sorry, at which point the lift doors opened, and M calmly stepped in.

As he turned back round to face me, I said in a calm and quiet voice but loud enough for him to hear, "You will regret what you have done for the rest of your sad life" the doors jarred to a close and he was gone.

That was the last thing I ever said to him. I stood there, deflated and upset. The ticket collector offered me his seat and asked again if I was ok. I thanked him and told him I was fine and that my friend was waiting for me back at the court, I apologised for swearing, he smiled and replied with a "Good for you Girlie."

Back outside the court Lucy stood waiting, I was physically shaking, but I had no shame, I had done what I had needed to do and that sat comfortably with me.

September 18th, 2014

The following day I contacted the Witness Care Unit (WCU) and was assigned a witness care officer named Debbie, who wasted no time in telling me what I already knew: that bigamy was an unusual offence which would very probably be heard in Crown Court and that the next available hearing dates were not until January 2015. How much longer was this going to go on for? That date was five months away; by then it would be one year since I had discovered The Facebook photograph. She also anticipated media interest and advised me not to engage with the press. I was relieved to learn that as Seb was under 18 years of age he could not be named.

As we spoke, I was conscious that my mobile in my desk drawer had pinged numerous times in close succession: 11 messages, all from local acquaintances and friends. Did I know my ex-husband was in the Liverpool Echo, the local Merseyside newspaper? I went on-line and there he was: a picture of him outside the court throwing his empty water bottle; I was unsure when the photo had been taken. The article included his full name and age and that he had attended Wirral magistrates court after being charged with bigamy and that the charge stated that *'during the life of your wife you went through a form of marriage with Suzanne Tracey Prudhoe.'* It named the Al Bustan hotel in Muscat and the date of March 30th the previous year as where and when the alleged marriage took place. It also said he gave an address in Muscat although he was formerly of the Wirral, that the case had been adjourned, that he was released on unconditional bail and that no plea had been entered, which was an accurate summary of what had taken place.

As I looked at that photograph of him tears welled up in my eyes, this was what we had become, this was how our marriage had ended. The article was on page 24 of a newspaper that had a printed circulation of 30,000 readers. I hoped that if there were any further articles, they would only rate accordingly and be found at the back of the paper, I was wrong many times in my assumptions during this journey, and this was most definitely one of those times.

Debbie had advised me to start to write my Victim Personal statement (VPS) as soon as possible; I had put the task off as I knew how painful it would be. I was acutely aware I could not put it off any longer, but first I needed to read up on what the statement was, and how it would be used. The information below was lifted from the online GOV.UK website reference guide:

What is a Victim Personal Statement?

1. A VPS is a statement given by victims of crime to the police (or any agency or organisation assigned to take the VPS on their behalf). It is important as it gives victims a voice in the criminal justice process by helping others to understand how the crime has affected them. It provides an opportunity for victims to communicate verbally and/or in writing the effects the crime has had on them (and also their family members). It is the victim's way of telling the court about the crime they have suffered and the impact it has had on them whether physical, emotional, psychological, financial or in any other way.

When assessing the nature and seriousness of the offender's actions, courts will take into account the physical, emotional and financial harm caused to a victim or his or her family. Whilst the court is aware of the likely impact of most offences, the VPS can help them understand better how they apply to the particular case before them. In other words, it can help them understand how the crime has affected the victim.

It would be difficult and painful to write but according to the guidelines if I wrote it well enough it would be worth the upset.

Chapter 16

September 24th, 2014

We returned to the court for the second hearing, in the expectation that we would be able to 'sit in' while the evidence that would determine if the case would be heard in the Magistrate's Court or go Crown Court was presented to the district judge by the CPS lawyer and Mr Q. This new CPS lawyer, my second, was great, he was engaging and enthusiastic and I hoped he would stay with us until the conclusion of the trial. He explained that we would not be allowed into the first part of the discussions but would be called in as soon as it was permitted. A short while later the usher escorted us to our seats inside the courtroom, a brighter and bigger room than the previous week. The district judge sat on a podium, the lawyers sat together to his left and the magistrate's clerk made notes. In this chapter all of District Judge X's remarks were recorded verbatim in our notes and reproduced in this and the following chapters as such.

I was impressed by District Judge X's attitude as he took time to explain the process to Lucy and me. We were told that they were trying to sort out the information pertaining to the case, a process made more difficult by my former husband's not being in attendance. M's solicitor had requested that he receive a suspended rather than a custodial sentence; he went on to explain that if he were to consider that option it would have to include community service, which meant the criminal gave so many hours, sometimes in the hundreds, working on a court assigned voluntary project. Mr Q interjected and reiterated the point, which we then understood he had already made in support of his suspended sentence request, that M would not be able to do community service as he was not resident in the UK.

I whispered to Lucy that that wasn't correct as he is a resident of the UK. The judge had seen me lean over to Lucy and I don't know whether he asked if I had something to say sarcastically as a reprimand for talking in his court, or if he was genuinely interested in what I might bring to the discussion. I said I wasn't sure if I was allowed to speak, he replied that he had "a very open court" and as such "believed everyone in attendance had the right to speak."

So, I explained how that was not true: that M was not a permanent Omani resident. He was employed as a contractor and therefore had the right to reside only for as long as his contract continued, and that his right to residency would be withdrawn, along with his work permit, once his time bound contract was completed. And that I knew this, not only from having spent time in Oman and being aware of the residency laws for expatriates, but also from having several close friends who resided there on the same basis. Don't ask me how but I had the presence of mind to add, in an attempt to impress, that from my experience as a diplomat with the Foreign and Commonwealth Office I could confirm with some authority that as a UK passport holder my ex-husband unquestionably retained his UK residency, irrespective of any temporary residency he may have overseas. Lucy had noted that Mr Q tapped his fingers against the desk non-stop during my recital.

District Judge X told me the information was very interesting and that it had been duly noted; he thanked me. I, in turn, duly noted that Mr Q looked incredibly angry. Discussion about changing dates on the charge sheet followed. This must have been relevant to the dialogue we had not been privy to; I sensed that it related to the new evidence. What did it mean? I was sure the nice CPS lawyer would tell us. The judge went on to ask how I had found out about the bigamy, and Mr Q supplied the answer "on Facebook."

I was taken aback by the judge's remarks when he stated that it must have been "a very difficult emotional journey" for me and asked if "all matters related to the divorce were over" I told him they were not and explained about the issue of M's uncollected possessions and the problems he had created around the remortgaging. I then went on to describe his fraudulent activities and his deliberate failure to engage effectively, in his efforts to conceal the bigamy during the prolonged divorce proceedings, and the large debt I had incurred as a result of his behaviours.

Surprisingly, the judge asked me to tell him more. While I welcomed the opportunity, I was aware that I probably had limited time, so I tried my best to be as concise as possible. I covered his abandonment and rejection of Seb and Seb's subsequent mental health issues, and how he had divided the children, and that I feared for their future well-being as a result. I added that as a result of his behaviour there had been no contact from Seb's paternal family, which further exacerbated the abandonment issues. He made no attempt to close me down, so I elaborated further on M's financial deception and fraud on the Form E; I even told him about the violence towards me and the attempt to run me over.

He responded by saying "it was very upsetting," and he was "sorry to hear this." I then brought the situation up to date and told him about the depth of my embarrassment in relation to the recent newspaper and online article and the professional humiliation it had already caused me. And how I anticipated that it would be a lot worse. I again mentioned that I still socialised and met professionally with some old FCO colleagues, and as such I had been made aware that the bigamy was currently being gossiped about worldwide and that I was mortified at the thought of that.

He said, "this is nightmarish," after he had audibly gasped at the parts related to Seb and at my legal fee debt, as did the note-taker whom I recognised from the previous week's hearing. He went on to say he was "very sorry to hear this" and that "it's been very helpful for you to give me this extra information." Well, he was certainly not going to get it from anywhere else. He said again "it is all noted" followed by "I will bear it all in mind when I deal with this" which I took to mean it would be used in his consideration of the sentence or his decision to send the case to Crown Court. Mr Q never looked at me once, but Lucy noted he had continued to tap his fingers on the desk throughout and looked increasingly perplexed. I am sure that was in part because he was not able to challenge anything I had said, and he would not have been used to that. District Judge X thanked us for attending and that was that – the second hearing was over. We waited outside for the CPS lawyer, who exited the courtroom with a huge grin on his face. He rushed over to us, it seemed he couldn't contain himself when he said

"What you have done is brilliant! The district judge will retain all you have said."

He also told us it was highly irregular for the district judge to have invited me to speak and that he had never seen that before. It was beginning to feel like it had been a successful day. He was also forthcoming about the new evidence: documentation from the British Embassy had indeed been received and it included a statement from the Consular Officer who it appeared, had married them, my husband at the time and Ms Prudhoe, at the Embassy and not at the Al Bustan hotel, as we had all been led to believe. I held onto Lucy's arm to steady myself and took a few deep breaths as I attempted to take control to prevent the looming panic attack from taking hold… I could not believe what I was hearing.

Oblivious to my inner struggle, he continued:

"If this information is correct, he will be in a bad position, there will be nowhere for him to go. He will HAVE to plead guilty."

M, he told us, was required to appear at the next hearing which had been scheduled for October 22nd, 2014 and he would have to enter his plea on that date. Given the evidence, the district judge could proceed to sentencing at that time if he pleaded guilty or, regardless of that, he could still choose to send him to Crown Court. We would not know until the actual date as to how he would conduct the hearing.

The CPS lawyer also told us that there was a technicality that Mr Q was hoping to use, although we were unsure how or even what it was. Lucy and I suspected it may be that he had been charged with bigamy on 30 March 2014, the date of the ceremony at the Al Bustan hotel. Whereas we now knew that the actual wedding had been 10 days earlier than that date, on 20 March 2013, at the British Embassy. What had now become clear was that M had planned to plead not guilty on the basis that the police were unaware of the Embassy wedding. He had not committed bigamy at the Al Bustan on 30 March because, in fact, by then he was already a bigamist, if the Embassy wedding had remained concealed, he would have probably got off scot free.

I asked the CPS lawyer if there was anything at all he could tell us about the Embassy wedding, but it wasn't possible, on the basis that if he supplied me with any further information, and if the case went to trial, it could prejudice the outcome or even worse cause a mistrial, which was the last thing I would want. He suggested that I could speak to the prosecutor after the trial and ask to see the paperwork, and I decided that that was what I would do. I was disappointed to learn that this nice CPS lawyer was not available on the next hearing date as he was on leave; he assured us, however, that due to the gravity of the case a senior lawyer would be appointed. He also stressed the importance of my VPS and the potential effect it could have on M's sentencing, especially, he said, after how well I had presented myself in the courtroom earlier. For that reason, he emphasised I should ensure that I read my statement on the day, and not have someone read it on my behalf.

I asked if he thought the additional charges of perjury or fraud would be laid against M, but his opinion was that further charges would not be made, but rather that they would increase the level of seriousness of the existing bigamy charge and cause him to incur a longer custodial sentence. Lucy and I thought the judge had acted fairly and as such I felt hopeful that, if he presided over the final hearing, he would take into account the fraud and perjury and that would result in a substantial custodial sentence as the CPS lawyer had suggested.

I recalled how I had suspected they had married prior to the Al Bustan in the light of Suzanne Prudhoe's vows *today I confirm my promise to take you* and Vicki's insistence that they would not have been allowed to be married at a hotel. It was a good feeling that the initial research I had shared with the investigating officers had contributed to his downfall.

As a result of these recent events, I was 'on a high' and felt highly motivated to write my VPS. It took me several days, I had to have frequent breaks; at points I found it too difficult to continue. I would come in from work and write and re-write several times over until the early hours of the morning. It was a traumatic experience and I shed what felt like bucket loads of tears. I think it finally brought home to me just what we, as our now new family of three, had gone through: the emotional turmoil and the psychological damage caused by the very same man who should have protected us and loved us as father and husband and not been the one man responsible for emotionally wrecking his own family.

I had resisted the temptation to review the emails and text exchanges between us from close to the date of the Embassy wedding but could not put it off any longer. Anticipating yet another emotional slap in the face I scrolled back through my phone: on the eve of his wedding there were 12 emails on the light-hearted conversation around his decision, that due to his excessive sweating he would now have his shirts and bed linen laundered. Laundered by whom I now thought, his new wife?

Emails on the day of his 'wedding' told me he had had a bad headache, so had stayed home in his apartment with the poor internet, which had been his excuse for not getting in touch. I doubted he wanted to interrupt what should have been the happiest day of his new life by messaging his wife. Yet the following day he was feeling better and had gone for a bike ride along the corniche and stopped at his regular Starbucks and predictably had ordered a cappuccino and low sugar apple cake.

It was beyond my scope of understanding then, and remains so now, as to how my husband, a man I had trusted and had absolute faith in to always do the 'right thing' for our family, functioned within a mindset of such pure deceit.

October 6th, 2014

I received a call from the female CID detective: Sharie. She was sure, in the light of the recently revealed evidence, that M's solicitor would advise him to plead guilty. In her opinion he had dug himself a bigger and bigger hole. She made reference to the counterfeit Decree Absolute issued, from a court "down south," which it later transpired was from Ilford County Court. The bogus order stated that the Decree Nisi had been issued on June 8th, 2009 and the Decree Absolute issued on July 22nd, 2009. I had to end the call at that point as I was so distraught, I couldn't speak. Sharie had no idea of the significance of the information she had just shared. M had, it seemed, submitted yet more fake documentation to support his application to marry at the Embassy. He had not chosen random dates or an arbitrary court location. My father lived in Ilford, and while that on its own may have seemed a coincidence I knew it was not. Because M had also chosen to use my dead mother's birthday of June 8th as the date of our legal separation on the Decree Nisi and he had used the day after my 50th birthday for the issue of the Decree Absolute – those dates were deliberately chosen. I could just imagine him telling people how the 'best 50th birthday present he could have given me was to divorce me' This began a pattern of intimidation that resulted 2 years later in a non-molestation order being issued against him, as repeated malicious actions were made against us, but only on dates that had significance to the two of us or to what had once been our precious family unit.

I don't believe I truly knew the extent of the wickedness and cruelty of M's heart and mind until then. These dates were deliberately chosen with the sole intent to wound and hurt me, as that would be my punishment if I ever discovered the bigamy and as a consequence discovered the premeditated actions he had to set in place to enable that final act of betrayal to happen. Did he hate me so much that he would want to kick me so much further down the road of despair than I already was? Or was it his need to control, that he had been unable to relinquish even as he planned to marry another woman and, as I was to discover, for the years that followed ?

October 15th, 2014

My VPS was finished, and I emailed it to the detectives, I was so relieved when it was done, it had been a harrowing process. DC Sharpe would forward it on to the CPS who would then hand me back the official version to read in court. He had also forwarded a copy to the Criminal Justice Unit and confirmed that they were aware of my intention to read the statement on the day in court. I also sent a copy as requested to Debbie at the Witness Care Unit (WCU) who told me it was considered to be one of the most powerful statements they had ever received. It had been read by a senior manager who asked if she could attend the court to hear me read the statement; they were interested to see the court's reaction to the anticipated influential content and, of course, I readily agreed. My mood was lifted by their positive response as I presumed that if it were so potent a document it would have the desired effect when it came to M being sentenced.

I still had awful problems trying to sleep; it seemed that disturbed nights had become the norm, I could not remember the last time I had had a good night's sleep. I would lie awake replaying events and trying to understand how my marriage has reached the point that it had, I found myself dissecting conversations that had taken place years before and trying to rationalise why he had said or done certain things, what clues had I missed to the real character of the man I had married?

It was during one of those sleepless nights that I had a sudden realisation that if they had married at the British Embassy, and as marriages are a matter of public record, the details of the marriage would be held on the database at the UK General Registrar's Office. Why had none of us thought of that earlier on? If anyone would have checked it might have saved months of waiting and uncertainty. The next morning, I made an online application and paid the fee to obtain a copy of their wedding certificate.

October 22nd, 2020

The day of the court hearing had finally arrived. I had been awake from the early hours of the morning; I knew that, in spite of taking care with my appearance, on that morning I still looked drained and exhausted. In my head I spoke to all of those who had passed and asked for their help today in guiding the judge's decision to ensure M received the retribution he deserved by being sent to Crown Court or if not then to prison.

We arrived early; we sat in a witness room and I was allocated a new witness care officer, Ray. After some time, we were introduced to the 3rd CPS lawyer assigned to the case; she had the title of Senior Crown Prosecutor, her name was Penelope and she was, I was told, a very senior lawyer but was not a 'people's person.' Not what I needed to hear at this stage as I needed a lawyer that would support me and explain what was happening, not someone who would find communication difficult. The detectives had told me to remind my lawyer on the day of my intention to read my VPS myself to the court, and she acknowledged that. District Judge X, the same judge from the second hearing whom we had already met, was presiding and Ray told us that he had the power to sentence criminals for up to one year but sentencing beyond that is within the realms of the Crown Court. Ray offered his opinion that the judge had a reputation of being firm but fair and that he agreed with his decisions "99% of the time," but he added, the previous day he had found him uncharacteristically harsh, as he had sentenced a security guard to two months imprisonment for an expired Security Guard Licence. A criminal record had the potential to ensure that the security guard never worked in security again.

Ray left the room to fetch us both a coffee, on his return he told us that both lawyers had been told to "go and do something" but it had not been revealed what the judge had tasked them to do. A few moments later Penelope, avoiding all eye contact, revealed that the judge had only just seen certain documentation, but she declined to elaborate on what that might be.

I guessed it was very probably the proof of their Embassy wedding but didn't let on that I knew about that. I might well have been one step ahead of them all, as only the day before I had received the marriage certificate. Opening the envelope had been difficult enough without having to look at the content, but I did, I finally had the proof of the bigamy there in my hand. The details of their 'marriage' on 20 March 2013, on that very same day I had been married to him for 17 years 7 months and 5 days; when they had been married for just one day, I had been married to him for 17 years, 7 months and 6 days and so it would go on. The bride's sister was a witness, as was another woman who, I discovered online, was also a PDO school teacher. I wondered if Suzanne Prudhoe wore her bride's dress for the ceremony and how they had celebrated? Where had they spent their wedding night? Which was just two months after he had been lying in our marital bed. It was no wonder I felt mentally and physically exhausted, it was no wonder I did not look or function at my best.

Two hours had passed since we had arrived; we had been scheduled for a 10.00 hours hearing. I was becoming anxious as time was passing – what was going on? Penelope re-appeared; a decision had been made. What decision? Was M going straight to Crown Court? Had additional charges, such as perjury or fraud been added? What was it? But it wasn't about M at all, it was about me, the object of my husband's crime.

Penelope stood there and with scant disregard for my feelings announced I was NOT allowed to read my VPS in court because it was too long. I immediately burst into tears; I couldn't take any more of this. I was aware it was a long document; I had said that when I sent it to the DC's, it was that length because I had a lot to say. Penelope told me it was not only too long, but that part of the content was inappropriate as it made reference to the recent divorce proceedings. Yes, of course it did! It had been a deliberately drawn-out process due to my ex-husband's efforts to conceal the bigamy, and so it was appropriate that the impact of his actions should be included in my VPS.

Memories of the FDR hearing in February flooded back, and how I felt when I realised that my legal team did not care enough about me or the boys to actually do the best they could for us; that was not going to happen again. I summoned up an inner strength even though I felt as if I had none left and I stood my ground, I told Penelope I insisted that I be allowed to read it. While wiping away tears, I questioned her: if there was opposition to its content or length it should have been raised earlier by the police, or the Criminal Justice Unit, or the WCU or the CPS and I asked her how they had all failed to do so? I told her I objected in the strongest of terms (whatever they were) and that I did not accept the decision. Rather dramatically I told her it was against my human rights to deny me the opportunity not to read my statement in court. But of course it was bigger than that, it was a point of justice and a point of freedom of speech, it was my right as a victim to be heard. How could my statement inform the sentencing process if it were not to be heard?

The Crown Prosecution Service Legal Guidelines: Victim Personal Statements does not specify a limit in length or word content of the VPS.

Chapter 2 Part A paragraph 1.11 states the purpose of a VPS is to:

Give victims a more structured opportunity to state how the crime has affected them – physically, emotionally, psychologically, financially or in any other way

Chapter 2 Part B paragraph 1:13 states that:

The court is responsible for notifying the Witness Care Unit (WCU) of the court's decision about whether, and what sections of the VPS should be read aloud and who will read it.

Chapter 2 Part B paragraph 1:14:

There is an additional obligation on the WCU which must, wherever possible, notify the victim of the court's decision so that the victim can make arrangements to attend court if necessary.

Annex A of the Crown Prosecution Services Legal Guidance on Victim Personal Statements in reference to who reads the statement and if it is read in part or complete states that *'the court should take account of the victim's preferences and follow them unless there is good reason not to do so.'*

I was devastated. I decided that, when we went into court, I would ask to be given the opportunity to challenge that decision; I was not going to be silenced. I did not understand how or why they were doing this to me, had I not been through enough already? Ray told us he had never heard of this situation before; it was in his opinion unethical. At a point shortly after my refusal to accept the decision I was informed, without explanation, that the decision had been reversed and I would be allowed to read my statement in its entirety. I would suggest that that would never have happened if I hadn't objected quite so strongly and been so determined to read it.

Ray was summoned by Penelope and returned to explain that the earlier mystery had now been revealed: the original date and location of the bigamy was still to be amended on the charge, hence the delay. Yet this information had been available to the CPS for over one month, the court had been aware of these changes since the second hearing so, given that they had had access to the correct information all this time, why were the changes being made on the day of the hearing? The case was rescheduled to 14.00 hours to enable the CPS to make those two simple changes of date and location. It was ludicrous, made even more so by the fact that I actually had the correct date and location in my possession before it was ever altered on his charge.

Ray proposed that, as the judge was keeping the case here, he must have reviewed the paperwork and advised that M plead guilty. He explained that, given the fraudulent documents received from the Embassy, if it went to trial at Crown Court it would not go in M's favour as he would find it difficult to defend his actions, especially under cross questioning. M had, as the second CPS lawyer said, nowhere to go now.

It seemed, according to Ray, who was the most informative person we had so far encountered, that M would get credit for pleading guilty. Credit? For pleading guilty, for acknowledging that he had committed a criminal act of which, until the new evidence came to light, he was insisting he was innocent? This made no sense to me, that a criminal be rewarded with freedom for admitting his guilt and the injured, innocently party be treated with such little respect.

Chapter 17

Lucy and I now had two hours to kill; we left the court and in the pouring rain, on a cold and windy day, walked the short distance to the nearby shopping mall. We sat in the Marks & Spencer café; I drank several coffees, my tuna salad sandwich remained untouched. A young couple sat at the next table. We later saw them in court, they were the Liverpool Echo and Mirror Group reporters.

When we returned to the court, we were told of yet another delay. District Judge X had decided to hear the other cases listed for that afternoon first, as the "Gibney case would take the longest" so we had two options: to sit in the room where we had already spent the whole morning, or to sit in the court and listen to the other cases. We chose the latter.

"Let's see how firm and fair DJ X is in action," I said to Lucy.

Ray escorted us to our seats, where we would remain the whole afternoon, with the exception of when I would be called to the stand to read my VPS. Ray took his seat next to the journalists next to whom we had sat at lunch; as our hearing time approached the remainder of the seats filled.

While in one way the situation now seemed real, the culmination of nine months of waiting and worrying, it also felt like I was an observer, detached from any personal connection, rather just going through the motions. I couldn't explain why I felt like that, maybe it was the state of nervousness I was in, but regardless of my feelings I could only hope that justice would be served that afternoon.

M was led to his place in the dock; he wore yet another grey suit and stood with his head bowed. He was asked to state his full name and address and he did so. The district judge read out the charge, the date had been changed and Mr Q was asked to confirm he acknowledged the amendment.

Then the moment I had been waiting for: M was asked to enter his plea "GUILTY."

He was told he could remain seated for the time being, so he sat with shoulders hunched and his head down. The district judge acknowledged the press's presence and stated that this was an "open court"; I knew what that meant, more newspaper coverage, but I had already resigned myself to it.

District Judge X stated that he had received three testimonials in praise of the accused's character. Mr Q was instantly on his feet to make an application that the parties be anonymised, and the content of their statements not read to the court. This, he stressed, was for their own protection as I had, he confidently said, pursued and harassed them all with emails and phone calls. I was taken aback by that allegation, stated as if it were a matter of fact, without any evidence to support it, as there was none. At that point I was oblivious as to who had even written the testimonials. How could he have stood there and accused me of such actions with no proof or without my having a right to respond to this slanderous allegation? He could only have been acting on his client's say-so, but surely, as a lawyer, he required evidence to support this false claim. I looked at Penelope, I shook my head and mouthed to her "that's not true." She just looked back at me, expressionless; she said nothing and did nothing in response. Lucy and I were shocked, was there a place in this court for my character assassination? I don't know whether the district judge saw our exchanged looks of incredulity or not, but he told M to stand and asked him if I had done what they claimed I had, had any of the witnesses reported me to the police?

For once, M told the truth, "No they had not."

At which point Mr Q withdrew his application, a clever tactic on their behalf, as I later realised; regardless of the withdrawal there would have remained a question of doubt over my integrity.

The district judge proceeded to read out the names: Stella, M's sister, had written to say how their elderly mother depended on M's financial support, Jane had also contributed and claimed that M still supported her and 24-year-old Jessica. It was claimed that if M should go to prison, then these three individuals would struggle money-wise as a result. The third testimonial was from Suzanne Prudhoe who had written to declare that she stood by her man. The district judge expressed his surprise to have received a supporting statement from her, whom, he stated, he also considered to be a victim of Maurice Gibney's crime. He went on to elaborate further that in his opinion, not stating whether that was his personal or legal opinion, that Ms Prudhoe was more of a victim than I, and his sympathies lay with her. The words that were unsaid and, I felt, would have completed his statement were 'with her, more so than with me.' Again, Lucy and I exchanged looks of disbelief.

Apparently, Mr Q had written a three-page mitigation argument. I did not understand what that meant at the time, and no one bothered to explain. It was in effect a process of mitigation used during the negotiations or at sentencing that allows the defendant to effectively present facts about themselves which would cause the court to impose a lesser sentence than that which was first considered. I can only suppose the testimonials must have been included in that.

It was finally time for me to read my VPS but Mr Q objected, this time on the grounds that parts of it were not relevant to the case. He went on to request that only matters admissible to the case should be allowed to be heard and emphasised, even at this late stage, that my VPS should be edited significantly. He then announced to the court that if I were permitted to read it in its entirety, he would cross-examine me on its content. I interpreted this as a threat to deter me and it worked, I felt threatened, I had not been prepared for this.

How could I be cross examined on my statement as if I were the criminal? Yet M, by having pleaded guilty, was exempted from any such questioning. How could this man question me on how I felt? How his client's crime had impacted on me and my family? Did he know what went on in my house, in my head, in my heart? Had he counted up the hours when I should have been sleeping but instead lay awake tormenting myself and beating myself up for not being stronger, for not seeing through his lies and manipulation, for maybe in part enabling his control? Was he there when my son told me about the voices in his head? His hallucinations? His anxiety? His inability to concentrate at school? He knew all of this so well, did he, that he would be able to tell me I was wrong?

Had he cried with me when Josh had finally found his voice and the courage to confront the years of psychological abuse M had inflicted on him as a child and how he lived with the threat of M harming me if he ever told the truth about the brutality and viciousness M had perpetrated against him? How throughout his childhood and then in young adulthood Josh had made a conscious decision not to tell me about M's behaviour in order to protect me? Mr. Q knew how that felt, did he? How Josh's young life too had been so torturous at the hands of his client? Was he, Mr Q, big shot criminal lawyer there, taking notes and gathering evidence, so that he could contest what I was about to swear as the truth?

All three of us had been in counselling and intermittently returned to it, as six years on we are still dealing with the fallout of M's actions on our mental health, but Mr Q, leading criminal defender of Liverpool thought he knew better. But I had to acknowledge that he would be acting with his client's permission. That was very difficult to even contemplate, let alone to accept.

Mr Q was advised by the district judge that he was not in a position to determine the personal impact of the crime, at which point Mr Q retracted his previous statement and informed the court that he would not cross-examine me. But in spite of the district judge's making the point that "these days the victims were at the forefront of the courts and their voices should be heard" Mr Q's promise was short-lived as was the judge's instruction to him. District Judge X then proceeded to tell me to read my statement in its entirety and to take my time in doing so.

Most of the content of this book is from notes, emails and letters written or taken from the time the incidents occurred; likewise with the recording of this court case. Both Lucy and I had notebooks with us in court, and as I read my statement reproduced below to those assembled in the court that day, Lucy made notes of her observations and in particular of M's reactions to what I read aloud. Her notebook entries are included here and follow the commentary M was reacting to. The comments made by his lawyer and the district judge were also recorded verbatim and are reproduced here.

I stood in the witness box; the Senior Prosecutor who had not engaged with me for even the briefest of moments so far looked straight at me, she seemed oblivious to the fact that she was to provide me with the official copy of my VPS. It was only when I extracted my own copy, from the manilla folder I had carried with me, that she produced the CPS copy for me to read, below is a copy of the actual VPS.

I am normally a confident speaker but at that moment I had to summon up all my courage and strength and find my voice, because this was my one opportunity to potentially influence the sentencing and to ensure that Maurice Gibney heard me. I wanted what I had to say to resonate and to stay with him for years to come.

When Maurice Gibney married Suzanne Prudhoe on March 30th, 2013, he was still married to me.

Until January 2013, although we had discussed the possibility of separation previously, Maurice gave me every impression that he was fully committed to our marriage.

M raised his eyebrows.

In late January 2013 he came home on leave from Oman and stayed in the family home as my husband and as father to our son Sebastian.

M looked at the ceiling, eyes closed.

Before that point, no legal action had taken place to initiate divorce proceedings. It was halfway into that last visit we argued over his recent unreasonable behaviour, Maurice was violently abusive and then attempted to run me over, an act I believe Seb witnessed from his bedroom window.

M shook his head.

I did not report this incident to the police in order to protect Seb. M left the house without saying goodbye to his son, and flew back to Oman the following day; this was the last time Seb saw his father.

In spite of my initial and considerable efforts to encourage communication between him and Seb after this date very little contact was attempted by Maurice. The last contact was a 2013 Christmas card, Seb has not heard from his father since.

The impact on Seb of his father's rejection and abandonment has been huge. In December 2013 Seb was referred to CAMHS – Cheshire adolescent mental health services – with a diagnosis of depression, anxiety and insomnia; he experiences auditory and visual hallucinations. He is under the care of a psychiatrist and has regular counselling.

M looks like he is about to cry.

He is learning to cope with his symptoms but this whole episode has had a devastating effect on his teenage life.

M is rubbing his chin.

At the request of his psychiatrist the exam boards gave permission for him to sit his GCSEs this summer listening to music through headphones, in an attempt to subdue the negative impact of the voices; this was only the second time in its history that the exam board had received such a request. Seb, who is dyslexic, also had to cope with the impact the anxiety episodes and insomnia had not only on his ability to concentrate and study and carry out normal daily activities but on his physical health too. Inevitably he did not achieve his predicted grades. At the matrimonial court in

February 2014 Maurice was presented with a letter from CAMHS detailing Seb's condition and yet he has at no point, ever enquired after his well-being.

M has his head down, rubbing his face.

I had no knowledge of Suzanne Prudhoe's existence or her relationship with my husband until February 2014, yet it appears that she announced her engagement to my husband on Facebook in May 2012.

M lets out a big sigh.

If Maurice had wanted a divorce, he could have started proceedings several years ago. All the pain he has inflicted on myself and our children has been completely unnecessary.

I feel that the intensity of his forethought and planning can only be seen as deliberate intent to injure his family: me, Josh and Seb.

A few examples of this intent (only some of the very many I could cite) are as follows:

M shakes his head.

Seb and I travelled to Muscat to celebrate Christmas 2011 with Maurice, but he had to unexpectedly travel into the desert for work from December 23rd to 26th. He actually arrived back in Muscat late on the 27th, which meant Seb, then aged 13, and I spent Christmas alone in the apartment. Seb insisted on waiting for his dad to return before opening his Christmas presents and to eat the Christmas treats, brought from the UK to share with his dad. The reality was Maurice had abandoned us and flown 3,700 miles back to the UK to spend Christmas with Suzanne Prudhoe and her family.

M shakes his head again.

Other planned family holidays during 2012, our trips to Muscat and Maurice's trips home, were cancelled at the last minute or downgraded to a few days from a few weeks, Maurice always said this was due to the pressures of work, although the reality was to conceal his relationship with Suzanne Prudhoe or to holiday with her instead. That year he returned to the UK on leave on at least 3 occasions unbeknown to us visiting his mother and siblings a few miles from our family home while still pretending to be in Oman.

M has his eyes closed and is still shaking his head.

At Christmas 2012, a few days before he was expected home, he told me he was very depressed, his mood was too volatile and that on the advice of a Relate counsellor he should not return home in case he became distressed in front of Seb.

M looks really angry; he is shaking his head.

We agreed he would return on December 27th, he told Seb of the plans he had made for their time together, but he never arrived or offered any explanation other than his state of mental health. I was naturally very worried as I thought he must have been very depressed to let us down in that way, Christmas was not good for us that year either. However, none of this was true, he actually spent that Christmas here in the UK with both his and Suzanne Prudhoe's family.

I started to find out about his secret visits in May 2103. As the ever-growing levels of deception and perfidy were revealed to me, I found it increasingly difficult to cope, just when I thought there could be nothing else left to hurt or shock, I would discover another appalling act of dishonesty. I tried very hard to mask my true feelings of distress but was ultimately diagnosed with depression and stress, prescribed anti-depressants and was unable to work for a total of 2 months. I was referred for counselling, feeling too low to wait for an NHS appointment. I saw a counsellor privately at a cost of £30 per weekly session for approximately 6 months, a cost I could not afford. But as Seb's sole carer I had to recover as soon as possible. I deeply regret that I was unable to conceal episodes of extreme upset and crying from him or our eldest son Joshua.

At mention of sole carer M looked at Yve and muttered.

Joshua was offered work in the US during this period but declined it as he was too worried about Seb and I to leave us, his decision to remain inevitably had a negative effect on his career progression, I feel very guilty over this too.

Through the process of counselling, I was able to examine my relationship with the accused, re-visiting incidences in itself caused me to relieve that pain. I carry guilt: that I couldn't have prevented the hurt caused to my children, at times I was full of self-loathing that I couldn't have seen through who he really was, that I allowed myself to be manipulated and controlled by him for so long. But I understand now for as long as I was compliant the relationship worked.

At the time of the bigamous wedding, we had been married for 17 years. I had believed in our marriage and that we shared the values that were inherent to it: trust, love and respect for each other with a sense of decency and morality. While it may not have been the most conventional marriage given the time we spent apart due to work, I loved him unconditionally and believed that love was reciprocated.

No matter how many times I have tried to write this part of my statement I just cannot get it right, because I just simply do not have the words to effectively convey the depth of pain and hurt or the sense of betrayal that I feel.

M shakes his head and looks at the judge.

I cannot adequately describe my emotional state when I found out my husband had 'married' another woman while still married to me. Most people refer to it as 'a life of duplicity,' but the connotations of that phrase for me means I have to accept that my husband was unfaithful to me: emotionally, physically and morally for a prolonged period of time culminating in the ultimate betrayal of 'marrying' another woman and having his family bear witness to that event: my stepdaughter was bridesmaid, my mother-in-law walked him down the aisle, my sister in laws and nieces were in attendance.

M shakes his head.

The day he entered into that bigamous marriage my own marriage and the whole history of it to me, became worthless. I cannot think of it in any other way. For Maurice to have carried out so many acts of dishonesty and deception and on so many levels against us, his wife and his children, I feel we surely could not have held any significance or value to him.

M is looking in disbelief, he is gesturing at his solicitor.

I had to stop here for a few moments and re-compose myself, I was given a glass of water by the court usher. I waited a few minutes before I could continue, I was overwhelmed by hearing my own words aloud and what they meant.

> *Yet at the time of the bigamous wedding, we were still in daily contact, predominantly by regular emails and additionally by text with at least a weekly phone call. The day prior to the wedding we exchanged 11 emails discussing the pros and cons of him having his bed linen laundered versus him washing it himself. The day after the wedding the text apologising for no contact the previous day saying he had had a violent headache and had spent the day in bed. Regular contact was maintained until he was again unwell (on the day of the ceremony at the Al Bustan hotel), texts resumed the following day when he told me he was cycling and had stopped for his usual Starbucks coffee and slice of low-fat apple cake. These examples epitomise his skill and power of manipulation over me. This has caused me such despair that I am unable to talk about it, his actions are such an abuse of my faith in the truth.*

> *I understand now that Maurice told all of his immediate family before the bigamous wedding that we had been divorced for some time, and that we had kept the divorce a secret to protect Sebastian. He also alleged I was 'crazy,' and he feared for his well being. He successfully persuaded them not to have any contact with us. Seb was very close to his paternal grandmother, his only living grandparent, she severed all contact with him in January 2013.*

M vigorously shaking his head.

> *My stepdaughter Jessica has always been a much-loved member of our family and she had spent some of her early years living with me, Maurice and the children in Nigeria. In 2012 she went travelling in Australia and was in regular contact with me. In February 2013 she had emailed her travelling plans for the following few months but did not include details of her trip to Oman for her dad's 'wedding' to Suzanne Prudhoe where she was bridesmaid. There has been no contact between Jessica and me since then and virtually no contact between her and her brothers.*

When talking about Jessica M rolls his eyes, with head back he looks as if he is going to explode.

We all presumed she was still in Australia, until August this year when Seb saw her by chance in Liverpool. In spite of not having seen his sister for over two years he was not able to approach her. He explained how upset he was by this but told me 'given the situation I felt I couldn't because I didn't know what dad would have told her.'

Seb has truly struggled to understand the loss of contact with his paternal family, in particular his sister whom he loves dearly. The accused, their father, has driven a wedge between all 3 children.

M shakes his head and mouths at Yve "that's you."

In time I hope this broken relationship can be mended, but it will never be as it was, the brothers and sister that were devoted to each other. I worry for Jessica as I ask myself how she will recover from this situation knowing how her father used her as a tool in his subterfuge.

I wiped away tears, all the while M glared at me from the dock. He was mouthing words at me: "It's all your fault not mine, it's you, it's you." He pointed his finger at me, accusingly. If I could see him and make out what he was saying so could the judge, why was he allowing this behaviour? The journalists caught my eye, they were looking from him to me, I didn't know them, but I knew what they were thinking, it was clear from their facial expressions.

In the course of the divorce proceedings, I tried very hard to maintain contact and to keep the relationship with Maurice as amicable as possible to facilitate a straightforward process. However, the majority of the information Maurice declared on the Form E were falsehoods and misrepresentations.

M shaking his head and says No.

He attempted to conceal the nature and whereabouts of the majority of his assets and possessions by submitting forged bank statements and denying and withholding other financial details. In the Matrimonial Court he admitted to providing false accounts.

When we started the divorce proceedings in February 2013 the standard divorce costs were quoted at £2,500, Maurice's failure to comply with the requirements of the divorce process, forced me to incur legal costs in excess of £40,000. It is apparent now that his actions were not only to withhold financial information which would have enabled a fairer divorce settlement but were necessary to conceal his relationship with Suzanne Prudhoe. The wedding celebrations at the Al Bustan hotel cost approximately £45,000, yet a month earlier Maurice had claimed he could not afford £200 spending money for Seb's school trip to Russia and contributed only £120. At this time, we lived off our joint account overdraft which Maurice refused to clear.

In June 2013 Maurice reduced his monthly contribution for the household maintenance by initially a 1/3rd then 2/3rds citing the termination of his contract and no immediate prospect of employment as the reason.

Mr Q turns to look at M in response to termination of contract, M shook his head.

The accused had told Suzanne Prudhoe we had been divorced for several years, his motivation for causing us such further financial hardship was I believe the need to conceal these payments from her. At this time, he informed me of his plan to return permanently to the UK to work and supplied an itinerary of job interviews and of local properties that he had arranged to view, and we agreed he should collect the second family car, which would remain a joint asset until the divorce. I later discovered he had no interviews or viewings planned, and that this was an elaborate ruse to obtain the car, he subsequently refused to reveal its whereabouts, and I have not seen it since.

M raises eyebrows and looks away.

Incidents such as these compounds the hurt as he would have been acutely aware of the impact of his actions particularly the financial threats that he made and carried out.

Maurice has been in continuous employment in Muscat since July 2011, earning a tax-free salary in excess of £85,000 pa. I am a nurse in the NHS and earn a quarter of his salary. In order to clear the overdraft and pay the bills, I extinguished my savings, sold my mother's inherited jewellery, and had to take on two additional jobs...

M shakes his head and Mr Q made notes.

… while trying to support Seb through his health crisis.

M lowers his head, holds his head in his hands.
The DJ was looking directly at Yve and then at M.

This huge financial debt has caused me considerable stress and financial embarrassment. I had to acquire credit cards to pay the bills, at times I could not make the monthly payments, and this has affected my credit rating. I have had to re-mortgage the house to pay off this debt, and yet have sustained even further legal costs due to Maurice's refusal to sign the re-mortgage papers and his refusal to collect his personal possessions from the family home, both contrary to the matrimonial court order.

I am an ex-diplomat having worked for the Foreign and Commonwealth Office as a Nursing Officer. Maurice and I first met when I posted to the British High Commission in Nigeria. The bigamous wedding took place at the British Embassy in Muscat, officiated by the Consular Officer there. Socially and professionally, I am in regular contact with current and ex FCO staff, a bigamous wedding is rare, as is the honour of getting married in an Embassy. This 'wedding' is being gossiped about at the FCO at home and abroad, and particularly in Nigeria where I still have many friends. I feel that my professional reputation is now tarnished, in addition to any future career prospects already being damaged by my recent sickness record and diagnosis of depression.

The court hearing on September 17th was reported with Maurice's photo at multiple online sites and was in the Liverpool Echo. I had kept our situation as secret as possible to protect myself and my children, but on that date, I was called by people I barely knew, and my friends had to field questions from others enquiring about my private life. I had been warned by the Witness Care Officer that there will be a great deal of media interest in this case, as it is so unusual, I am dreading this.

I am to be publicly humiliated, through absolutely no fault of my own and I am so fearful that my son's details may appear in the media and of the potential consequences that may arise from that.

M looks on in utter disbelief.

I have lost count of how many times I have tried to understand Maurice's actions and motivations for even thinking about this crime, let alone planning it, committing it and going to such extremes to conceal it and to convince all concerned to believe in his version of the truth of it.

How could he have denied us as his family? I have struggled to understand. If he wanted a divorce, he should have taken action to achieve it instead of causing so much heartbreak.

Dealing with all of this has been difficult enough. Yet I recently learnt that the content of the forged Decree Absolute was also designed to wound. The date of the Decree Nisi is my dead mother's birthday.

M has a look of disbelief on his face.

And the date of the Decree Absolute, a day after my 50th birthday. Now knowing his modus operandi – I think these are not random dates but were chosen to punish me if I ever discovered the Decree Absolute which would mean I had discovered the bigamy.

It will take a long time to fully accept what has transpired, even at this stage of the proceedings. There is a lot of grieving, the loss of the family in such abhorrent shocking circumstances remains very difficult to deal with and has caused me and my two sons insurmountable and overwhelming psychological distress. I doubt we will ever be able to come to terms with his cruelty and his total absence of remorse or contrition.

At this point, Lucy's notes make reference to the female reporter: looks totally upset and disbelieving, both reporters are staring at M.

This is our lives, our emotional baggage and this is the emotional legacy he has given all three of our children.

Reading this statement here today has been very difficult: to share such intimate details and to feel so exposed. But I am aware of the power this statement holds, and I trust the courts to use the knowledge I have shared today to inform a decision that gives justice.

Phew, I had done it, I had read my Personal Victim Statement and I had made him listen to every word of it, and that was what I had needed to do.

Chapter 18

Reading a Victim Personal Statement and in particular one as emotive as mine in a public forum in front of the perpetrator was a harrowing experience. My distress had been further exacerbated by my ex-husband's behaviour from the dock. He had gesticulated, grimaced and mouthed insults at me, repeatedly tried to attract his solicitor's attention but at no point had he been asked to modify his behaviour by the district judge. Yet, earlier in the afternoon during one of the cases Lucy and I had observed, a defendant who had fidgeted repeatedly from what looked like possible substance withdrawal was removed from the court, at District Judge X's instruction, as he was not prepared to tolerate his inability to keep still in the dock.

I was given no time to recover from my emotional ordeal when, contrary to what had been agreed, Mr Q stood up and prepared to question me. I hadn't expected this as I was under the impression it had been decided there was to be no cross questioning. I turned to look at Penelope, silently imploring her to intervene, she raised an eyebrow as if to say what now, what's the problem? Mr Q asked questions about when I had first instructed solicitors in relation to the divorce, but these questions led nowhere, I didn't see the point of them, maybe they were just a warmup exercise for what was to come.

He moved on to the bigamous wedding celebrations and said according to Lucy's notes: "You mention the cost of the celebrations, how do you know the costs?"

I explained that I had contacted the Al Bustan Hotel's wedding planner, that I had pretended to have been a guest at the Gibney/Prudhoe wedding and wanted exactly the same wedding for myself the following year, and as such was provided with the costings.

"So, you received this information from a sales rep who was trying to sell you something?"

No, I repeated how I had gained the information. He smirked as he began his next scathing attack in which he implied my gullibility had got the better of me in accepting over-estimated costs purely to suit my purpose.

How dare he. I didn't know if it was his arrogance, his attempts to belittle me in front of the court or his own contempt for me for whatever reason, or maybe that was just how he played the game to maintain his reputation, but I had had it. I was not prepared, courtroom or no courtroom, to be bullied and intimidated by an individual who knew better. After all, it was not me that was on trial, I had done nothing wrong. I was the victim.

The Ministry of Justice Code of Practice for Victims of Crime point 3.3 refers:

> *The CPS (Prosecutor) will treat witnesses in court respectfully and where appropriate, will seek the court's intervention where cross-examination is considered by the prosecutor to be inappropriate or aggressive.*

Penelope sat and watched Mr Q attack me as if she were a casual bystander and not a senior representative of the CPS with the responsibility for my protection and to ensure the proceedings were fair and appropriate.

So, I asked him why he was asking me these questions, questions to which he knew the answers to. He had already read my VPS, along with all the supporting evidence for all the claims I had made, which I had included when I submitted it, and which contained the emailed correspondence between myself and the Al Bustan staff. I asked him if he had mislaid that evidence because if so, I had copies here in my file, at which point I reached down and picked up the file which I then waved in the air. I looked to Penelope for help again, she looked right through me, just as Mr Q had done at our first encounter. Maybe it was a trait perfected by senior criminal lawyers, but it was not an impressive one.

I wanted to shout at her, 'Will you just do your bloody job and help me out here!' I was trying hard not to cry as I stood there in that witness box feeling intimidated, feeling anxious, and feeling lost.

Mr Q told me to put down my file and that my behaviour was inappropriate for the courtroom, he appealed to the district judge to caution me over my behaviour, and he wasted no time in doing just that. Mr Q then went on to question me about the re-mortgaging of the house and had the audacity to tell me that M had also had to pay off the overdraft that I had referred to. I replied by telling him that we had paid off 50% of the overdraft each, despite the fact that M earned four times what I did. That line of questioning did not go any further either.

He went on to ask about M's failure to collect his personal possessions and inferred that I had been obstructive and that I had prevented M from attending the FMH to collect his belongings. He obviously expected me to say this was a self-imposed restriction, so I took some pleasure in telling him that the police had advised, given that I was a victim and possible witness in this on-going investigation, that M was not allowed to attend personally, which as a criminal lawyer he would have known anyway. He did not pursue that line of questioning either.

Mr Q continued to question me, and when he finally withdrew, he had not been able to prove me wrong on any of the supposed contradictions or issues he had raised. I later learnt that the WCU had not warned me that I might be cross-questioned on my VPS because it was such a rare occurrence in Magistrates Courts. In fact, the WCU staff had never known it to happen at Wirral Magistrates Court before. So, it seemed I was the first, I still wonder why that was?

The police had advised that I apply for a restraining order against M. Not only was I fearful of retaliation for reporting him for bigamy and anticipated further retribution if he went to prison, but there had been incidents that summer that seriously perturbed me and which I had reported to the police. A used and partially filled condom had been tied to my car aerial and on several occasions, I had been aware that my house was being watched, by a young man who looked very much like M's nephew. I surmised M was behind it and I knew why: the Golf Open championship had just been held at the nearby golf course and I had offered parking spaces on my driveway to a male work colleague and a friend of a friend, who was a particularly good-looking man who drove that year's Lexus; they were spectators at the competition. I was sure M had been by the house and probably spotted either man or car or both and in spite of loathing me and being divorced from me, he would still have been enraged at the thought of another man in the house with me.

The CPS prosecutor had so far failed to mention the request for such an order, and it seemed even to my untrained self that the proceedings were rapidly coming to a close. So I had to ask the district judge if I could talk to Penelope, meanwhile Mr Q moved position to ensure he was within earshot of our conversation. Lucy had made notes to that effect.

Penelope finally entered into the proceedings to make my application, albeit rather half-heartedly. Mr Q opposed it and the district judge denied it, on the basis that he felt there was in his opinion "little risk of contact as it seemed that Mr Gibney had distanced himself from this family"

He continued that he got "the impression he wants to get well away from you." That was a hurtful statement and said almost mockingly, it was inappropriate especially given the circumstances. As such he had decided he was not inclined to issue a restraining order.

Not only did I find his comments tasteless and patronising, but his statement made it abundantly clear to me that he had failed to take on board anything I had said in relation to M's deception, manipulation and disregard for us. To the extent that it seemed he did not think M capable of further attacking our security and well-being in any way other than face to face.

District Judge X went on to advise that there would be a victim surcharge of £85. This is a payment used to fund victim services through the Victim and Witness General Fund, and the amount of surcharge is based upon the length of the sentence. Which forced me to consider that, as the order I am writing in is the order the case progressed in, according to our notes, the sentencing had already been decided before Mr Q made his plea for leniency or my statement was heard.

Mr Q stated that there were no guidelines for a case such as this, which puzzled me as I had researched and read up on several bigamy cases, in anticipation of sentencing; what aspect of this case was without guidelines in law? The issue was not elaborated on other than Mr Q stating that cases should be assessed on their own merit. He confirmed M accepted that false documents had been produced and that this 'aggravated the breach,' again no explanation was offered so we had no idea what he was referring to or what that comment meant, but at least the deception had finally been acknowledged.

Mr Q reverted back to the no guidelines issue and proposed that in the absence of formal directions, (whatever they were), credits should be taken into consideration. And thus, he presented a self-effacing and glorified version of his client's life achievements: he had left school aged 16 years old and supported himself throughout college and then university where he graduated as a quantity surveyor in 1993. He stopped at this point to make the district judge aware that I was making notes, but was told:

"Mrs Gibney can make notes on anything she likes."

He regained his flow and told the courtroom there will be areas of the world that M, given the possible sentencing, would not be able to work.

He was "a great supporter to various members of his family and has shown responsibility and been willing to support them in whatever way he can."

Having to listen to this tale of self-sacrifice was galling, surely the way he had treated his own son and his stepson was the real example of his commitment to supporting his family? He continued to say he could not speculate how a criminal conviction would affect his future job prospects.

I wondered when the Crown Prosecutor would make her contribution to the sentencing discussion as surely time was running out. But she remained seated throughout and appeared to have no involvement whatsoever in what appeared to be a one-sided debate.

It was now over to the district judge to declare his sentence; I did not know how this was going to play out. I had lost confidence in him, the odd supportive comments including that I had read my VPS 'with great fortitude' he had made to me were meaningless when put into context of a possible custodial sentence. I had to listen hard and stay focussed, my heart was pounding so loud in my chest and echoing in my ears. He ruled out a conditional discharge, well, how could that have even been a viable option? He said he was not in a position for a curfew, that option seemed ridiculous anyway and not in context of the crime. Nor was a community order appropriate, although I believed that M's eligibility for community service had been clarified at the second hearing. Nor was he prepared to accept a financial penalty as suitable. Lucy and I held tight onto each other's arms, surely this is where he pronounces a custodial sentence?

It looked like it was going that way when the district judge announced that he was very sorry if the sentence inhibits his future employment, but he has found himself in this position because of his own actions.

"You initiated into a bigamous marriage, you knew precisely what you were doing at the time you did it, there was no hiding it. You entered into a bigamous marriage. There are plenty of marvellous testimonials on your behalf, but they can't save you."

Lucy and I exchanged smiles; we were so hopeful. M stood hands in pockets, head bowed, the district judge pronounced sentence:

"Six months suspended sentence for two years."

I was unsure what I had heard, or rather I could not believe what I thought I had just heard, Lucy had to repeat it for me. It seemed the rest of the court given the shocked looks on the faces of those in my line of vision and the instant murmuring that filled the courtroom, were equally as surprised as we were at the leniency of the sentencing. Ray came to collect us and led us back to the room we had spent the morning in to give us the chance to compose ourselves. I was tearful. Ray was very vocal in his astonishment at the sentence M had received, especially given the judge's reputation and the seriousness of the crimes M had committed.

We left the court via the same entrance I had followed M through a month earlier. I was aware the reporters on the opposite side of the road were taking my photograph. I approached them and through tears begged them not to use my picture, but they told me that was not an option as the story was scheduled for publication the following day on the front page. This was a rude awakening for me, as I had not realised, I would have no control over what the press published, nor had I even considered that they would be interested in me.

Lucy drove me home, we got changed and went straight to a local bar where we met Cal, another friend who had supported me from the beginning of this traumatic journey. All three of us drank a lot of Prosecco that night. We tried hard to find a positive in the outcome, but other than the fact that M would now have a criminal record as a result, there was none. My phone pinged constantly with messages of outrage and astonishment at the pathetic and grossly inadequate punishment issued by the court.

Sleep eluded me that night as it had for so long. I lay there wondering if the stress and aggravation of the last nine months had been worth it; maybe I too should have chosen to ignore the bigamy as my legal team and the divorce court judge had done.

I went to work the next day depressed and hung over. It was late morning when Cal called, the story was in the Liverpool Echo, in fact it covered the whole of the front page. I pretended my photo was not looming out from the newsstand in Morrison's as I tried to appear nonchalant at the till when I bought several copies on my way home.

As I came through the front door my landline was ringing, an ITV producer introduced herself and invited me to do an interview for the 6 o'clock news that evening. I did not know what to say other than to ask her why? She explained she had read 'my story' on-line and anticipated it would be in the 'nationals' tomorrow so pre-empting the interest they were keen to speak with me. As she and the cameraman were Manchester based, they could be at my house within the hour. I was out of my depth, before committing to the interview I spoke to Ruth, a TV producer friend who suggested that the interview might go some way to diminishing the interest in the story, but there was also a chance it could go the other way...

I would take my chances. So, within two hours of our brief conversation, I dressed in the most slimming dress I owned, made up and was poised on the edge of the sofa while sympathetically being questioned about the trial and the outcome. They were a lovely team who later told me they had expected anger and bitterness instead of the disappointment that I had expressed towards the criminal court and family law systems. I had also stated that I did not believe the outcome was either fair or just.

It was a surreal experience to watch myself on the local ITV news and even more so when throughout the evening the interview was promoted in between programmes and then repeated on the prestigious News at Ten. This level of interest was a precursor of what was to come, The story of Maurice Gibney's bigamy was reported in all of the national newspapers the following day, both in print and online.

By mid-morning there were journalists gathered at my garden gate and a pile of business cards and letters posted through the letterbox, with offers of cash incentives to tell 'my story.' I ignored the continuous ringing of the landline and politely asked the journalists to leave. After taking further advice from Ruth, I understood that I would be best placed, given that 'my story' would be told anyway, to work with a reputable agency who would literally sell 'my story' to the highest bidder. Taking this option would also give me the opportunity to have some control and hopefully ensure accurate reporting, having already read what was clearly made-up information.

As a result, the forthcoming Saturday was spent in the company of a Daily Mail journalist, Angella. We got on very well in spite of the fact I am not a fan of the Daily Mail, nor was I representative of their readership, but such was the power of the story. None of my dresses were suitable to be photographed in so we had to go shopping, a makeup artist arrived and after I was dressed, coiffured and photographed, I was unrecognisable to myself but clearly, I sported a familiar image to attract the Daily Mail reader.

The story ran as a double page spread on October 26th, 2014 the headline read '*My Husband's Secret Wedding Makes Me Look Like a Trusting Fool,*' which I was not happy with, but it was the editor's choice, and was not up for discussion. However, the article was representative of what had taken place and displayed both 'our' wedding photo and 'their' Facebook page wedding photo as well as a snippet of their 'marriage certificate' described as 'The Oman wedding certificate listing him as divorced.'

The final paragraph of the article read '*ironically it is the internet that has been the means for revenge. It is, she says, the only potent weapon that she has left.*'

The story is going viral with people getting in contact with me from all over the world. At least he's been publicly shamed, and everyone now knows what kind of heartless person he really is.

I was paid a few thousand pounds for that article, and the whole amount went straight towards reducing my credit card debt accrued to pay off the huge legal bill from the divorce.

Another article that was later brought to my attention included a comment reported on from the court and was made by District Judge X and it deeply troubled me. It was a derogatory remark made after I had read my VPS to the court and was the only observation he had made about my statement:

"You can tell just how bitter she is about it, I'm not here to sentence you because she feels bitter, I'm sentencing you for what you have done."

I do not believe it was appropriate for the district judge to have made such a condemnatory comment about me or within the context of my VPS. That declaration was reproduced in the global media and as such publicly humiliated me, which in turn added to my distress surrounding what I considered to be unreasonable management of the case. His remark was an insult to my integrity and, I felt, also undermined the content of my VPS. I had every right to feel bitter but that was not conveyed in the text of my statement and I would challenge anyone to identify any part which can be considered as such. But if the District Judge had genuinely interpreted some of my comments as bitter, why did he only focus on that one element? Why did he allow it to overwhelm the profoundly personal and emotional components and make the term bitter acceptable as the primary descriptive label applied to my pain and suffering as a result of my ex-husband's crime?

According to the Judiciary UK Criminal Practice Directions this is the circumstances in which my VPS should have been referred to and how the content should have been actively used to inform sentencing. It should be noted there is no reference to the judge forming a personal opinion of the victim's feelings included.

Annexe A – CPD Sentencing F: Victim Personal Statements states:

F.3 If the court is presented with a VPS the following approach, subject to the further guidance given by the Court of Appeal in R v Perkins; Bennett; Hall [2013] EWCA Crim 323, [2013] Crim L.R. 533, should be adopted:

c) The VPS and any evidence in support should be considered and taken into account by the court, prior to passing sentence.

d) In all cases it will be appropriate for a VPS to be referred to in the course of the sentencing hearing and/or in the sentencing remarks.

e) The court must pass what it judges to be the appropriate sentence having regard to the circumstances of the offence and of the offender, taking into account, so far as the court considers it appropriate, the impact on the victim.

The pain of my husband's betrayal in love and marriage, his premeditated destruction of our family and the ease with which he rejected his parental responsibilities had gone unpunished. The distress I had experienced at writing my VPS was insurmountable, yet it seemed it had all been for nothing. District Judge X had been dismissive of its content and indifferent to the suffering I described, and he was contemptuous in respect of M's annihilation of our children's future happiness. Did that man take anything I had described into consideration in his sentencing? Did he take into account the deception, the fraud, the perjury, the breach of bail conditions and being placed on the Police

National Computer alongside the charge of bigamy into consideration? NO, I do not believe he did.

While I had been portrayed as 'a bitter woman' by the district judge, in contrast, the Senior Crown Prosecutor Penelope had portrayed M as misguided in his actions and almost as 'an accidental bigamist.' On October 23, 2014 she had posted the following on the Crown Prosecution Service website:

> *Gibney claimed that he thought he could marry his second wife because divorce proceedings from his first wife had begun. This is not the case. Until a person receives a decree absolute, they are still legally married. He may also have thought that the rules didn't apply to him because he married abroad but this isn't the case either."*

Yet this so-called 'claim' was not heard or submitted in his defence in the court hearing.

If M had believed he was free to marry as she claimed, why had he submitted the fraudulent Decree Absolute at the British Embassy to obtain the Certificate of No Impediment to Marry?

Or why did he declare himself as divorced and swear an affidavit to that effect, which resulted in his status being described as divorced on the Marriage Certificate issued at the British Embassy on March 20th, 2013?

Divorce proceedings had not even begun when he started the process of organising the marriage at the Embassy, nor were we even legally separated when they had the bigamous wedding.

The Crown Prosecution Service describes itself thus: *'Our duty is to make sure that the right person is prosecuted for the right offence, and to bring offenders to justice wherever possible. Prosecutors must be fair, objective and independent.'*

I could not understand, therefore, how the CPS considered the published statement to be credible as there was no evidence to support the claim. The only available evidence clearly contradicted it. So why was it posted on their website as a true representation of the facts of the case when it was pure conjecture and as such distorted the actualities, specifics and seriousness of the case?

In early November I was invited to appear on the Lorraine Kelly show and Lucy accompanied me. We were provided with the train tickets to London, overnight accommodation at a Hilton Doubletree with dinner and breakfast and whisked everywhere by a chauffeur driven car. This was just the welcome break we deserved. It was a pleasure to meet Lorraine who had been briefed by her researcher and who referred to M in not the politest of terms, which instantly made me warm to her. I wasn't as nervous as I thought I might be as Lorraine made me feel so comfortable. The interview filled a whole segment, and I would have quite happily sat there for the rest of the show. I felt so relaxed. I was recognised by a few women on the train journey home who were very kind in their comments as was the feedback I received on social media too.

While complete strangers had sent supportive messages, M's family remained incommunicado. While I would never have expected or wanted to resume relationships with any of them, with the exception of Essi, I had anticipated that after the dust had settled, we might have been sent a note of apology or an explanation to account for their behaviour. Such as, that they too, had been duped into believing we were divorced which accounted for their actions, but that was not to be. I can only conclude their lack of remorse to be indicative of their character and moral standing.

I had sent this email to the detectives:

I just wanted to say firstly a huge thank you for all of your support throughout this case and for believing in me!

I was initially disappointed that Maurice did not get a custodial sentence but after all the media coverage it's better he is not hidden away in prison. I doubt any of us could have ever anticipated the media would be so interested.

Once again, thank you.

I did receive the nicest reply to my email from the CID detectives, they wished me well and hoped I could now move on with my life.

The thought of moving on and reclaiming my life without the threat of legal documents, demands, court cases, debt, or fear of reprisals and everything else that came with it, hanging over us and dragging us down was certainly an appealing one. But once I had a chance to start to recover from this ordeal that had preoccupied my life for what seemed forever, I realised that if I were ever going to begin to heal or even to reach some type of closure, for me, it would not happen until I had achieved a sense of justice. And also, not until I could prove that gender bias, financial, class and social inequalities coupled with the bigotry that exists in the system of family law and criminal law were responsible as much as my ex-husband's deceitfulness and criminality were for the position we now found ourselves in. Yes, I would be moving on with my life but not in the way I had initially anticipated.

Maurice Gibney would return to Oman and live his life as he did before the trial began, yet our lives were shattered. I was determined to pick up the pieces and change the outcome for the better, we were one step closer to that already as we were free of HIM.

Chapter 19

September 2014

Prior to the second court hearing, I had contacted Essi's mother, Jane. The last time we had seen each other was three years earlier at Essi's 21st birthday celebrations, in a Japanese restaurant in Liverpool. I seriously doubted M would have told her or anyone else in his family group about the bigamy charge, but she had a right to know, to enable her and Essi to be prepared, especially if there was a chance of media coverage. I had texted her a deliberately ambiguous message about M to pique her interest in the hope that she would reply. Although we had known each other since 1995 and I had, for some years, shared the parenting of her daughter, we had no relationship to speak of. I couldn't anticipate how receptive she would be. I was pleased to receive a response but once we had we confirmed a date and time to call I began to question my actions. Was I right to assume that she knew nothing of his crime? Maybe Essi had told her what she already knew? I guessed Jane was still in contact with M?

The conversation began well, and I felt comfortable; we exchanged general pleasantries and then got to the point of the call. What did she know about M's court appearances? It was immediately apparent that she had no idea what I was talking about, or was it? I no longer trusted people so easily, especially those with a connection to M. So I tried to prepare her, not knowing if she would even believe me, because what if M had told her his version first? She would most definitely believe him over me, but I could only try. So I explained the recent history of events: our divorce and his deceitful behaviour, the bigamy discovery and the subsequent charge. And to bring her up to date, I told her I was about to attend court for the second time and that a third hearing was planned in October which would be followed by his appearance, I had been told, at Crown Court. I made her aware of the local press coverage and that I had been warned by a sympathetic journalist that the story might 'go national' as everyone was interested in bigamy because it was a rare crime. Plus, it ticked all the right boxes for public interest: broken lives, deceit, betrayal and even more compelling in this era of social media, my finding the proof of his 'other marriage' on Facebook.

Her surprise at these revelations seemed genuine. I suggested she make Essi aware of what to expect. Here lay further uncertainty, as I was unaware of how much Essi knew about the forthcoming trial, if anything, but it was clear that whatever she might know she had not shared with her mother. Jane told me she doubted that Essi had any knowledge of her father having committed bigamy at all let alone being charged for it. I didn't tell her that I had written to Essi in Australia in the February about M's bigamous marriage or that Josh had also emailed her to tell her the reality of the situation in March, after the first visit to our house by the CID detectives. As Essi was coming to visit her that weekend, we agreed the best plan was that she would discuss the situation with her then and she would call me back to let me know how it went. I sent her the links to the local press stories to read for herself. I was relieved that the first step was over. I felt for her though; I knew how distressing the news must have been to hear, and how ugly it must have sounded. I had no idea how she was going to broach the subject with Essi.

For me, this was yet another example of M's destructive influence, as Essi knew about the bigamy and the police investigation, because she had responded to Josh's email. Yet she had, it seemed, chosen not to believe it, or if she did, her father's powers of persuasion had convinced her otherwise. Her failure to respond to us or contact us was the clearest indication of where her loyalties lay, and to a point I could understand that, but for her not to have shared what she knew with her mother? Not even a hint of it. In my opinion that pointed to her having doubts about the truth of her father's behaviour and having concealed it from her mother, possibly to protect him, regardless of the cost to her own conscience. It cannot be easy to accept that your own father had manipulated you, played you, used you as a prop to support his dishonest and devious lifestyle choices. She would have had to acknowledge that he had been dismissive of the harmful consequences of his behaviours and the impact they had had on her: the decisive actions of losing your brothers and your step-mum and having to live with that. To an extent, he had groomed her all her life for this role; he had caused her, encouraged her, to conceal truths and mislead us, and me in particular, from as far back as I could remember.

Jane and I spoke again the following week, I had called her, as she had not called me as agreed. The reason she gave for not doing so was that both father and daughter had warned her against it and told her not to get involved

This call lasted over two hours with a break in the middle when Jane became too distressed to continue. I welcomed a breather as I was horrified at what had come to light during our conversation. After our very first call, she had spoken to M, who she claimed had made derogatory statements about me and accusations about my unstable mental health. Jane told me she knew his comments were unfounded, as she was far too familiar with his accusatory behaviour and how he would say anything to protect himself. He would say or do whatever it took she told me as everything was always about him, and that he was 'such a liar.'

However, it was what she said next that revealed to me that my 19-year relationship with him had indeed also been a lie, not only from the very first moment we met but until the very bitter end.

It emerged that the man I had fallen in love with all those years ago, in the very first week of my new life in Nigeria, and in which he had rapidly become such an important part, had lied to me from that very first magical moment in the Canadian club. What was it in his psyche that led him to deceive from the very first step he took toward me? Why did he choose to misrepresent himself, to make me believe he was available to me from the utterance of the first word he spoke to me? Just as he had done to Suzanne Prudhoe when he had met her in the bar of the Intercontinental Hotel in Muscat.

I can still hear Jane's voice telling me that "if it hadn't have happened to you it would have happened to me, well, it almost did."

I didn't understand what she meant so I asked her to explain. It appeared that, when he had married me on 15 August 1995, he was at the very same time engaged to be married to Jane, three months later, in the November of that same year. The wedding was to take place in the church where both she and Essi had been christened and would be carried out by the same vicar who had baptised Essi. When I met him they had been together for over seven years and had been engaged since before their daughter was born. He had gone to work in Lagos to earn that extra bit of money to kickstart their married life together. Yet, in May 1995, we were already inseparable and we were living together in my house in Lagos.

She went on to reveal the history of their relationship. This was the first time I had heard the honest account of a relationship that I thought I had known everything about for the last nineteen years. She began by telling me that she had lived with him in his house in Liverpool and she thought they had been happy together. They had planned Essi's pregnancy but, as it progressed, she became acutely aware of his reluctance to engage. He had eventually told her that he was not keen to be a father as he was too young; they were both 25.

Inexplicably, he had insisted that she had to conceal the pregnancy from his family. She had even had to stop visiting Isabel, whom she was fond of, once the pregnancy had begun to show. This confirmed the only part of their story that was familiar to me, and that what my mother-in-law had told me as true, that none of his family knew about her pregnancy until Jane had actually gone into labour.

I was so stunned by the revelation of their engagement and planned marriage that I didn't think to ask her why she had been forced to conceal the pregnancy or why she had gone along with his request? What possible motivation could he have had and why would she have complied with such an unusual demand? Jane continued: she had thought he was scared of being a father and suspected he would leave her; as such, she had been forced to plead with him to stay with her until the birth. A few days after their baby daughter was born, he had been unashamedly unfaithful to her.

Shortly after the birth, she moved back to her mother's house. Three months later she returned to M's Liverpool house with Essi to visit M. Despite her repeated knocking, M had refused to answer the door to them. When he eventually relented it was apparent why he had been reluctant to let her in. Tracey was there, wallpapering the hallway. In that short period of her absence, Tracey had moved in. At that moment Jane's suspicions were confirmed; he had been having an affair with Tracey throughout the pregnancy and probably long before. Jane believed that that was his real reason for sabotaging their relationship.

Some months later, M had gone back to Jane and implored her to return to live with him again. He had told her that he wanted to be a proper dad. Once she and the baby were settled in the house, he moved to Derby to study at the university there. He would come and go, not always as reliably returning at weekends and holidays as he should have. She told me she had a nagging feeling that she still could not trust him, so had put her name down for a housing association house in Chester, so she would be nearer to her mother, 'just in case.'

When he left for Lagos, Essi was nearly five years old, and while they were still together, she was now living in her new home in Chester. Unbeknown to me he had called her every week from Lagos and they had written to each other every week via his work postal address. In June 1995, as he was on an eight and two-week rotation, he returned to Liverpool on home leave. To enable me to meet him at the airport on his return I had to organise British High Commission transport to pick him up, as due to the security situation we were not allowed to travel to the airport without an armed guard. I had missed him so much and was desperate for him to be back, to be close to me again. I can still remember how excited

I was to see him and what I wore: high heeled black strappy sandals, a short bright green skirt, a sleeveless black top with a high collar, with my long hair in a high ponytail. I had big silver hoop earrings in my ears and silver bangles on both wrists.

During his time away he had played happy families with his fiancée and daughter, he had taken Essi swimming, they had gone on day trips to the coast and had visited his family. Further plans for the wedding were made and Jane expected her husband-to-be to return home again in August; and he did indeed travel back in August, but not alone; he was with me, and five days later we were married. I had married her fiancée.

On our way south from Scotland after our wedding we had stayed at his house. On that Saturday, day five of married life, I had taken the train from Liverpool down to London. That afternoon he went to watch Liverpool play at Anfield and he was then, or so he had told me, going to meet Jane to tell her we had married. He would reassure her that the marriage would not change his relationship with Essi, in fact it would enhance it, as she would have a brother less than a month apart in age. We were to meet up again on the Wednesday in London and that is exactly how I recollect it happening.

However, Jane had an entirely different account of that time. She recalled that, on that same Saturday, his sister Teresa was hosting a birthday party for one of her daughters and Essi had been very excited to see daddy, but he had arrived late, after the football. He had taken Jane for a walk to Stanley Park, opposite Everton's ground, and while sitting at a picnic table, and without any forewarning he had told her, she said that he could not commit to her any more, that he planned to stay on in Lagos and that he knew she would never move to Nigeria. He went on to tell her that he had made a new life for himself in Lagos and he was happy there, that he did not plan to come home as often as she would like him to anymore. "So, we are not going to get married anymore, our engagement is off." She asked the usual questions in these circumstances, including whether he had met somebody else, which he had emphatically denied., Maybe she should have asked him if he had married someone else?

At that point, her voice had begun to falter, it was obviously still a painful memory for her. She told me how she had not been able to believe what she was hearing. She had shouted at him, reminded him that they were engaged, they were getting married in just a few months' time, that they had a five-year-old daughter.

She went on to describe how she knew her pleas for him to reconsider were futile, as the moment he had said that it was over, it was over. He had made up his mind and he wasn't going to change it just because she was shouting at him, as he always got his own way. She had told him, "to go to hell" and had stormed off. She had collected Essi from the party and had cried the whole way home.

Besides the hurt, she had to deal with her wrongly perceived shame and embarrassment in having to explain to family and friends that the wedding was off. He was back on home leave from Lagos again in the October and had spent time with Essi; that must have been an exceedingly difficult experience for Jane. He had still insisted, in response to her repeated questioning, that he was single and was not involved with anyone else.

At the beginning of December of that year Josh and I had come back to London as my mum was ill, and sadly passed away within a few days of our arrival. We remained with my dad on compassionate leave until early January. The week before Christmas, once M was home, we had driven to Chester to pick up Essi as we were taking her and Josh to Euro Disney for a few days. Jane told me how clearly she remembered that day. She had looked through the lace curtain to wave her daughter off and had seen me sitting in his green BMW, the car that she used to drive.

She had wanted to call out, "you fucking bitch; you have taken my man and there you are sitting there, in what should still be my car."

It was only then that she realised he had lied, that he was with someone else, he had not even had the decency to tell her that we were together and that all four of us were going on holiday, that it wasn't just him and Essi.

She told me how she hated me, hated me with a vengeance, not just then but for years and years afterwards. According to her I was the woman that took her man away and that was the only way she could think of me.

We were on the paddle steamer ride in a snow-covered Euro Disney, when Josh and Essi had started to argue, as Josh had told her that M was married to me, while Essi had insisted he was married to her mum. Who knew then how close to the truth that statement could have been? We were, or so I thought, both under the impression that Jane had told Essi that we were married, M appeared as taken aback as I was by Essi's insistence. I suggested she had probably struggled to process the fact, as she had the childhood ideal of what relationships between parents should be. It had fallen to me to explain how, even though I wasn't married to Josh's dad, his dad loved him just as much as her dad loved her, and that parents did not have to be married to love their little girl or boy as much as married parents did. I told her how we had got married in an old castle and how romantic it had been, appealing to her girlie side. Neither she nor Josh referred to the issue again.

The part about the castle must have appealed to Essi's imagination as she told her mum when watching a TV programme that involved castles that Boxing Day that daddy and Yve had married in a castle. That was how Jane had found out I had married 'her man' three months prior to the date of what should have been her own wedding day to that very same man. Her reaction had been to run out of the house screaming, she was hysterical, she told me she could not understand what had happened, how had he married me? She was heartbroken. At this point she broke down in tears; even though this had happened 19 years ago. She would call me back as she was crying too much to continue.

I welcomed the break. I poured a large glass of wine, followed by another in rapid succession. I too was crying. I could not grasp what she had just told me, how could he have lied and deceived me for so long, and worse still, from the very, very beginning of our love at first sight whirlwind romance. According to M, when he had told Jane about our marriage in the park in Everton, she had been reassured by his insistence that it would make no difference to his relationship with Essi or the financial support he provided for her. He said she had been upset when he had shared our brief relationship history, but accepting, and why would I not have believed that? After all, they had not been together for at least five years; well, that was according to his version of events from when we first met.

Their relationship had begun when he and a friend had met Jane and her friend in a club. They had double dated, and while the other couple had not gone beyond a few dates, they had stayed together for over two years. The relationship ended, so he told me, due to his repeated cheating. Hang on, had that been him being honest? Or was it an attempt at reverse psychology, to affirm his honest nature and that he could own his mistakes? Later they got together again on a more casual basis at Jane's request, and two months after that she had announced her pregnancy, hence his declaration that she had 'trapped him.' However, they had remained good friends with Essi's best interests, their shared mutual goal. Yet, on that day in the park, that pusillanimous coward had deceived both of us. He had denied me, his newlywed wife, my existence, and he had denied Jane the truth. He had dumped his fiancée, the mother of his child, a couple of months before their wedding, having been unfaithful for the previous four months. How distressing must it have been for her to find out that he had married me, and that he had not had the strength of character to tell her. How could he have shown her such little respect?

Jane called me back, she sounded a bit drunk, I had poured my third large glass of white wine, I needed it, and was probably not far behind her. She told me she always thought one day we would get together and talk about it. It was important to me that she accepted that I had not known the truth of the situation until she recounted her narrative. She told me she did believe me. I had no reason to doubt her then or ever since on the topic of him and Jane – it would take me some time to come to terms with the newly discovered truth which was an added burden on top of the fallout from the bigamy. We spoke about his skills of manipulation: she and I had spent some time together over the years, but our conversations had never been meaningful in any way. It was obvious how he had surreptitiously controlled our contact and the situations where we met, underpinned by the aim to prevent us from talking about those early days.

I was pregnant with Seb when Essi came to live with us in Lagos. At my insistence and against M's reluctance, Jane had come out to stay for a week to see Essi's new school, the house we lived in, to experience the diplomatic, expat lifestyle and all that we could offer, to reassure her what a wonderful opportunity it would be for Essi. I recalled the only time I had spent alone with her was when we went shopping to the Awolowo Road for a kaftan for her to wear at a pool party that weekend, hardly time for a heart to heart.

I so appreciated her candour when she told me that she would "never have dreamt in all the years he and I had been together that he would ever disrespect me."

She told me she always thought he "loved me immensely." She had been very shocked when things started to take a different turn, as she never expected him to be without me or to meet someone else, let alone ever get married again. We had hosted Essi's 18th birthday party at our house, and a large group of her friends and family had attended. Close members of Jane's family had commented to her how much in love we seemed and how we were the 'perfect couple.' She admitted, even though at that time she was with her long-term partner, to a twinge of jealousy, still thinking 'that could have been me.'

As a result of our conversation, Jane had checked out the photographs of Suzanne Prudhoe online including the group schoolteacher picture on the PDO School website. She was adamant there was no way M would have been attracted to Suzanne if she looked like she did in the photo when she had first met him.

She speculated that she must have thought herself "incredibly lucky to have met a lovely rich guy, this is my new life now," hence the weight loss, the hairstyle, the makeup.

Essi had told her what 'a huge shock' it had been when she first met Suzanne Prudhoe and equally so when she was told about the wedding. She had been informed she was to be bridesmaid at short notice by email. I asked when Essi had first met her or when she had first heard Suzanne's name, but she couldn't recall, but Essi had mentioned her as being a 'lovely lady.' When the two of them had come to collect Essi from her house, Jane had made a point of not being there; she told me was adamant she did not want to meet her.

So, after our first conversation, Jane had called M to ask "What the hell is going on? Tell me."

His reply followed his standard line, that I was crazy, that I only wanted to get information from her and to cross-examine her about him and Suzanne.

He denied to her that he had attended court, or that he had been charged with bigamy. She told me he had told her not to reply to my text or call me back, to have nothing to do with me, and apparently Essi had said the same. Jane told me that Essi did not want to see me, and that hurt. She told me she had her reasons, I wondered what they were.

Essi, she told me, had also said in reference to her dad that "she doesn't want to think about it but if he goes to prison there's nothing she can do about it anyway."

I expressed concern: "I hope she's OK, she is going to struggle with the fallout of his actions."

She said again that she had her own things to deal with.

I was surprised when she told me that Essi now knew about her pregnancy and all that had transpired including why her parents did not marry, and that she also knew about Tracey. Essi had, she said, told her that she knows her dad has problems. But he is her dad, and she will support him one hundred percent even if she knows what he has done is wrong.

So, Essi had never known the truth. She had never known that the pregnancy had to be concealed, she had never known that her father did not want her. Or how he had cast her and her mother aside and destroyed her mother's dreams of a married life with him. How he had disrespected and shamed Jane by marrying me while still engaged to her. Essi was now 25 years old and had just learnt the truth of her family history, I appreciated how upsetting it must be and why Jane would not have told her earlier. Poor, poor Essi.

She continued; she thought his "parents were not on this planet."

I agreed; from what I knew of his father he had not been a nice man. It was unavoidable that his upbringing would impact on his own parenting skills. But just how bad had his childhood been to make him so inept and inadequate as a father?

She would not mention this call to either Essi or M. I recognised the risk she was taking by compromising herself in speaking to me, and so openly. I sensed she needed me at this point as much as I needed her; to whom else could she talk about 'our man's' double-crossing? She hoped that maybe in a year or two, if not sooner, she would be able to tell Essi that she needed to hear the truth of what had happened and not just her father's side of the bigamy story, but she explained she was not able to do that at the moment.

"I just can't get involved" she repeated that phrase three or four times. I wasn't sure if she was relaying somebody else's message or her own; it was possibly both.

Chapter 20

November 2014

Three weeks after the final court hearing, the media coverage had finally subsided, although if I googled my name the screen instantly filled with articles describing the bigamy case in multiple languages in global locations. Meanwhile I was trying to establish a new sense of normality in our everyday lives.

Unexpectedly, I received a call from Jane. She asked if I wanted to meet for a drink; while we had mooted the idea last time we had spoken I actually didn't expect her to follow up on the plan. However, I jumped at the chance and we made a date for the following week in a bar in Bold Street, a popular meeting place in central Liverpool. I wondered why she wanted to see me; did she consider me her friend? Did she have information for me? Was I reading too much into this, maybe she probably just wanted to talk?

I, on the other hand, did have an ulterior motive: I hoped she might innocently reveal something that might be useful in my search for evidence to prove that M had concealed monetary assets in the divorce proceedings. She might even unravel some of the mystery around the bigamous marriage and their relationship during the time that led up to it, of which I remained ignorant. While the criminal case was over, I still struggled on a personal level to understand the actions of my false-hearted husband, and how he had consciously and so very deliberately set out to destroy our marriage. There were plenty of questions that I sought answers for, so I packed a notebook just in case and the scene that unravels here is written from those notes and from memory. I need to stress that what I have written here is what I was told, I cannot confirm the accuracy of any narrative other than my own .

She was already there when I arrived, sitting on one of the oversized Chesterfield sofas, with several large Primark bags on the floor next to her. She was talking to a tall, gaunt looking man, whom she introduced as her partner. They had been looking at local properties as they were planning to move in together. He had a London accent which I thought would be common ground to start a conversation, but he was not interested. He promptly drained his pint and told Jane he would be across the road at the Wetherspoons pub and told me to "look after her." He had lit up a roll-up and inhaled deeply before he had even gone through the door.

I bought us a large Chardonnay each and sat down facing her on the sofa. She inquired after Josh and Seb and I updated her. I reciprocated with questions about Essi, and learnt she was still living in Leeds with her boyfriend and enjoying her work. She didn't mention if Essi had gone back to university to do her Masters, which we had discussed in her last email to me the week before she had flown to Oman to be bridesmaid. So I guessed that that hadn't happened. I didn't ask her about it though, as it was one of the last things Essi and I had shared, and I felt possessive about it. It was early evening; I hadn't eaten and rapidly felt a bit tipsy, having nervously swigged my wine far too quickly.

Jane reminded me that I must not tell Essi or M that we had spoken or met, but as I had no contact with either of them there was little chance of that; I think she just needed me to say it and to hear it for her own reassurance. After M's sentencing, she had had a brief telephone conversation with him in which he had "forbidden her" to have any contact with me. What right did he have to forbid her? Essi, she told me, had since also threatened that she would never speak to her mother again if she spoke to me.

"But why would she say that?" I asked.

"Well, after all that you've done."

"But what have I done?"

Maybe I should have asked her what it was that I was meant to have done, what was it that I was being blamed for now? Was it wrong of me to have reported M to the police for a crime he had pleaded guilty to and had been convicted of?

She told me everyone was angry with me because I had taken the story to the press, and I had made them say all those awful things about Maurice. So, I explained how the Liverpool Echo journalists had been present in court during the hearings and that I had had no control whatsoever over the story being published. I told her how I had cried outside the court and had literally begged them not to publish and to destroy the photograph they had taken of me, but to no avail. Of course, they had to publish, it was news, and news that everyone would want to read about and that was their job. The district judge, in declaring the case was being heard in an open court, had facilitated their reporting of conversations, documents and discussions during the court session. That was how, I explained, parts of my VPS had been quoted in the press along with the district judge's closing and sentencing statement.

I reminded her that these were the same journalists who had been good enough to warn me that the outcome of the trial had the potential to be front-page news, which was why I had contacted her in the first place, to tell her just that. But she insisted I should not have done it. She seemed incapable of grasping what I had just clarified. But she had very probably already been convinced of the harm I had caused to M, by M, as opposed to his taking responsibility for his actions and for having put us all in this position in the first place.

I admitted I had willingly taken part in the recently published Mail interview as it had given me the opportunity to tell my side of the story, and to counteract some of the untruths that I had read about myself and our family situation. I was honest and told her I had received a few thousand pounds fee and that I had used it towards paying off my legal bill. She was surprised at the fee; she was under the impression it would have been at least £10,000. I could only guess at who had persuaded her of that outlandish figure.

She continued to tell me that Essi would always take her father's side no matter what he did. She believes whatever her dad tells her, he can't do anything wrong by her; she told me bluntly that she would always believe him over me.

She continued, "Let's face it, he has always been a good father to her, he has always been the best" she added.

How could she have looked me in the face and said that, in all honesty, he had been a good father to Essi? He had used her as a pawn in his sham marriage and set her up as bridesmaid to validate his authenticity to marry. He had made her a vital and especially important part of his lie. Why could Jane not see that?

Roll back the clock: he had had a one-night stand within days of Essi being born, he had had an affair with Tracey during Jane's pregnancy and had then chosen Tracey over her and their new-born daughter. He had told me that Jane had tricked him by getting pregnant and that when Essi was conceived they were not even a couple, but the reality was that they were engaged, and the pregnancy had been planned. In Nigeria, when a week-long football tournament 450 miles away clashed with the arrival of seven-year-old Essi's stay for the Easter holidays, he had prioritised the football event and therefore missed the first week of her stay, in spite of not having seen her since the Christmas break.

Yet, she considered the man who had hoodwinked his children from the moment they were born to be a good father; I did not understand her thought process at all. Unless she was referring to the financial support rather than to the absence of any emotional support, nurturing, love or the 'being there' for your child, all of which are inherent traits in the majority of parents, but not him.

As we drank our second glass of wine, I asked if her idea of a good father was him throwing money at Essi, as it seemed to me that whatever she had asked for she had always been given. He had paid a generous monthly maintenance and, in addition, gave Essi a separate allowance, but it was never enough, there was always some other 'necessary' item that required extra funds. He indulged Essi far more than he did the boys with, let's face it, what was our money as opposed to just his.

"Because he gave her money all the time? Is that what you mean? Does that compensate for the abandonment and guilt, do you think?" I asked her.

"Well, he's a better parent than you are" she snapped back at me.

Wow, where did that come from! I might not be the perfect parent, but I have always tried my very best, to make that comparison was outrageous and unsubstantiated. What was wrong with this woman that she, who knew him so well, could say such a thing to me?

It seemed, according to M, that I had prevented Seb from maintaining contact with him, as he had told her he had written numerous letters to Seb and, at one point, allegedly had even sent a letter a week but had never received a reply. He had also apparently messaged and phoned Seb, but I had cruelly prevented Seb from responding to all forms of communication with his father. Could she really imagine M writing a letter I asked, let alone going to the post office to post it. I told her how he had told me there was no reliable postal service in Oman.

"Surely, he would have emailed him or texted Seb rather than written a letter, don't you think?"

I explained to her that I had no control over Seb's accounts and that his passwords were private; if M had contacted him it would have been Seb's decision if he chose to respond or not. This accusation was particularly infuriating as during the first few months of our separation I had tried my absolute best to encourage contact between them both until I realised, and had to accept, that it was not what M actually wanted. I told her the exact date M had last seen or spoken to his son, which at that point was 21 months ago. Jane could not understand why he had broken contact with Seb, yet to me it was obvious. Seb had to be sacrificed in order to maintain his relationship with Suzanne Prudhoe, because how would he have explained his mistress/fiancée away to Seb?

In stark contrast, and this was soon to become the conversational pattern for the evening, she went on to tell me how good a stepmother I had been to Essi. Although she did remind me that on first knowledge of me, she had an instant hatred for me and that when she used to call the house in Lagos to speak to Essi she had to stop herself from telling me just that. She had remained jealous of me and my family life with "her man and Essi and Josh for years."

Shamelessly, she continued, instead of its abating over time, her jealousy had peaked when I was pregnant with Seb, which was three years after he had rejected her and their long-standing wedding plans and married me. She went on to tell me how she had desperately wanted a second child with him. That she had wanted M to father a child with her after how cruelly he had treated her was incomprehensible to me. Was she honestly telling me that she was still emotionally and physically attracted to him?

However, during Essi 's teenage years, nine years after the two of us had first met, she had finally grown to like me, but she added that that was based purely upon Essi's enthusiasm for me. She said that after spending time with me Essi would return home and tell her, "Yve taught me this, took me there, bought me this."

Reluctantly, she had slowly accepted that I loved her daughter and realised how much her daughter loved me back. I used the opportunity to ask if she knew when Essi might agree to speak to me or meet me.

"No she did not" She was not willing to elaborate further.

But now that Essi knew the details of her parents' early relationship, her father's affair with Tracey, coupled with his bigamy, she had no doubt had enough to deal with, and I told Jane so. I hoped we would be able to talk in the future once she had got through this upset. Jane assured me that we would. I knew I could have helped Essi through this difficult time, but that was not going to happen, he had made sure of that.

Randomly, Jane repeated how Essi had been so shocked to meet Suzanne Prudhoe and to hear about the wedding.

I asked, "How was she introduced? As his girlfriend, friend? How did he explain her to Essi?"

Essi had stayed with M in Oman in November 2012, seven months after their engagement had been announced on Facebook, so she must have been aware of their relationship and their forthcoming marriage plans. Jane ignored my questions; maybe she preferred not to answer them, or maybe she didn't know how to?

Instead, she said "Suzanne knows about you and Seb and Josh you know?"

I had already surmised that, as it would have been very difficult to conceal our existence, although I am sure if it had been possible, he would have done just that. But the risk would have been too great, given that his family members might have mentioned us at some point, by accident, even though he would have instructed them not to speak about us.

She told me she did not even know the two of us weren't together when she first heard about Suzanne from Essi and had presumed M was having an affair with Suzanne. Puzzled, she could not work out where Suzanne fitted in as, if he was having an affair with her, he wouldn't have introduced her to Essi.

But that was exactly what he had done. We were indeed together at that time, just as we were when they got engaged, and in fact we were still a married couple for exactly one year after he had 'married' Suzanne Prudhoe. The Decree Absolute which confirmed our divorce had been issued just ten days before their first wedding anniversary. So yes, I could say with confidence that we were still together when Essi first met Suzanne Prudhoe, at whatever stage of their relationship that might have been.

Jane went on to tell me how his behaviour had always been impossible to predict. She was in full flow, I didn't want to interrupt her, I had to be patient, and wait for the right moment.

"When Essi told me that she was going to be a bridesmaid I asked her if she had spoken to you about it; she told me she hadn't. I asked her why not? She said Maurice had told her not to, because when you had found out he was seeing Suzanne you had gone crazy and were set on destroying their relationship. So that was why he said you weren't to know anything about the wedding because, apparently, you had threatened to harm Suzanne. I asked her about Seb, and how he would go to the wedding if you didn't know anything about it?"

Essi, she continued, had asked M the same question and been told that under no circumstance could Seb be told anything about the wedding, as I would never let him attend anyway. So, to protect both Seb and Suzanne she had to ensure she kept it a secret.

He had, she said, strongly stressed the point that Suzanne would be put at risk if I knew anything about it. He had apparently told Essi that she knew what I was like; I did not know what he had intended to imply by that comment. He had apparently also claimed that, if I knew about the wedding, I would probably turn up and try to stop it, and had emphasised that she, his own daughter, would not want to be responsible for that.

Oddly, none of what Jane had just relayed surprised me, it further demonstrated how scheming and manipulative he was, how determined he was to use and abuse even his own daughter to protect himself and his treachery. Essi had also told her she thought it would be out of character for me to threaten Suzanne or keep Seb away from the wedding, which would have been true under different circumstances.

Jane continued on another and welcome tangent, She explained how she had told Essi that she should not have accepted to be bridesmaid until she had spoken to me. She acknowledged that we were close, and she knew how much she loved me, and that she should respect me regardless of what her father said. She had told Essi I was the last person she would want to hurt and that she should get my permission to be bridesmaid.

Essi had told her she would think about it. At this point my eyes were filled with tears; thank you Jane, thank you. It seemed Jane had been the only person throughout this whole sordid affair that had even considered me and my feelings. How ironic was that?

Jane had asked Essi if we had got divorced, and she had told her she didn't know, as her dad had not mentioned it. "When I asked her what you had told her about it, she said when you two had met in London, you had told her the pair of you were going through a rough patch, but that you had definitely not mentioned divorce."

Jane mentioned Essi's 18th birthday party at our house again and 'how together' M and I had appeared, and that we seemed to be the 'perfect couple' in everyone's eyes. She had mused over what had happened to change that. Essi's 18th was in 2008. That was when, as I later found out during the ensuing years of investigation into his many duplicitous lives, that while we looked like the 'perfect couple,' he was screwing his bestie, Tracey.

From the moment Essi had told her about the wedding, Jane explained that something had not seemed right to her, so she had called M and challenged him to explain: why had he not told her that we were separated? When and why had we got divorced? Why had he not told her about his plans to remarry? She had remained puzzled by his response as he had told her we had been separated for a long time but were not yet divorced, but their conversation had taken place just a month before the Al Bustan wedding. He had agreed with her he was "cutting it fine" but insisted he knew the date the divorce was to be finalised and had reassured her it would happen "just in time."

He had also told her not to discuss the wedding with anyone, and most definitely not with me, as knowing he was to remarry would upset me, and he was concerned about that, he wanted to protect me.

She had also asked M about Seb attending, and had told him how much Essi wanted him to be there, that she had offered to look after him too, but his response had remained a firm no. He had also stressed to her that neither Seb nor I were to know for our own self-preservation. She recalled how his tone had become increasingly aggressive to force the point home to her, and he had made her actually repeat aloud that she would not under any circumstances contact me. She thought it all very odd, that he was so adamant, especially as she hadn't independently contacted me since Essi was a child.

"Something wasn't right, but I didn't know what it was, I couldn't work out why Maurice was so angry."

She had contacted Essi again and asked if she had spoken to me. She had said no, and that she wasn't going to, because she didn't want to be the one to tell me about the wedding.

She had gone on to share her concerns with Essi that 'something wasn't right.' She had told her that her father should not be asking her to lie for him and that that was wrong. Essi had promised her that once it was all out in the open, she would get in touch with me to explain her actions and to ensure Seb and I were OK. Well, that day has certainly been a long time coming, as we are still waiting for her to do that.

So, it seemed, he had told Jane one story about our divorce and Essi another. Had he been caught off-guard and was ill-prepared for Jane's questioning? It was unlike him to have made such a simple and easily recognised error. I didn't think to ask at that time if she had relayed to Essi that her father had said we were not yet divorced.

I ordered another round at the bar and was asked to tell Jane to keep her voice down as she was being too loud. To be honest, I had been too engrossed in what she had been saying to notice, but when I sat back down I realised that she was drunk, she must have been drinking before we had met. I thanked her for sharing, I had no way of really knowing what had taken place other than what she had told me.

We were in a unique situation. We were both drunk and talking about our ex-partner's bigamous marriage, on the first occasion that we had been alone socially in each other's company in the 19 years that we had known each other. Yes, she agreed, it was indeed an odd situation.

Then looking up at me, she told me not to forget, "I fucking hated you" she said, again a bit too loudly, and she had moved in a bit too close.

The expression on my face at that moment must have given away my total confusion at her behaviour. I looked around at the bar, embarrassed; other customers were staring at us, I gestured "sorry" and asked her to keep her voice down.

What is described below is as I recall it and from the notes I made from the meeting. The words that I have recorded as Jane saying are not verbatim but are as close to her original statements as I can recall. The comments are her comments, I have recorded them here in the way I have described.

"I did though, I hated you. You stole everything from me, my man, my car, you stole my life. But you weren't as bad as Tracey, I hated her in a different way."

She spoke in a calm but still louder than normal voice, her expression was neutral for someone who spoke such venomous words:

"I'll always regret stopping him from strangling her!"

What? What was she talking about? Was she telling me that M had tried to strangle Tracey? WTF!

She wasted no time in illuminating further, in what was one of the most incredible conversations I have ever had and, given the places where I have worked, that is really saying something.

It transpired that prior to asking her and Essi to return to live with him, he had kicked Tracey out as the relationship was over (temporarily as I later discovered). He had been responsible for ending it as he had told Jane, he wanted her and Essi back so badly. Some months later she had woken late one night on hearing a noise in the house and then footsteps on the stairs. She woke M and, as he jumped out of bed, the bedroom door opened and there, illuminated by the hallway light, stood Tracey.

"He grabbed her and pinned her against the wall, one hand round her throat."

Tracey was clutching a bunch of keys in her hand, she had let herself in, Jane said, further setting the scene.

"With his other hand he had prised the keys out of her hand; she was clutching them really tightly, she obviously didn't want to let them go. He snapped open her fingers. I thought he was going to break them, but she still hung on to the keys really tightly; I don't suppose she wanted him to have them."

"She couldn't talk, she was trying to, but he had her too tight, he was shouting at her, calling her a fucking bitch, a fucking whore. I thought, yeah, you tell her fucking bitch, fucking whore. But then I could see it looked like he was really going to strangle her, because he took one hand off her neck and pressed it over her mouth to shut her up, even though she wasn't saying anything, well, not what I could hear anyway."

Jane was so loud, but I did not want to try and quieten her as I needed to hear the rest of her story, but I felt uncomfortable not knowing what was coming next. Out of the corner of my eye I could see the three young women to my right staring at us in disbelief, they had no conversation, no need, they were listening intently to Jane.

She continued, oblivious to her growing audience. "I told him to let her go, I tried to pull his arm down, but he was too strong, like super strong. I had to do something, so I started screaming. I thought he was really going to kill her. I woke the baby up, she was screaming as well, that's what made him stop, not me, the baby. He got Tracey by the arm and sort of dragged her down the stairs, I heard two bangs, one I think might have been her head against the wall, the other was the front door slamming."

I was conscious of how quiet the bar suddenly seemed, the only sound I could hear was Jane. I looked around, even the bar staff were staring at us. The barmaid who had told me to tell Jane to quieten down was now hanging on to her every word, no longer caring about the noise she was making now, as she entertained the drinkers present.

She continued, "I remember I was shaking; I had never seen him so angry! If I hadn't been there, I think he would have killed her. I had to feed the baby, so I stayed upstairs, but I wanted to be out of his way anyway. He didn't come up for ages; when he did, he just said, 'she won't be back' and got into bed and fell asleep."

I actually heard a sharp intake of breath from the table to my right; the women sitting there exchanged looks of incredulity between themselves. Jane seemed oblivious to the impact her narrative was having.

"After, when I knew he had started seeing her and sleeping with her again, I thought I should have let you strangle her, well I don't really mean that, but I sort of do."

"You know what I mean?" she asked rhetorically.

"I hated Tracey in a different way, not like I hated you."

Her voice had got louder as her level of excitement had risen, I tried to shush her, no one should be listening to this, no matter how much it seemed they all wanted to.

I was speechless, I am sure my mouth was fixed wide open, I was in a state of shock. I couldn't believe that he had tried to strangle Tracey just as he had done me, this was too much to take in, especially coupled with Jane telling me that in one way she wished he had strangled her.

My head was reeling. How could she sit there and describe his assault on Tracey so casually? Her concerns were not directed at the ferociousness of his attack but rather that Tracey had walked free. Was that how, if she had witnessed his attempt to strangle me, she would have described it, while sat comfortably drinking a glass of wine in a bar? With its customers listening in.

That day and that vicious assault when he had attacked me had been the turning point for me, although I am now fully aware that I should have reached that point a lot earlier. But what I could not understand was how Tracey could have gone back to him after that, the anger, the aggression, his need to control, the humiliation? But I had stayed with him and I had experienced that same violence, his need to dominate, his abuse, but surely that scenario, as described by Jane, would have been one step too far? Especially as they had no family ties, no children, she was not dependent on him, well, not financially anyway. But evidently that had not been the case. Tracey had chosen yet another path to bring them closer together some time later. A path I now know they had stayed on together for many years to come.

One of the bar staff came over with an odd look on her face; I guessed she did not know what to make of us. We were told that if Jane raised her voice one more time we would be asked to leave. I apologised; I wanted to say "but you didn't mind her being that loud when you are listening to our conversation," but I didn't. Instead, I apologised and told her that Jane was upset, and that it would not happen again. Who knows what they thought of us, particularly given all they had just heard: listening to her describe such a vicious attack? I asked her to keep her voice down; I did not want to leave. I needed to keep her there; she was drunk, but given her recent revelation I was desperate to hear what else she might reveal.

In a quieter voice, she reverted back to her hatred of me. I understood why she would have resented me so much, and Tracey too, but what she had failed to understand was that M was the antagonist in all of this, and that he was the one to whom her anger should have been directed, particularly at this point in time of our shared history, and not at me. But she could not see that and still insisted that it was all my fault.

She accused me of having deliberately targeted him all those years ago in Lagos. That I had seen this attractive guy with a good job, a good salary and as a single parent had made a beeline for him, to entrap him, not caring that he was engaged or that he had a child of his own. So, it was no wonder, according to Jane, that Essi didn't care enough about me to tell me that she was going to be bridesmaid.

This tirade was concluded with the statement that, "He should have married me, not you or Suzanne, and now Essi knows that. Why would she want to see you or talk to you after all you did?"

She must have bottled up these emotions for years, and they were probably further exacerbated by the so-called 'second marriage.' I was sure she had fantasised about telling me exactly how she had felt in the early days, but now, I did not want to hear it, not again, it had all happened so long ago. No matter how overdue, I wasn't having it, especially as none of it was true. But while I felt it, I somehow couldn't be bothered to tell her that.

I had been hurt by her reference to Essi, though, and I was annoyed at her inability to acknowledge that M was responsible for it all; past and present and future, whatever that held, it would be in his hands. Jane was so full of contradictions, I could not help myself, I retaliated. While I didn't want to upset her, I had to shock her out of the blame game and show her how the culpability for all of the heartbreak stood firmly with M and no one else.

So I told her how, that summer, Seb, out with friends, had walked down the very same street that we were now sitting in and had spotted her out shopping. How she had called down the street to a young woman who turned to walk towards her and how then Seb had recognised the young woman as his sister. I told her how he had watched them go into a shop together, just a few meters away, across the narrow street from him. Seb's friends had asked him what was wrong as he was visibly shaken, and he had told them he had just seen his sister whom he thought was in Australia. One of his friends had said he didn't even know he had a sister.

He hadn't approached them, he hadn't crossed the road to hug the sister he hadn't seen for over two years, because he said, "I didn't know what dad would have told her, I didn't want to upset her."

"Can you believe that?" I asked. "He didn't know what to say to her, his own sister, because of what their father had said or done to them both."

I was welling up at that point and tears trickled freely down her face too as she told me how much Essi loved Seb and how badly this had all turned out, how sad it was that the boys and Essi were estranged from each other. At last, a mention of Josh; he and Essi had been inseparable during the Nigeria days.

Included in my VPS was the line, "This is our lives, our emotional baggage and this is the emotional legacy he has given all three of our children." Sadly, there was no better example than this.

At this point her boyfriend came back, an unwelcome intrusion, as we had just begun to recover lost ground. On seeing her wipe away tears, he leaned over the table and, far too close to her face, said:

"I told you she was trouble, I said you shouldn't come to meet her, they were right, she's a nasty piece of work."

I ignored his negative comments and attempted to reassure him that we had both been upset as we were talking about the children, he had nothing to worry about, we were getting on very well. He looked towards her for confirmation, she smiled the lopsided smile of a drunk.

He responded by saying "I'm going, I've had enough, the beers are too bloody dear across there."

I wondered where he normally drank if the beer was too dear in Spoons. Jane meanwhile watched him walk out of the door; she didn't say anything for a minute or two. I sat and waited, unsure what to do or say. She turned to face me and smiled,

"Does Seb want to come to my 50th next week? I'm having a birthday party; Essi will be there?"

After what I had just told her? I explained why I did not think that would be a good idea right now, she did not disagree. She then asked where the toilet was. I directed her towards the stairs; as she walked, she left a trail of little droplets on the floor. I noticed her seat looked damp; I patted it dry with a couple of tissues from my bag. I suddenly felt overwhelmed by a sadness for her, maybe it was misplaced, maybe it was the effects of the drink, I don't know. For a split second, I thought of the two of us as M's cast-offs, drunk together in a bar in Liverpool, but that's not the truth of it, it was just a lull in my mood and no doubt alcohol-fuelled. I went to the toilet straight after her to wash my hands and suggested our next round should be soft drinks, or a coffee. I planned to leave shortly after as I had had too much to drink and felt I could not take much more of this. But there was one more question that I wanted an answer to: it was the most pressing question of all.

"Do you know if they are still together? Did Suzanne stay with him after the bigamy trial?"

"How stupid can she be?" She sniggered.

I was very interested. "What do you mean?"

Trying not to sound too keen, "she's stayed with him then?"

"Well, how many times can he marry her?" she replied.

There was a pause while I processed what she had just said, was she telling me that they had now married LEGALLY?

"Have they got married? Properly? I mean since the trial, has he married her for real?" I could not believe that was what she was implying.

She withdrew, and told me she shouldn't have said anything, I was to forget it, she shouldn't have told me.

Oh no, she was not getting away with that, I had to know all the details. When, where, was she sure? She relented; he had phoned Essi to tell her straight after the ceremony. I still could not believe what I was hearing.

She had just told me they were now legally married. What on earth was wrong with that woman, I thought?

But I tried to stay calm and not sound too desperate "Where did they get married?"

She remained tight-lipped, reluctant to say, but I insisted she tell me. I told her as I now knew they were married she might as well tell me what else she knew. Without realising the significance of what she was about to say she told me that they had married at Gretna Green in Scotland. Gretna Green, the very same place that he and I had originally planned to marry. Gretna Green was a mere 17 miles away from Comlongon where we had had our wedding.

Immediately, in spite of being drunk and in a state of shock and bewilderment, I knew the choice of destination for their wedding had a hidden meaning, and one that only I would be aware of. This too was part of my punishment, his revenge for unmasking him as a bigamist. Yet, as time has passed, and I discovered so much more deceit and bizarre and extreme behaviour, I am sure that if he had been able to, he would have taken Suzanne Prudhoe to Comlongon Castle, where we had married, and married her there too.

It seemed they had married as early as they could after the trial, without family or friends present, only strangers as witnesses. I couldn't help but smile – what a comedown from their original weddings in Oman: the first at the British Embassy, followed by the extravagant ceremony at the Al Bustan hotel. What story had he told her, how had he convinced her to marry him for real after he had treated her so abysmally? Or maybe, crazy as it sounded to Jane and me, maybe she hadn't needed convincing?

I had to get out of there, a pervading sense of gloom and anxiety had come over me. The choice to leave, however, had been taken out of our hands as Jane was now quite agitated, and loudly announced she had been wrong to meet with me. Her boyfriend had been right, I was a "cow." I had no idea where this had come from, but I knew where we were going, out of the door, as directed by the bar staff. I apologised as best I could while gathering up her bags and helping her on with her coat. I was so, so embarrassed; it takes some doing to get thrown out of a bar in Liverpool!

She wouldn't walk with me, so I followed her down the street, as I was concerned as to how she would get home. She put her bags down, waited and turned to look at me. With both hands she reached up and grabbed either side of my face and held it tightly, I could feel her nails digging into my skin.

"I fucking hate you, I always have and always will, now fuck off."

Fair enough, I did exactly that. I walked away, I no longer cared how she got home. At the station in an effort to soak up the alcohol I bought an egg mayonnaise sandwich and a diet coke. I couldn't wait to get off the train to call Lucy to tell her they had married legally, although I still couldn't believe it.

Early the next morning I woke to a text from Jane; "hope you got home safe. Love to the boys. Take care."

I knew I wouldn't be meeting Jane again. I felt that maybe I had taken advantage of her, given that she was drunk, but then I rationalised it, as so was I. And she had used the opportunity too, to vent after all these years and that had to be a good thing, but now, there was nothing more to be said.

I couldn't get the thought of their marrying again out of my head. I could not deny it, I was upset at the thought of it. I had wanted M to be rejected, to be alone, to be shamed, not to be happily married. I could not understand why Suzanne Prudhoe would have agreed to marry him, again, and for real this time. To regain her dignity perhaps? Years later, when I told a counsellor friend the story, she said "Dignity? What dignity?"

There was Jane, to whom M was engaged to when he married me, three months before he was due to marry her, and from whom he chose to keep our marriage a secret. Yet, he had told Jane in confidence of his planned marriage to Suzanne Prudhoe and requested that she shield me from the details in order to protect me. And, yet in spite of their history, I was convinced that Jane would welcome M back into her life if the opportunity ever arose, because I don't believe she ever stopped loving him.

There was Suzanne Prudhoe, whom he had deceived from the very first moment when, still married to me, he had portrayed himself as a free and single man and as a consequence betrayed her trust in his love for her. When he was found guilty of bigamy, she was humiliated in social media and on the front pages of newspapers around the world. Yet she, too, must have still loved him; after all, she married the bigamist for the third time to finally become his legal wife.

And then there was me.

Three women who had been 'love rivals' for a man who had tricked his way into our hearts and lives and caused us all so much pain and hurt. The difference was that I had stopped loving him a long time ago. I was not like the others, I wanted nothing from him other than what I knew to be rightly mine. I now knew without a doubt that not only had he cheated on me in love he had also deceived me financially which meant our divorce settlement had been made under false pretences and was based upon erroneous claims. In effect, he had stolen from me and Josh and Seb. It was apparent that any appeal through family law or indeed the criminal justice system, based on my recent experience, would be futile so, I decided once again, with the help of my 'Lady Detective' friends both at home and abroad, that I would take back what was rightfully ours.

The task was greater than I could have ever anticipated. It took four years and during that time I discovered the expected financial fraud and the unexpected: the women who had co-existed in my marriage, and shared my husband, a long time before Suzanne Prudhoe came on the scene. I am sure there are many more women that had a fling, a one stand, an affair, a relationship, a flirtation, or whatever you want to call it, with my husband than I am aware of. Perhaps one of them was you?

I also had to ask the question who was the real Maurice Gibney? Because I had married an imposter. It seemed he was many characters to many women: a boyfriend, a lover, a fiancée, several times over, all while he played the role of my loving husband.

But above all, I should have known that HE would not relinquish his power over me; he could not walk away from me, he could not let me go. I knew how much he despised me but that did not impact on his need to control me.

I had to involve the police, the CPS, my MP and the Ministry of Justice, I even had to engage lawyers in Oman to defend myself against him and to protect my family, and to expose the truth. Through my first-hand experiences of further attendances in the UK courts I became even more acutely aware of the inequalities and injustices embedded in our legal system All the while though, M continued to hold the power, his manipulation and dominance throughout the court cases that followed was never challenged, nor was he ever held accountable for his actions. That was until, with the help of a powerful, female legal team I finally won my case against him, and had my divorce settlement set aside and renegotiated in April 2018.

It had been a very long journey and, as the truth of my real married life unravelled, it was an emotionally devastating one. But I had not sought revenge; I had needed to redress the balance, to change what was wrong and to make it right, and I did. I finally succeeded in achieving a sense of justice while most importantly. maintaining my integrity and, above all, my dignity, throughout.

Printed in Great Britain
by Amazon